THE CONTRACT

ELIZABETH KELLY

THE CONTRACT

How far will she go to keep his secret?

I'm not Liam Knight's type.

Not that it matters.

I'm his PA, and sleeping with your boss is the quickest road to unemployment.

Still, I can't seem to control my lust for him. And now that I've stumbled on to his dirty little secret, my lust has become a fiery, irresistible burn.

He's offering me a contract to keep his secret.

A contract that will bring my wildest fantasies to life…

* * *

CHAPTER 1

"It's your turn, Mae."

"My turn for what?" I gave Ida, the HR manager, an innocent look.

"Don't even bother pretending, Mae. You know for what."

I stared out the window of her disgustingly neat office. I had worked for the law firm of Knight and Associates for over a year and, so far, managed to avoid being Liam Knight's personal assistant. I knew my luck would run out sooner or later, but I had hoped my perceived fragility would have netted me a few more months.

"You know how it works. All the PAs have to take their turn helping Mr. Knight."

"I know." I gave her what I hoped was a trembling smile. "It's just, you know, he scares me."

"He scares everyone," Ida replied. "Yesterday, he had Roxie sobbing hysterically in her office."

"Is that why it's my turn?" I said.

Ida shrugged. "Roxie's been his PA for nearly four months. We need to switch it up before she quits on us."

I groaned and sat back in my chair, crossing my legs and

straightening my skirt. Knight and Associates was one of the largest law firms in the city. Liam Knight had started the company at the age of twenty-five. He hired a legal assistant and a receptionist and went to work. Ten years later, thanks to hard work and a good head for business, Liam Knight had propelled his company into a multi-million-dollar enterprise. It boasted a staff of over fifteen lawyers, multiple legal assistants, and other administrative staff.

It wasn't just the company that garnered a lot of attention. With his utter ruthlessness in court and his brooding good looks, Liam Knight quickly became popular with the local media. He spent most of his weekends at various charity events or high-profile business functions, always with a different woman at his side.

"I won't try to tell you it's not as bad as you think because it's probably worse." Ida shuffled the pile of papers on her gleaming desk. "You've been here long enough to know that Mr. Knight is demanding of his PA and expects a great deal from them."

"Yeah," I said, "blood, sweat and tears."

Ida laughed. "I've seen a lot of sweat and tears from his PAs over the years, but no blood yet."

"Great. I'll probably be the first. Listen, Ida, have you ever considered hiring a permanent PA for Mr. Knight? There must be someone out there who can handle him on a regular basis."

Ida shook her head. "Don't you think we've tried that, Mae? All that happens is the PA quits after a few months, and we're back to square one. At least with our current system, we don't have to constantly retrain someone on Mr. Knight's likes and dislikes."

I sighed again. A few years ago, Ida had, in desperation, come up with the system we currently used. Every few months, the PAs in the office were shuffled among the lawyers. I frowned to myself. More accurately put – Mr. Knight's PA was shuffled.

Mr. Knight was nearly impossible to work with, and after a bevy of PAs had quit, one after the other, Ida came up with the brilliant idea of using the PAs who were currently employed. Knowing that they only had to put up with Liam Knight for a few hellish months before Ida took pity on them and moved them stopped the steady flow of PAs quitting.

My ability to avoid being his PA was a combination of luck and timing. Two days after starting at the firm, my fiancé called off our engagement. I was devastated and found it difficult to keep my emotions in check, even at my new job. The fact that I spent the first few months randomly bursting into tears convinced Ida I was too fragile to work for Mr. Knight. She pulled me out of the pool of revolving PAs and assigned me to work for Kevin Thornton, one of the more easy-going lawyers in the firm.

The truth was that I wasn't nearly as fragile and emotional as the office believed me to be. But once I learned how difficult Liam Knight was to work for, I'm not ashamed to admit I worked the fragile and emotional bit for all it was worth. Unfortunately, it seemed its usefulness had worn off, and now I had to find a new angle.

"Kevin's not going to be happy," I warned Ida. I had a great working relationship with Kevin, and I hoped he might go to bat for me.

"Kevin already knows," Ida said breezily. "He's upset but understands how it works around here."

"This is ridiculous," I grumbled.

"It's only for a few months, and then we'll move you to one of the other lawyers," Ida replied. "It's only fair, Mae. Some of the other PAs have noticed and started complaining."

"Fine, but when I'm crying hysterically in the bathroom, you'll feel terrible, Ida."

She grinned. "Oh, probably. I usually do. But don't think crying hysterically in the bathroom on your first day will get you moved, Mae. You have to put in at least a few months."

Before I could reply, there was a knock on her door, and the subject of our conversation walked into her office. I swallowed and glanced out the window. I would die before I admitted this to anyone, but it wasn't just Liam Knight's cruelty that made me nervous about being his PA. I'd had a crush on the aloof and distant Mr. Knight for the past six months, and I was growing increasingly aware that no matter how cruel my boss was, I was more than a little interested in sleeping with him.

I snorted to myself. I was as far from Liam Knight's type as you could get. The women who graced his arm at every business function and charity event were always tall and willowy with blonde hair and blue eyes. They walked like models – hell, half of them *were* models – and had perfect skin and oodles of money.

At 5'4", I barely reached Liam Knight's chest, and my dark hair and eyes were depressingly boring. Even at twenty-nine years old, my skin occasionally acted like it belonged to a teenager. More times than I cared to admit, I would wake to find a pimple had erupted on my face in the night.

None of that mattered, though. Even if I was tall and blonde, there was still the small matter of my weight. Or, more accurately put, the large matter. As my mother liked to point out gently, I was pleasantly plump. Truth be told, I didn't mind all that much. My breasts might be large, but they were perky enough, and the roundness of my belly could usually be hidden with some control-top underwear. Besides, as my friend Allie liked to tell me, plenty of chubby chasers were out there.

Of course, I certainly wasn't finding any of them if there were. I hadn't gone on a single date since my dickhead fiancé Neil broke my heart. For months, the only thing between my legs was my hand or my trusty vibrator "Paul". That was probably why I got so hot and bothered whenever I was close to my boss.

Or maybe it was because the man was a walking, talking, and extremely lickable sex god. He was at least a foot taller than me, and the broadness of his shoulders sent me into very uncharacteristic swoonville. Although I had never seen him in anything but a tailored business suit, I was positive that under his clothes was an abdomen of steel and a chest rippled with muscles. His dark hair and cold grey eyes were an odd combination, but they worked for him.

I risked a glance at him and shivered when I realized those cold grey eyes were staring right at me. He stared unblinkingly at me until I blushed and looked away.

"Hello, Mr. Knight." Ida smiled at him. "What can I do for you?"

"You need to do something about Ms. Falkner. She keeps crying in her office. It's impossible to get any work done with her blubbering away in there," he said.

"Actually," Ida stood, and I did the same after hesitating, "this is good timing. I just told Mae she'll be your new PA starting tomorrow."

As Mr. Knight looked me up and down, from my dark hair piled in an unflattering bun on the top of my head to my cheap black heels, I forced myself to smile at him.

"I'm looking forward to working with you, Mr. Knight," I lied brightly.

"No."

"I'm sorry?" I frowned at him.

He turned to Ida. "I'm not working with her."

"Why not?" Ida looked as flabbergasted as I did.

"She's too emotional. She'll never survive being my PA, and you know it, Ida," Mr. Knight said grimly.

"She'll be fine." Ida glared at him.

I was always impressed by the way Ida handled Mr. Knight. Maybe it was just her personality, or maybe because she was his first assistant when he started the business, but she never seemed to have a problem telling him what for.

"I said no, Ida." He gave her a warning look that Ida pointedly ignored.

"Well, that's too bad, Liam, because, at this moment, she's the only PA in the pool willing to work with you. The others all need a break."

He snorted disdainfully. "Maybe we should look at hiring PAs who understand this is business and nothing personal."

His gaze slid to me as he spoke, and the contempt in his eyes brought my usually well-hidden temper busting out.

"I can assure you, Mr. Knight," I said icily, "that I will not cry in my office." I figured since my emotional fragility was no longer working as a barrier to being his assistant, I might as well drop the act.

He cocked his eyebrow at me, and I drew myself up to my full height as he strode across the room to stand directly in front of me. "We both know that's not true, Ms. Temple."

He stared down at my flushed and angry face, and when his gaze fell on my breasts hidden beneath my cheap suit jacket, I poked him in the chest.

"Up here, Mr. Knight," I said quietly, and he had the good grace to flush a little. I rolled my eyes. The man was standing in the office of the HR manager, for God's sake, and he had just blatantly ogled my tits. I ignored the little rush of heat that tingled through my girl bits and glared at him.

"I think you'll find I'm more than capable of handling your insane workload demands."

"Insane?" He looked back at Ida, who shrugged.

"Yes, insane," I replied. "Some of us have a social life."

I wasn't one of those people, but the man standing before me, currently trying to burn a hole in my skull with his gaze, didn't need to know that.

He stared at me silently for a few minutes and then sighed harshly. "Fine, Ms. Temple. But the first time I catch you crying in your office, you're reassigned to another lawyer. Do I make myself clear?"

"Perfectly," I retorted.

He turned and left the office. Ida gave me a look of admiration. "You might not get eaten alive after all, Mae."

CHAPTER 2

"How have your first few days been, Mae?" Roxie asked softly. I studied the blonde woman as I ate my salad in the lunchroom. She had a timid and nervous personality, and I wasn't surprised that she had spent most of her tenure as Mr. Knight's PA crying in her office.

I shrugged. "Oh, fine. It's nice having my own little office."

Unlike the other lawyer's PAs, who had desks outside their assigned lawyer's office, I had my own office as Mr. Knight's assistant. Of course, it was connected directly to Mr. Knight's office, and I had to walk by his desk and hot gaze every time I needed to use the bathroom, but it had a window with a spectacular view of the city.

"Trust me, after a month of working for Mr. Knight, the office will start to look like a prison," Christine, another one of the PAs, said.

"So far, I haven't done anything more than type correspondence. He's been in and out of the office for the last few days." I opened the yogurt container and spooned some into my mouth, cursing when a bit dropped onto the front of my pink blouse. It left a noticeable splotch, and I dabbed futilely at it as Christine pointed her fork at me.

"Just wait until you're getting instant message after instant message from him. Ms. Temple, I need the file for this case. Ms. Temple, I need you to photocopy these files right now. Ms. Temple, I need a coffee."

"Four sugars, no cream," Christine and Roxie finished together.

"God, I hate getting that man coffee." Christine stabbed a piece of chicken and stared at it before popping it into her mouth.

Still swiping at the yogurt stain, I said, "It doesn't bother me if he wants me to get him coffee. I get paid whether I'm bringing him coffee or typing files."

"Speak of the devil," Christine muttered as Mr. Knight entered the lunchroom. He stared silently at us for a moment before looking pointedly at his watch.

"If you've finished your lunch, Ms. Temple, I require your assistance in my office." He left without waiting for my reply.

I rolled my eyes and hurriedly packed up my lunch. "Later, ladies."

* * *

"Do you understand my instructions, Ms. Temple?"

"Yes."

"Are you certain? It would take less time to explain it again now than later," Mr. Knight said.

"I've got it." I had to fight from rolling my eyes again. What he wanted done was so simple a monkey could do it.

"I don't appreciate sarcasm, Ms. Temple."

"Well, we're going to have a difficult working relationship then, Mr. Knight," I responded sweetly.

I had already decided that now that I was his PA, I would

stop hiding who I really was. Frankly, it was tiring and had become increasingly difficult over the months anyway. He raised one eyebrow at me, and I was thankful he was sitting and I was standing. It gave me a sense of power that I suddenly desperately needed, whether real or not.

"Are you deliberately trying to provoke me?" His deep voice, usually so cool and distant, was filled with anger, and I flushed a little.

You need this job, Mae. Stop being a smartass just because you want to prove you're not the fragile little doll he thinks you are.

I didn't know why, but the idea that he thought I was weak bothered me. I pushed that aside and made myself apologetically smile at him. I had a student loan to pay off, rent due, and it would be nice to buy groceries this month.

"Sorry, Mr. Knight."

He nodded, and I gathered the papers he was holding out and escaped to my office. I sat behind my desk with a soft sigh and stared blankly at the computer screen. My legs trembled, and my heart pounded in my chest.

It was being so close to him. I could try and deny it, but God, I wanted him. Just standing next to him and feeling his body heat turned me on. I thought it was difficult working in the same building as him, but my lust had increased substantially the moment I moved into the small office adjoined to his.

The hell of it was, I had no idea why I was so attracted to him. He was a powerful, alpha male, and I liked my boys on the submissive side. Of course, I mused thoughtfully, it would be just short of terrific to have a man like Liam Knight on his knees before me. My pussy throbbed at the thought, and my clit swelled with anticipation. I squeezed my thighs together as the instant messenger on my computer dinged softly.

Coffee, please, Ms. Temple. Four sugars, no cream.

I stood and took a couple of deep breaths before I left the safety of my office and entered into his. He stared at his computer and paid no attention as I left his office and headed to the kitchen.

* * *

I STRETCHED AND YAWNED TIREDLY. IT WAS AFTER EIGHT, AND I was more than ready to go home. A switch seemed to have flipped in Liam Knight's brain, and I had spent the last four days working my considerable ass off for the man.

I sighed wearily. The man was a goddamn machine when it came to work. I quickly realized that he worked crazy hours, and as his PA, I was expected to work the same hours. I hadn't been home before seven in the last four days. From the look of his calendar, that wasn't about to change any time soon. I shut down my computer and listened intently. I was pretty sure Mr. Knight had left his office. Now was the time to sneak out before he found just one more file for me to work on.

I gathered my purse, slung my coat over my arm, and walked quickly toward my office door. Steps from the doorway, the heel of my shoe gave out, and my ankle turned. Screeching, I pin wheeled my arms madly to stop from falling. It didn't work. I hit the ground with a thud that shook the pictures on the walls. I cursed loudly as my head banged off the doorframe. I lay in the open doorway, my head throbbing and my ankle screaming at me. Tears threatened, and I blinked them back fiercely as I sat up and reached down to rub at my ankle.

"Fuck!" My ankle was already swelling and throbbing with a sick kind of pain, but I was more horrified by my shoe. They were my only pair of heels, and I stared miserably at the left one. The heel had snapped off and dangled limply by a few threads. I pulled off my shoe and cursed again.

I rubbed my head where I had banged it against the doorframe and sniffed. The tears I was holding back were starting to drip down my face, and I shrieked in surprise when Mr. Knight crouched beside me.

He flinched and rubbed at his left ear. "I'd appreciate it if you didn't deafen me, Ms. Temple."

"I'd appreciate it if you didn't sneak up on me!" I said.

"Why are you sitting on the floor?"

"Oh, you know, I was tired and thought I'd take a quick five-minute nap." I rolled my eyes. "I fell and twisted my ankle. Maybe I should be applying for WCB."

He had snagged my broken shoe and was examining it carefully. "Or stop buying cheap shoes."

I flushed and gave him a dirty look before holding out my hand. "Help me up."

He stood and, ignoring my outstretched hand, hooked his hands into my armpits and lifted me easily to my feet. My pulse sped up as he looked me up and down. I flushed when I realized that my skirt was rucked up so high my control-top underwear was nearly showing. I shoved the skirt down to hide my chunky thighs from his gaze and straightened my top.

"Can you walk?" he asked.

"Yes," I said.

I took a step, my ankle rolled, and I would have fallen again if Mr. Knight hadn't caught me neatly. Sighing with annoyance, he lifted me into his arms and carried me to my chair. He set me in it and knelt at my feet, examining my ankle. I hissed with pain when he poked at it, and he looked up at me.

"Did that hurt?"

"Yes!" I scowled.

He continued to poke and prod at my ankle. If it hadn't hurt so much, I would have laughed. Earlier, I fantasized about having my boss kneel at my feet, and now he was doing exactly that.

Of course, I had pictured me wearing sexy lingerie and him wearing nothing at all, but a girl couldn't have everything she wanted. I let my eyes drift over him. Even though it was eight at night, the man hadn't even loosened his tie. I was both impressed and envious of his ability to look so damn good after nearly twelve hours in the suit.

I realized he was looking up at me, and I flushed again. "What?"

"Are you crying?"

I quickly wiped the tell-tale moisture off my cheeks with the heel of my hand. "No."

"I believe we had a deal about you crying in your office, Ms. Temple."

"It doesn't count when a broken ankle causes it," I argued.

He suddenly grinned at me, and I nearly slid off my chair. My boss was hard to resist when he walked around with a perma scowl. He was downright dangerous when he smiled.

My underwear suddenly felt too tight, and my bra chafed my hardened nipples. I straightened in my chair and gave myself a pep talk.

Keep it in your pants, Mae. Your underwear is always this tight. It's supposed to be, remember? They wouldn't call it control-top if it didn't keep everything sucked in.

"Fair enough, Ms. Temple." His gaze returned to my foot, and he absentmindedly started to rub the bottom of it. I couldn't hold back my moan of approval. After twelve hours, my feet were killing me in my cheap heels, and his long fingers felt amazing.

Without looking at me, he rubbed my foot and said, "I

don't think it's broken. It's swelling, but I'm pretty sure you just sprained it."

He was holding my nylon-clad foot, his fingers rubbing and pressing against the bottom of my heel and without thinking, I blurted out, "Higher."

He slid his fingers to my instep obediently and rubbed firmly. I gave another groan of approval as he shifted slightly. Still looking at my foot, he moved his hand higher. He rubbed and pulled on my toes through the nylon with his right hand as his left continued to massage my insole.

I sighed with pleasure and barely heard him when he said, "Are you finished your work for the day, Ms. Temple?"

I fought the urge to run my fingers through his thick, dark hair. "Yes."

He stopped rubbing my foot, stood, and quickly turned away. I decided my overactive imagination only made it look like the front of his pants was tented.

"I'll help you to your car. Just give me a minute to shut down my computer." He left the room. I stood and gingerly put some weight on my injured foot. It sent pain shooting through my leg, and I cursed and lifted my foot.

I stood there patiently until he returned. He eyed my raised foot. "Can you walk at all?"

"Yes," I lied.

He grabbed my purse and coat from the floor and helped me into the jacket. I clutched my purse in one hand as he stood beside me and bent slightly.

"Put your arm around my shoulders."

I hooked my arm around his broad shoulders. Even with him bending, I had to stand on my tiptoes. I knew I looked absolutely ridiculous, balancing on one foot with my other stuck up like a chubby stork.

"Ready?"

I nodded grimly and forced myself to hobble forward. My

hand squeezed his shoulder unconsciously, and a small whimper of pain slipped out from between my lips with every step I took.

He grunted with annoyance and then swept me up into his arms. I tapped him lightly on the back. "Put me down, please. I can walk."

"It'll take us forever to get to the parking lot. I want to get home and eat before midnight," he said as he strode through his dark office and into the hallway.

"You can't carry me the entire way to the parking lot," I said.

"Why not?"

"Because I'm too heavy," I protested. "I'll be fired for sure when the office finds out you died of a heart attack carrying me to my car."

He laughed, and I trembled at the feel of it rumbling through his broad chest.

"One - you're not too heavy, and two – I work out for two hours every morning. My body is in incredible shape."

"You know, I don't care what the others in the office say – I don't think you're arrogant at all," I said.

He laughed again, and my cheeks warmed at the sound.

"I work hard to maintain my body. There's nothing wrong with being proud of that fact."

By now, we were in the elevator, and I reached out and pushed the lobby button. I expected him to set me down, but he only shifted me in his arms and leaned against the elevator wall. We spent the short ride in silence. He was staring at the elevator doors with a bored look on his face, and I was using every bit of willpower I possessed not to bend my head and lick his throat like a cat.

As he strode through the lobby, he nodded to the security guard behind the desk. "Good night, Jim."

"Have a good evening, Mr. Knight." Bless his heart, Jim

didn't raise an eyebrow at the sight of me, wearing only one shoe, being carried out into the darkness by one of the most influential lawyers in the city.

I waved at Jim over Mr. Knight's shoulder, and he nodded slightly. Maybe my boss always carried women out of the building, and that's why Jim didn't seem that surprised. Frankly, I wouldn't be shocked if he did. He had the alpha male thing down to a science. I swallowed thickly and reminded myself I didn't care for the caveman type.

Mr. Knight paused in the parking lot to scan the nearly empty lot and then carried me directly to my car. I tamped down my embarrassment as he set me down gently next to my old and rusted Honda.

"How did you know this was my car?" I asked.

"Is this piece of junk even going to start?" he said.

"Yes," I bristled. "Just because I don't drive a fancy sports car doesn't mean my car is a piece of junk."

"You're right, I apologize. Your car isn't a piece of junk. It's a walking death trap." He squinted at the lemon-yellow duct tape holding a piece of the front bumper firmly in place. "Is that... duct tape?"

I fished my keys out of my bag and quickly unlocked the door. Still holding up my foot, I opened the door. "Thank you very much, Mr. Knight. I appreciate your help. I'll see you tomorrow."

He stared into my car's interior and cursed before grabbing my arm. "You drive a stick."

"Nothing gets past you, does it?"

He ignored my snarky comment. "How will you push the clutch in?"

I shrugged. "I'll manage."

He shook his head. "No, you won't."

Before I could protest, he slammed my car door shut and

picked me up again. His shoes clicked on the hard pavement as he carried me toward his car.

"What are you doing?"

"I'll give you a ride home."

"How am I supposed to get to work in the morning if my car is sitting here in the parking lot?" I said.

"Take a cab and expense it. I'll approve the expense form," he replied dismissively.

I sighed inwardly. I lived nearly forty-five minutes from the office. With rush hour traffic, taking a cab would be at least forty bucks. Unfortunately, I had precisely twenty-three dollars in my bank account until payday, and my credit card was maxed from paying my student loan payment with it.

I wasn't about to tell my boss that, though, not when he was currently sliding me into a car that cost more than four of my cars combined.

"You drive a Jaguar. Shocking."

He grinned, and I pushed down the little shiver that went through me when the back of his hand brushed my breast as he clicked my seatbelt into place.

"Listen, Mr. Knight, it's late, and I know you're anxious to get home. Why don't you drop me off at the train station? I live pretty far from the office."

He shook his head as he climbed into the driver's seat and started the car. "I don't mind, and call me Liam."

I licked my lips. With the way I was lusting after him, calling him Liam seemed far too intimate for me. It was safer to stick to Mr. Knight.

"Which way to your house, Mae?" He raised his eyebrow at me. I ignored the liquid pool of desire that grew in my belly at the sound of my given name crossing those gorgeous lips of his.

"Take your first left," I said. I stared into the darkness as he navigated the car through the streets. I wasn't looking forward to having my boss see my dingy apartment building in the bad part of town, but there didn't seem to be much I could do about it.

* * *

"THIS IS WHERE YOU LIVE?" MR. KNIGHT PARKED HIS CAR IN front of my apartment building and stared at it distastefully.

"Yes." I could feel my cheeks heating up with embarrassment as I unbuckled my seatbelt.

Mr. Knight had made one stop on the drive home. He had pulled into the pharmacy's parking lot, instructed me to stay put, and disappeared into the brightly lit building. He reappeared less than fifteen minutes later, carrying a plastic bag and a cane.

"They didn't have crutches." He stowed the items in the minuscule back seat.

"You didn't have to do that." I gave him a tentative smile. "Um, how much do I owe you?"

He shrugged. "Don't worry about it."

"Oh no, I can't let you -"

"I said don't worry about it, Mae." He'd given me a terse look, and I'd wisely shut my mouth.

I pulled the cane from the back seat and smiled at him. "Thank you again, Mr. Knight. I'll see you -"

He was already leaving the car, and I sighed and opened my door. My hope that he would just drop me off was dying quickly.

He helped me out of the car and plucked the plastic bag from the back seat before shutting the door. Handing the plastic bag to me, he picked me up again and carried me up the steps of my apartment building. I had my keys in my hand and quickly opened the door while he held me. I shoved it open, and he looked around the old and dirty lobby with another look of distaste.

"What floor are you on?"

"The third," I replied. We entered the elevator, and, like before, he held me instead of setting me down.

"How many times have you been mugged?" he asked suddenly.

I blinked at him. "I've never been mugged."

"I find that surprising, considering your neighbourhood," he said.

"It's not *that* bad. Besides, I carry mace in my purse and know how to use it," I informed him.

He set me down in front of my apartment door, and I smiled nervously. "Thank you again. Good night."

He waited while I opened the door and peered into the dark apartment. "Is your boyfriend not home?"

"I, um, I don't have a boyfriend." His comment surprised me into answering.

He sighed and picked me up again, wincing slightly when the cane I carried banged against his shin.

"Sorry." As he carried me into the apartment, I flicked the light switch by the door. He shut the door with his foot, and I stretched behind him to turn the deadbolt and put up the chain.

"Not that bad, huh?" He gave me a pointed look, and I flushed.

"I just believe in being cautious."

"Uh-huh." He peered around my tiny apartment. It was a bachelor apartment, and I blushed again at my unmade bed and the breakfast dishes in the sink. I kept my apartment fairly tidy, all things considered, but I was terrible at making the bed.

I chucked my purse and keys on the table as he carried me

to the door leading to the small bathroom. "Here, get changed into your pajamas. I'll wait for you out here."

I almost giggled at hearing the word pajamas come out of my hot boss's mouth, but I smothered it fiercely as he took the bag and the cane. I hopped into the bathroom. I shut the door behind me and stared at myself in the mirror above the sink.

My cheeks were flushed, and I had dark circles under my eyes. I groaned and leaned closer to the mirror, scrutinizing my face. At least I was zit free. My hair was falling out of my usual bun, and I quickly pulled out the hair band. I shook it, tried to fluff it up, and watched as it turned into a fuzzy giant halo around my face. I quickly scooped it up into a ponytail. Moving awkwardly, I struggled into my shorts and t-shirt. When I opened the bathroom door, Mr. Knight stood in the kitchen staring into my fridge.

"What are you doing?"

"You don't have much food in here." He shut the door and crossed the room to pick me up. I breathed a prayer of thanks that I had shaved my legs this morning as his hand curled around my thigh. Unfortunately, I could do nothing to hide the cellulite. I wished I had a pair of yoga pants in the bathroom instead of shorts.

He put me on the bed, and I jammed my pillow behind my back before leaning against the headboard. He sat down beside me, and I cleared my throat nervously. He stared silently at me before shifting down the bed and taking my injured foot in his hand.

"How does it feel?"

"Uh, it's okay," I squeaked out. I was lying. The damn ankle was throbbing and burning, but curiously the pain seemed to recede at the feel of his warm hand on my foot. He rummaged in the plastic bag he set on the floor and came up with a tensor bandage.

"This will help," he said. He quickly wrapped my foot and ankle in the tensor bandage and secured it firmly.

"Where did you learn to do that?"

He shrugged. "I had a lot of sports-related injuries when I was younger."

"I take it your body wasn't as incredible back then as it is now?" I teased.

He laughed. "Let's just say I didn't have a lot of regard for personal safety when I was a teenager."

"I once put my back out playing mini-golf," I volunteered.

"Really?" He gave me a skeptical look.

"Yeah. Apparently, I'm too top heavy to swing a golf club."

His gaze dropped to my chest, and I suddenly wished I had kept my big mouth shut. Why the hell I felt the need to bring attention to my tits, I'd never know.

His hand still cupped my ankle, and I gasped in pain when it suddenly tightened on the swollen flesh. He dragged his eyes to my face and let go of my ankle.

"Sorry," he muttered.

"Don't worry about it," I said as he stood and walked into the kitchen.

"I was going to make you something to eat, but all I can find is some carrots and a very suspicious looking package of chicken."

"I'm not hungry.

"You need to eat something," he insisted.

"I'm really not hungry at all," I repeated. "But could you get me a glass of water?"

He nodded and rummaged through the cupboards, looking for a glass. I took a deep breath. Tonight was turning out to be the weirdest night of my life. My boss, a powerful, well-respected lawyer, was searching through my kitchen cupboards. He pulled out a plastic glass with a picture of a Disney princess and raised his eyebrow at me.

I blushed but didn't say anything, and he filled it with water from the tap before opening the freezer. He found a bag of frozen peas and carried it and the glass of water back to the bed. He handed the glass over, reached into the plastic bag, and brought out a bottle of Advil. He shook three of the pills into his hand.

"Take these. It will help with the swelling and the pain."

I swallowed the pills obediently as he placed the bag of frozen peas on my ankle. "Keep this on your ankle for twenty minutes, okay?"

I nodded and took another drink of water. He studied me before saying, "Are you sure you're not hungry? I could order something in for you."

"No, that's fine. You've already been very kind. Thank you, Mr. Knight."

"Liam," he reminded me.

"Thank you, Liam." I swallowed nervously as he stood and walked to the door. I struggled off the bed and used the cane to limp my way to the door.

He pulled back the chain and unlocked the door. He peered into the hallway, his face wrinkling with disgust. "Good night, Ms. Temple."

"Good night. Thank you again."

He nodded and left, shutting the door. I turned the deadbolt and put the chain across the door before resting my head against the cold wood. I sighed and limped back to the bed, resting the frozen peas on my ankle and staring at the ceiling.

CHAPTER 3

"**D**ammit!" I muttered as I slipped and nearly landed on my ass on the lobby floor.

"You okay, ma'am?" Jim was back at his post, and he hurried around the desk and took me by the arm.

"Just fine." I smiled at him even though I wanted to scream in frustration and pain.

Without enough money to take a cab, I was forced to take the train to work. The usual fifteen-minute walk from the train station to the office took me closer to forty, and I was now half an hour late for work. To make matters worse, the sun shining merrily when I left my apartment had disappeared during the train ride. A sudden and surprisingly cold thunderstorm soaked me to the bone as I hobbled and limped from the train station to the office.

I was half-tempted to turn around and head straight back to the train station. I was soaking wet and tired, and I could only imagine the look on Mr. Knight's face when I showed up a half hour late. My ankle throbbed with renewed pain, and I sighed wearily. There was no way I could walk back to the train station like this. Hell, I'd be lucky if I could limp to it after resting it for the day.

I said a silent prayer that Mr. Knight would take pity on me and get his own damn coffee for the day before I made myself smile at Jim again.

"Forgive me, ma'am, but you don't look all that great," he said, not unkindly.

That made me laugh. "Yeah. It's been a bad morning."

He stared at the cane in my hand, my purse hooked awkwardly over my chubby body, and the water dripping from my pants and top to puddle on the smooth granite floor of the lobby.

"Do you need help up to your floor?"

"Oh no, I'll be fine," I said as my cell phone chirped at me. I dug it out of my bag and stared at the text.

"Where are you?"

The number was unfamiliar, and I quickly texted back.

"Who is this?"

"Your boss, Ms. Temple. Are you working today or not?"

I groaned to myself, and my fingers trembling a little, quickly texted back.

"I'm in the lobby. See you in a few minutes."

I smiled at Jim as I hobbled toward the elevator. "Have a good day, Jim."

"You as well."

Ten minutes later, I limped into Liam Knight's office.

"Good morning. I'm sorry I'm late," I said cheerfully as I headed toward my office. He looked up from his desk and cursed before standing and crossing the room.

"You look like a drowned rat," he said.

"Gee, thanks." I tried to duck around him.

He sighed and, ignoring my gasp of surprise, picked me up.

"I'm soaking wet. Put me down!" I squeaked out.

26

"Why are you so wet?" he asked, carrying me into my office.

"Because it's raining out?" I pointed out the window where the rain was still pouring down.

"I know that, Ms. Temple," he said impatiently, setting me in my chair. "Did you have the cab drop you off a mile from the office?"

"I took the train to work."

"I told you to take a cab and expense it," he snapped.

I didn't reply as I eased myself into my chair. I didn't want to tell the millionaire I was so broke I couldn't afford a lousy forty bucks for a cab ride.

"Well?" He stared at me expectantly, and I sighed before turning on my computer.

"It wasn't raining when I left my apartment."

"I have an engagement after work tonight, so I won't be able to drive you home. Can I trust you'll listen to me this time and take a cab home?"

I felt a flash of annoyance. I didn't like being told what to do, and his alpha behaviour was getting on my nerves.

"I'll think about it."

"Do you have an aversion to cabs, Ms. Temple?"

I lost my temper. "Not all of us are lucky enough to run their own company and have money practically falling out of our asses, Mr. Knight. Cabs are expensive, and if I have to choose between taking a cab or limping my ass home on the train so I can afford groceries, I'm picking the train."

He blinked in surprise, and I stared down at the gleaming surface of my desk. Christ, was I trying to get my ass fired?

"Sorry," I said. "I didn't sleep well, and my ankle is sore, but that's no excuse for my behaviour."

He didn't reply, and I swiped the water that had dripped from my hair and shirt off my desk. I hadn't worn my jacket, something I deeply regretted. Maybe I could go to the bathroom and try to dry my clothes with the hand dryer.

I glanced up at him. He didn't seem angry and was, in fact, staring at my chest. My wet shirt was clinging to my breasts. I didn't need to look down to know that the cold rain had turned my nipples hard enough to be seen through my bra.

"Stay there," he instructed before turning and striding from the room.

"Where else am I going to go?" I said as I pulled my top away from my chest. I was digging through my purse for my compact - I wanted to see how badly my makeup had run in the rain - when he returned carrying a navy blue shirt.

"Here, take off your shirt and pants. You can wear this until they dry." He nearly shoved the shirt into my hands as I looked up at him in astonishment.

"I – I can't wear this," I sputtered.

"Why not?"

"Because I'm at work. Generally speaking, they prefer their employees to wear pants."

"I own the firm and don't care if you're wearing pants." He ignored the flush in my cheeks. "It's preferable to having you drip water all over the office equipment."

"Mr. Knight, I can't wear just your shirt. The first time I go to the kitchen for your coffee, Ida will have heart failure."

He rolled his eyes. "You're not doing anything today but sitting in your chair with your foot up. The Wenton case is heating up, and I'll need you typing the correspondence for most of the day."

"Fine," I said. "Why do you have an extra shirt anyway?"

He shrugged. "I always carry an extra suit and shirt in my office."

"Oh."

He stayed where he was, and I stared at him. "Um…I was going to change here, so uh…"

His cheeks flushed a little. "Right. Call me if you need help."

He turned and left the office, and I stared down at his shirt before struggling out of mine. My bra was wet, but I'd be damned if I was taking it off. I was more than a little worried that his shirt wouldn't fit, but I shouldn't have been. He was so large that the shirt floated on me, even with my plus-size body. I stood and pushed my pants down. I winced a little at the pain in my ankle before easing out of my running shoes and carefully pulling my pants off my legs.

His shirt fell to just below my knees and was luxuriously soft. I doubted I had ever had anything this expensive grace my body before. I suspected that his shirt alone cost more than my entire wardrobe. I petted the silky material for a moment before removing my damp socks.

"Ms. Temple?" he called from his office. "Are you decent?"

"Yes," I replied.

He walked back into my office carrying a towel in his hand. Without speaking, he gathered up my shirt, pants and socks and carefully spread them on the back of the two extra chairs crammed across from my desk. I almost laughed as I watched him rearrange my socks. It seemed so out of character for him to be fussing over me. Although, I reminded myself, I really knew nothing at all about Liam Knight.

He moved behind me and pulled the elastic out of my hair. I had my hair up in my usual top bun, and the hair tumbling down around my face was wet and cold.

"Hey!" I protested.

"Hold still." Using the towel, he roughly dried my hair.

"Thank you." I reached for my elastic, but he pulled it away.

"Your hair looks better down."

"Said every man ever." I plucked the elastic out of his hands and quickly pulled my thick, dark hair back into the bun.

He stared disapprovingly at the tensor bandage on my ankle. "Did you wrap your ankle in the dark?"

"There's nothing wrong with it," I said.

It was true, but he dropped to his knees beside my chair anyway and quickly unwrapped the bandage. He made a sound of disapproval at the swelling and bruising on my ankle and lightly probed at it.

I hissed with pain, and he frowned up at me. "Maybe you should get x-rays."

"Nope," I said immediately. "It's just badly sprained. It'll be fine."

If it's not any better in the next couple of days, you're going," he replied.

I stared down at his dark hair as he rewrapped my ankle. My boss was kneeling at my feet for the second time in as many days. This time, I wore just my underwear and his shirt. I decided this was an improvement in my fantasy.

I allowed myself to imagine taking his dark head in my hands and guiding it under his shirt. I wondered how it would feel to have those large hands slide my panties down my body so that he could bury his face between my legs. My pussy dampened at the thought of having one of the most powerful men in the city on his knees before me and doing whatever I told him to.

With a tingle of dismay, I realized that he had finished wrapping my ankle and was staring at me. My cheeks flamed bright red, and I cleared my throat.

"What were you thinking about?" He gave me a curious look.

"Um, nothing. Why?"

"You had a strange look on your face."

I just bet I did. Contrary to what the office thought of me, I had always been bossy in my day-to-day life and downright demanding in the bedroom. I knew exactly what I wanted, and having control over a man in bed turned me on like a house on fire. Fantasizing that the big and powerful Liam Knight would submit to little old me made me so wet I could have come right there.

"I should probably get started on my work." I cleared my throat again. "Thank you for the shirt and for wrapping my ankle."

"You're welcome." He stood and walked to the door of the office. "Do you want a coffee?"

I gave him a surprised look. "Oh, um, that's nice of you, but you don't have to -"

"Do you want one or not?" he asked impatiently.

"Yes, please. Two sugars and one cream."

He nodded and left my office.

* * *

I STRETCHED TIREDLY. IT WAS CLOSE TO FIVE, AND I WAS unbelievably happy to be going home. It was a strange day. I was busy enough, but I couldn't describe how weird it was to be wearing my boss' shirt while he brought me coffee not once but twice and showed up at noon with a sandwich and soup from the deli down the street.

Mid-morning, Mr. Knight appeared in my office and scooped me out of my chair without speaking. He carried me into his office to the door to his private bathroom. He waited patiently while I used it and then carried me back to my desk.

I shook my head and smoothed my wrinkled shirt. My clothes were still damp, but I had put them on mid-afternoon before stuffing Mr. Knight's shirt into my purse. I would pay to get it dry cleaned and then return it to him.

Mr. Knight had stuck his head into my office only ten minutes ago. "I'm leaving for the day." He hesitated. "I'd tell you to stay home tomorrow, but I'm afraid I need your help with the Wenton file."

"It's fine. My ankle is feeling a lot better."

He gave me a dry look, and I waited nervously for him to bring up the cab again. To my surprise, he didn't, just told me good night and left.

I picked up my cane and slowly left the office. Ida met me in the hallway. "How's the ankle?"

"Fine," I said.

"How's it going with Liam? Any blood yet?"

"That depends – mine or his?"

She laughed. "Well, he hasn't complained to me once since you started. That's a good sign."

"Is it?"

"Yes. Normally, he's sending me an email once a day complaining about the incompetency of his PA."

I didn't say anything, and she grinned at me. "Maybe I should make you his permanent PA."

I gave her a look of horror, and she laughed again. "Just kidding. Listen, I know that shit-heap car of yours is a standard. Do you need a ride home?"

I hesitated. Ida lived on the opposite side of the city, and I had already decided to try to drive my car home. It was late, and I was tired. I figured it would be worth the pain to drive.

"That's okay. Thanks, Ida."

"Are you sure?"

"Yep." I made myself smile cheerfully at her. "My ankle's quite a bit better. I'm going to try driving my car home."

"Well, if you can't drive it, just leave it in the lot again and take a cab home. You can expense it. I'll sign off on it."

"Will do. Thanks, and have a good night." I smiled at her.

CHAPTER 4

I waved wearily at Jim as I limped across the lobby. He returned my wave, and I pushed through the large glass double doors. I stopped and stared in surprise at the parking lot. My car was missing. I scanned the lot, positive I had to be mistaken. I wasn't. My rusty Honda, always noticeable among the gleaming new cars of the rest of the employees, was not there. I groaned, unable to believe that the damn thing had been towed. It looked like I was taking the train after all.

"Excuse me, Ms. Temple?"

I turned to see a man about my age, dressed in a black suit and standing beside a silver car, smiling at me.

"Yes?"

"My name is Russ. I'll be driving you home tonight."

"I'm sorry?" I stared blankly at him.

"I'm your driver for the evening."

"Um, I think you have me mistaken for someone else."

Russ stared at my bandaged ankle and the cane gripped firmly in my left hand. "No, ma'am. Mr. Knight asked me to drive you home this evening."

My mouth dropped open, and I stared silently at him. "How much is this going to cost?" I finally asked.

A small smile crossed Russ's face. "No cost, ma'am. I'm Mr. Knight's driver. Mr. Knight pays my salary."

He opened the door and indicated for me to get into the back seat. "Shall we go, Ms. Temple?"

"Um, yes. Thank you." I hobbled to the door and climbed into the seat. The seats were leather and deliciously comfortable. I settled into the seat and sighed happily. This was much better than the train or my piece-of-shit car.

Russ pulled smoothly away from the office building and into traffic.

"Do you need directions?"

"No, ma'am. Mr. Knight has already given me directions."

"Okay. And please, call me Mae."

His brown eyes met mine in the rear-view mirror. "And you can call me Russ. It's nice to meet you."

I stared silently out the window for a few minutes before clearing my throat. "Russ?"

"Yes?"

"Why does the car smell like chicken?"

He grinned at me in the mirror. "Mr. Knight asked me to pick up some dinner for you."

"He did not!"

"He did," Russ said.

I shook my head in disbelief and stared out the window again.

Once we reached my apartment building, Russ walked with me to my apartment. He carried my purse and dinner and kept up a steady stream of chatter. By the time we reached my apartment door, I knew he was from a small town in the west, was an aspiring actor, and had a boyfriend named Steve.

He placed the food on the table and unpacked it. My mouth dropped open at the sight of all the food.

"Good God! How much food did you buy, Russ?" I asked.

He shrugged. "Mr. Knight said to buy lots."

"I'll never eat all of that. Have you had dinner? You're welcome to stay and join me," I offered.

He hesitated. "Well, Steve is working tonight. I was going to grab a pizza, but if you're sure?"

"I'm sure," I said. "I'd like the company."

"Cool." Russ took off his suit jacket and loosened his tie as I grabbed a couple of plates from the cupboard.

"Here, sit down. I'll dish it up." He grinned at me.

Ten minutes later, we were digging into the food and chatting like old friends.

"How long have you worked for Mr. Knight?" I asked.

Russ shrugged. "Two years or so. It's a pretty good gig. I mostly work evenings and weekends. The one time I got a commercial, he was good about letting me take the time off to do it."

"I didn't even know he had a driver. He always drives his car to work." I chewed on some roasted potatoes.

"I mostly drive him to and from the various business functions and charity events he attends." Russ stabbed a piece of chicken with his fork. "Drive him to the airport, that sort of thing."

"What does Steve do?" I took a sip of water.

"He's a bartender at Night Play," Russ said. "Have you been there?"

I shook my head. "Not yet, but my friend Allie has been bugging me to go for months."

"You should go. It's a great club," Russ said enthusiastically.

"Maybe I will once this stupid ankle heals," I said.

"I'll give you my cell number. Text me when you plan on going, and I'll ensure you get in."

"That's really nice of you, Russ. Thanks." I patted his arm.

He leaned back in his chair and stared at my apartment. "No offense, Mae, but your place sucks."

I laughed and ate some more potatoes. "Yeah, I know."

"Why do you live here?"

"Being a PA doesn't pay much, and I've got student loans to pay off."

"What did you take in school?"

I took a deep breath. "Nursing."

"Working as a PA in a law firm is about as far away from nursing as you can get."

"I worked as a nurse for about six months."

"And then what?" Russ prompted.

I shrugged. "I decided I didn't like it." I speared a piece of broccoli and ate it. I was acutely aware of the redness of my face, and I wondered if Russ could tell I was lying.

"So," Russ stared around my apartment again, "ever been mugged in this rat hole?"

I laughed. "No. Why does everyone keep asking me that? It's not that bad of a neighbourhood."

"Are you kidding me? It's a terrible neighbourhood. When I leave, I'll be lucky if the car still has its wheels."

I snorted laughter but sobered when I remembered my impounded car. I had no idea how I would pay the fees.

"What?" Russ asked.

"My car was towed from the office parking lot. I was thinking about how much I'll owe in impound fees by the time I can afford to get it out of there."

"Oh shit!" Russ slapped himself in the forehead. "Mae, I'm sorry."

"Sorry for what?" I gathered the two plates before limping to the sink and rinsing them clean.

"Your car wasn't towed. It's at Mr. Knight's mechanic's shop."

"What?" I turned around and stared at him. "He has his own mechanic?"

"Well, yeah, sort of. I mean, the guy takes other customers, but he drops everything when Mr. Knight calls him."

"Of course he does," I muttered to myself. "Mr. Knight says jump - we say 'how high'."

"What was that?"

"Nothing."

Russ grinned at me. "Mr. Knight has a collection of vintage cars. He kind of does need his own mechanic."

"I still don't understand why my car is at the shop. Or how you got my car key?" I said.

"Mr. Knight gave me the key. I tried to start it earlier this afternoon because I was instructed to drive it back to your place. Only I couldn't get it to start. I phoned Mr. Knight, who told me to take it to his guy. So, I did."

I groaned. "Russ, you have to use the right technique to get her to start. She's old, and she's fussy. You can't just expect her to fire right up without pumping her a bit."

"I'm confused. Did you want me to start your car or make it horny?"

I snickered before sitting back down at the table with a loud thump. I propped my foot on the chair beside me and gave Russ a stern look.

"You have to pump the gas pedal exactly three times and pop the clutch. Then she would have started for you, no problem."

He laughed. "Of course you do. Why didn't I think of that?"

He pulled a business card from his pocket. "Speaking of which, here's Dale's number. He said to call him in a couple of days, and he'll let you know if your car is ready to go."

I took the card and set it on the table. I would call Dale first thing tomorrow and hopefully catch him before he started work on my car. I couldn't afford any of the repairs it undoubtedly needed.

My cell phone rang, and I dug it out of my purse. The number was vaguely familiar, and I shrugged at Russ before answering it.

"Hello?"

"Ms. Temple, I assume Russ drove you home this evening?" Liam Knight's deep and honey-coated voice gave me a shiver.

"Oh, um, hi. Yes, he did. Thank you very much. That was kind of you."

"Did he pick you up some dinner?"

"Yes. We're just finishing eating it now," I said.

"We?"

"I invited Russ to stay for dinner, and he said yes."

Russ was shaking his head frantically at me and mouthing the word no as the tone of Mr. Knight's voice turned icy.

"Did he now? Pass your phone to him, please."

"Why?"

"I need to speak with him."

"Why do you need to speak to him?" I glanced at Russ, who dropped his head to the table and banged his forehead against it.

"Ms. Temple, hand your phone to Russ now."

Obviously, my boss didn't like his employees talking. By opening my big mouth, I had just gotten a perfectly lovely guy into trouble, and I felt terrible about it.

"Promise me you'll be nice to him," I demanded. Even I could hear the bossiness in my voice. Russ lifted his head and stared wide-eyed at me. I shrugged and gripped my cell phone tightly as Mr. Knight's irritated sigh drifted over the line.

"Ms. Temple, I -"

"He didn't want to stay," I said. "I asked him to stay because I was bored and lonely. He was doing me a favour. Promise you'll be nice, or I swear I'll march into your office tomorrow morning and quit."

Russ did a face plant into the palm of his hand. I wasn't quite sure what had gotten into me. Being bossy wasn't unlike me, but I'd never acted this way with an employer. Not to mention that my threat to quit was ridiculous. One - I needed the job, and two – PAs were a dime a dozen. Ida would have a new girl in my chair and fetching Mr. Knight his coffee before my chubby ass made it out of the building.

There was another sigh of irritation, and then Mr. Knight said, "Yes, Mae, I promise I'll be nice."

"Thank you." I smiled at Russ and handed him the phone.

"Hello, sir," Russ said and then listened quietly.

"No, sir. Yes, I understand, sir. Of course, sir." He returned the phone to me.

"Hello."

"Russ will be picking you up for work and driving you home the rest of the week," Mr. Knight said tersely.

"Thank you," I said. "Did you steal my car key the night you gave me a lift home?"

He hesitated. "I didn't steal it, Mae. I just borrowed it so I could arrange to have it driven back to your place. When it wouldn't start, I asked Dale to look at your car. You shouldn't be driving a car that uses duct tape to hold it together. It's dangerous."

"Mr. Knight, my car is not your problem. Besides, it's not that dangerous."

"I told you to call me Liam, and yes, it is."

I opened my mouth to argue again, and he must have

41

sensed it because he snapped, "I'll be out of the office until the end of next week. I'm emailing you a list of work I need finished by Monday."

"Yes, sir. See you next week," I said snarkily and quickly ended the call.

Russ stared at me. "Jesus, Mae, you've got balls of steel."

"Was he nice to you?" I said.

He nodded. "Yeah."

"I'm sorry. I didn't mean to get you in trouble."

"I know." He stared consideringly at me. "I've never seen Mr. Knight do that before."

"Do what?"

"Be nice just because someone told him to be."

I shrugged. "Maybe it's the first time someone's ever asked him to be nice."

He laughed. "You didn't ask, Mae – you demanded. God, you're a bossy little thing, aren't you?"

"I'm not bossy. I'm... assertive." I winked at him, and he gave me another one of those careful looks.

"Maybe that's why he's different."

"What do you mean?" I took a drink of water and shifted in my chair.

"I mean, I've seen him with dozens of women over the last two years. He has never asked me to drive them back and forth to work."

I laughed. "It's only because he doesn't want me hobbling into work late."

"I doubt that." He scanned me up and down. "You look so different from his usual type."

I scowled at him. "One – I'm way smarter than his usual type and two -"

"That's for sure," he said. "They may be tall, blonde, and super-hot, but a good three-quarters of the women he's dated are dumb as rocks."

"And two," I gave him a dry look. "Mr. Knight has no interest in me."

He shrugged before standing. "Maybe, maybe not. Listen, I'd better get going. I'll pick you up at seven-thirty tomorrow morning, okay?"

"Okay." I struggled to my feet. "Thanks again, Russ. I appreciate it."

"No problem. Good night, Mae."

CHAPTER 5

"You looked at it already? But it was just dropped off yesterday afternoon." I stared blankly out my office window as I held the phone to my ear.

"Yes, ma'am. Mr. Knight asked me to look at it right away," Dale said.

I sighed. "How much do I owe you?"

"Oh, nothing. Mr. Knight is taking care of the bill."

"No, he isn't," I said. "I'll come by on the weekend and pay the bill." Friday was payday, and I crossed my fingers that I'd have enough to cover the repair bill.

"Mr. Knight has already paid for it," Dale said. "Besides, it wasn't that expensive. There wasn't a whole lot we could do with it."

"Fine," I said. "I'll pay Mr. Knight in person. I'll pick up the car on the weekend if that works for you."

"Actually, ma'am," Dale hesitated, "your car isn't road safe. I can't in good conscience allow you to drive it."

"Are you kidding me?" I groaned. "It's not that bad."

"It is," Dale said. "The clutch is about to go, your transmission is on its last legs, and," he hesitated again, "your duct tape is not nearly as sticky as it used to be."

"Dammit," I said. "Listen, Dale, can you please do me a favour and not tell Mr. Knight any of this?"

"Too late, ma'am. He called me last night," Dale said. "He told me to go ahead and junk it."

"You didn't!" I gasped in horror.

"Of course not. But I'm under strict instructions not to allow you to drive the car out of the garage," Dale said.

"Ridiculous," I said.

"Why don't you come by on the weekend and pick up your items from the car. I'll arrange to tow it to the junkyard after," Dale said.

"Yeah, I will. Thank you, Dale."

"You're welcome."

I hung up the phone and stared out the window again. If my boss thought he could control my life, he had a big surprise coming to him. I was picking up my car on the weekend, and no one was stopping me.

* * *

'DALE'S AUTO BODY AND REPAIR SHOP' WAS NOTHING LIKE I imagined. I had expected a modern, sleek, shiny garage with a receptionist who looked like a model and a bevy of expensive cars lined up and waiting to be serviced. Instead, it was a small, non-descript garage in the industrial area of town. There was no statuesque receptionist in the small and dirty reception area. A short, balding man in a blue work shirt with the name 'Dale" stitched into it above his left breast pocket came out from behind the desk.

"Hi, Dale. My name is Mae Temple. We spoke on the phone earlier this week." I held out my hand, and he pulled a rag from his pocket and quickly wiped the grease from his hand before shaking mine firmly.

"Hello, Ms. Temple. It's nice to meetcha'. I'll take you to your car so you can grab your things."

He led me into the garage. After four days, my ankle was much better, and I followed him easily with only a slight limp.

"Well, here you are. If you want to grab your stuff, I've got some paperwork for you to sign to send it off to the junk yard."

"Actually," I said, "I'll take my car home. Could I have the keys, please?"

"Aww shit, ma'am, you know I can't do that," Dale groaned.

"Of course you can," I said.

"Mr. Knight instructed me specifically not to let you drive this rustbucket out of here." Dale pounded his hand on the hood of my car. Rust flakes drifted to the ground, and part of the duct tape holding up the front bumper peeled off. The bumper sagged nearly to the ground, and Dale gave me a knowing look.

"See?"

I glared at him. "I'm gonna need to use some of your duct tape, Dale."

He laughed. "Ms. Temple, it's not safe. I'd feel real bad if I let you drive this car out of here and something happened to a little girl like you. I've got a daughter about your age, and trust me, I'd be grateful if she had someone like me refusing to let her drive a car like this."

"Dale, I appreciate your concern, but I'm taking my car home today."

"Here's the thing – Mr. Knight is my best customer, and if he finds out I let you drive this car home, he'll pull his business. I've got a mortgage, a wife who refuses to work, and six kids to feed!" Dale said desperately.

"Really?" I asked.

He shook his head. "Fine, my wife works, and I've only got two kids, but Mr. Knight's business does help keep this place afloat. That's the truth. If I lose the work he gives me, it's entirely possible this place will fold."

"I'm not a bleeding heart," I said with an indifference I definitely wasn't feeling. "What do I care if your place goes out of business?"

He grinned at me. "You're also not very good at lying, Ms. Temple."

"Goddammit!" I slammed my fist onto the hood of my car and flinched when, with a loud squeal, the entire front bumper fell off and landed on the oil-stained floor.

We stood silently for a moment, and then Dale said, "So, should I get that paperwork while you clear out your stuff?"

"Yes," I said.

* * *

"GOD, MAE, HURRY UP!" ALLIE'S VOICE, IMPATIENT AND WITH just enough whininess to set my teeth on edge, floated over the telephone line.

I rolled back my chair and leaned to see into Mr. Knight's office. "I told you, Allie, I have to wait until my boss is gone."

"God, it's after nine. Why the hell is he still there?" Allie said.

"Because he's been out of the office for nearly two weeks. I knew I'd have to work late tonight."

"It's Friday!" Allie griped.

"Yeah, I know. Listen, he's gone. I'll be down in ten minutes."

"We still have to go back to your place so you can change,"

Allie moaned. "Didn't you tell that Russ guy we'd be at the club by ten?"

"Yes." I stood and grabbed the large bag I had stashed under my desk. "I brought my clothes with me."

"Thank God," Allie said. "Hurry up, okay?"

"Yeah, yeah," I grumbled. "Keep your nylons on. I'll see you in ten."

I ended the call and carried my bag to Liam's private bathroom.

I frowned. Just thinking of him as Liam was difficult. Earlier today, he was cross with me when I called him Mr. Knight. Frankly, I was still pissed at him about my car and didn't want to call him Liam. Mr. Knight suited me just fine. Because of him, I'd spent the last week taking the train to and from work, adding an hour and a half to my commute. I should have pretended my ankle still hurt and had Russ drive me this week, too.

I shimmied out of my pants and shirt and pulled the dark green dress out of my bag. I had hidden my irritation with Liam about my car. Partially because I was already rude enough times to the man that he had reason enough to fire me and partially because he'd been trying to be nice.

I pulled the dress up my legs to my waist and left it bunched there as I quickly changed into the push-up bra I had brought. It was black and sheer and barely contained my breasts. I did my makeup, giving myself the ever-popular smoky eye look before painting my lips a dark red. I took down my bun and added some volumizer to my hair, bending over and shaking my head before flipping my hair back.

I shrugged. It was a bit wild, but I didn't have time to do anything else. I spritzed my favourite perfume between my ample breasts, readjusted them once more for good luck and slipped into my flat shoes. My ankle was still a little weak, and I had no intention of falling on the dance floor and spraining the stupid thing again.

I was pulling up my dress when a sharp inhale sounded behind me. I whirled around and stared straight into the shocked face of Liam Knight. His eyes dropped to my breasts, and I squeaked in alarm and yanked my dress up over my chest. I shoved my arms into the short sleeves and hurriedly tucked my breasts out of sight. I tugged nervously at the low neckline of the dress as Mr. Knight leaned against the door jamb.

"What are you doing here?" I asked as I pulled at the hem of my dress.

"What am I doing here? This is my office and my bathroom. I think the better question is – what are you doing here?" he said.

I flushed. "Sorry. I used your bathroom because I'm in a hurry, and my friend is waiting."

I grabbed my bag and tried to brush by him. His large body nearly filled the doorway, and I stopped abruptly when he put his arm up and blocked my exit route.

"Excuse me," I said pointedly.

He leaned down, and I shivered at his warm breath on my ear. "A friend or a date?"

"Why do you want to know?"

"Just curious." He was so tall, and I was so short that I knew he was looking straight down my dress. "Your outfit would suggest it's a date."

"Maybe," I lied.

"With Russ?"

I couldn't stop the grin from crossing my face. "He is a nice guy. I got to know him pretty well when he was driving me back and forth to work."

His nostrils flared. "How well?"

"Well, enough." I grinned impishly at him, but the grin

dropped from my face like a stone when he reached out and traced the tops of my exposed breasts with one long finger.

"Has he touched you here?" His finger dipped between my breasts, stroking my skin, and I couldn't stop my quiet moan.

"None of your business," I whispered as he leaned closer. His lips were almost touching my ear. I was this close to turning my head and kissing him when Allie's voice echoed through the office.

"Mae? For Christ's sake, girl, what the hell is taking so -"

She stopped talking as Liam pulled away from me.

She looked him up and down before smiling at him. "Why, hello there. I'm Allie."

"Liam Knight." He shook her hand when she held it out.

"I know who you are," she purred.

I tucked my bag over my shoulder. Allie was exactly Liam Knight's type. She was tall and blonde with a tiny waist and large boobs. Surgically enhanced, I reminded myself as I watched Allie press those surgically enhanced boobs against Liam's arm.

He was smiling at her, and I snorted to myself. I was crazy if I thought my boss was hitting on me in the bathroom. He might have almost, kind of, touched my tits, but it didn't mean he was attracted to me. All the women he dated were stacked on top. The man just liked boobs. With my low-cut dress and push-up bra, my tits were practically screaming to be touched.

"Come on, Allie." I took her arm and pulled.

"It was so nice to meet you, Mr. Knight." She smiled over her shoulder at him. "Maybe I'll see you again some time."

"Nice to meet you as well, Allie." Liam smiled again at her, and she flushed prettily. "Have fun at..."

He trailed off, and before I could drag her from the office,

Allie said brightly, "Oh, we're going to Night Play. Have you been there before?"

"That club isn't exactly his type of establishment," I said through gritted teeth. We were at the door to his office now, and I practically shoved Allie out into the hallway.

"Good night, Liam. Have a nice weekend," I called out as I hurried Allie towards the exit.

* * *

"OH MY GOD!" ALLIE SQUEALED SO LOUDLY INTO MY EAR THAT it felt like an ice pick had been drilled into it.

"What is your problem?" I snapped. I immediately felt guilty. I had been a real bitch to her since we had arrived at Night Play. I told myself it wasn't because of the way Allie had been flirting with my boss.

"Look who's here!" Allie dug her perfectly manicured fingernails into my arm. I looked in the direction she was staring at, and my stomach dropped.

"Are you fucking kidding me?" I groaned.

"We should invite him over to our table for a drink!" Allie squealed again.

"No goddamn way!" I pushed her arm down when she waved at Liam. I couldn't believe my boss, his thousand-dollar suit standing out like a flashing beacon among the other patrons, was walking into Night Play.

"C'mon, Mae," Allie wheedled. "I think I might have a chance with him. I'm totally his type. You know I am."

I shook my head as Russ joined us. "How's it going, ladies? Enjoying your first time at Night Play?" He dropped a kiss on my cheek as I glared at him.

"Russ, why did you invite Mr. Knight?"

He blinked in surprise. "What are you talking about, Mae? I didn't invite him."

"Then what the hell is he doing here?" I jerked my head in Liam's direction, and Russ gazed at him, his eyes widening.

"Well, would you look at that? Who would have thought Mr. Fancy Pants would come to a club like this?" Russ laughed.

"Russ, invite him to our table for a drink," Allie pleaded.

"If you do, I'm leaving. I swear to God," I said immediately.

"Dammit, Mae!" Allie pouted dramatically as Russ draped his arm over my shoulders. I leaned against him, and we watched as a large, burly man approached our boss. The man had gold chains around his neck and a hideous Hawaiian shirt covering his upper body.

Russ whistled under his breath. "I can't believe Dick even knows who Mr. Knight is."

"Who's Dick?" I asked.

"He's the owner of the club," Russ replied.

We watched as Dick shook Liam's hand. The two men chatted briefly, and then Dick guided Liam across the crowded club and toward the large spiral staircase at the far end of the building.

"Where are they going?" Allie asked.

"VIP area," Russ said. I followed his gaze upwards.

The staircase led to a large room with a balcony overlooking the rest of the club. I could just make out the couches and armchairs that dotted the room. It was completely empty.

"Dick doesn't let just anyone up there. Half the time, it stays empty. Although I'm not surprised that Dick offered it to Mr. Knight. He's been trying to turn this place into a high-roller nightclub. Mr. Knight would be just his type of client. He'll be schmoozing our boss all night, Mae. Guarantee it."

Liam paused at the base of the staircase, and a shiver went through me when his dark gaze landed on mine. He stared impassively at Russ and me, and I shivered again. Russ tightened his arm around me.

"What's wrong, Mae?"

"Nothing," I said. I grabbed my drink and tossed it back, looking for a little liquid courage as Mr. Knight walked up the staircase. "Do you want to dance?"

"Hell yes, I want to dance!" Russ's eyes lit up, and he took my and Allie's hands and dragged us to the dance floor.

* * *

"You want another, Mae?" Steve leaned over the bar and smiled at me.

"Yes, yes I do, you beautiful, sexy man," I said.

He laughed and turned to Russ, who stood beside me. "Want to watch her do a blowjob?"

Russ shrugged. "I'd rather watch you do a blowjob."

"Later tonight, baby." Steve laughed, and I pounded my fist on the top of the bar.

"What happened to that drink you promised me?" I hiccupped and then giggled.

"Shit, Mae. You are so wasted." Russ grinned as Steve turned away to make my drink.

"I am not!" I said indignantly. "I've had hardly anything to drink."

Russ laughed. "Please, you've been out-drinking that Canadian lumberjack at the other end of the bar."

I squinted down the bar at the bear of a man sitting at the other end. He wore a cowboy hat and a plaid shirt, and as his dark brown eyes met mine, I briefly considered seducing him. He was good looking in a rough kind of way, and he looked big and strong. I felt a bite of lust. My experience was that five times out of ten, the big ones were more than happy to let me tie them up and have my way with them.

I had a fifty/fifty chance that the big boy at the end of the bar would be submissive. I was just wondering if it was worth the effort to find out when a woman wearing a matching plaid shirt sat down next to him and put her hand on his meaty thigh.

"Dammit," I said.

Russ laughed. "You were too little for him anyway, Mae. You'd barely come up to his navel."

"Yeah, the boys like that about me," I said cheekily.

Russ laughed again as I looked around the bar. "Where's Allie?"

"Exactly where she was when you asked me ten minutes ago." Russ pointed upward, and my gaze narrowed when I saw Allie sitting on the couch next to Liam. Her lean body was pressed tightly against his, and she talked animatedly into his ear as he sipped at his drink.

A few other people were milling about the room, some leaning over the balcony to gaze at the rest of us, and I felt my irritation grow. They were all exactly like Allie and Liam – beautiful, rich, and perfect.

I sighed irritably and patted my hair. The dancing and the heat in the club had turned it into a limp mess, and I was pretty sure that most of my makeup had been sweated off. Russ loved to dance, and we had spent considerable time on the dance floor, grinding and swaying with the other dancers on the crowded floor.

"You sure you don't want to go up there, Mae?" Russ asked as Steve set down a shot glass half full of whipped cream before me.

"Positive. Why the hell would I want to party with our boss?" I said sulkily. "I see enough of him at work."

"Fair enough." Russ pointed to my drink. "Your blowjob, m'lady."

I eyed the drink and licked my lips before reaching for it.

"Whoa, whoa, whoa." Steve grabbed my hand and brought it to his mouth, kissing my knuckles lightly. "No hands allowed, beautiful."

I squirmed closer to the bar. "Fine."

Russ, Steve, and the skinny guy sitting on the other side of me watched as I bent my head, wrapped my lips around the top of the shot glass and sat up, tipping my head straight back. The fiery liquid and the sweet taste of the whipped cream mixed in my mouth, and I swallowed it down before bending my head and dropping the shot glass back on the bar.

I licked my lips again and grinned at Russ and Steve. "Well?"

"Not bad for a girl," Steve said. I smacked Russ on the chest when he laughed.

"Cork it, both of you." I gave them a mock scowl as I felt the slow burn of the alcohol spread through my body. Russ was right. I was drinking too much, but seeing Allie flirting and giggling with Liam was bugging me. I needed something to take my mind off of it.

I grinned at Steve. "What's next, gorgeous?"

CHAPTER 6

"Mae, are you seriously going up there?" Russ asked.

I nodded and slid off the bar stool, tugging my dress down as I weaved unsteadily. "You bet your sweet, tight ass I am, Russell."

He snickered. Another two hours had passed, and he was finally as drunk as I was. "I thought you saw enough of our boss during the day. That's what you said earlier."

"True," I conceded. "But earlier, my ass wasn't numb from sitting on these goddamn bar stools." I whacked the seat I had just vacated. "You'd think they'd make these things a little more comfortable."

Russ giggled and took another sip of whiskey as I squinted up at him. "Are you coming with me or not?"

"Nope. I'm sitting right here on these uncomfortable bar stools and staring at Steve's ass. It's the best ass in the place."

"Good plan. I'll talk to you later, okay?"

He nodded, his eyes already on Steve's jean-clad ass. I gave it my own long look. I had to admit that Russ's boyfriend did have one fine ass.

"Hey! Eyes off the prize, lady. He's mine." Russ smacked

me lightly on the arm. I giggled and wrapped my arms around his neck.

"You're a lucky man, Russell," I said solemnly.

"I know, right? And you should see the size of his cock. Christ – it's enough to make a grown man weep with joy," he said just as solemnly.

I planted a warm, wet kiss on his mouth. "Good for you, honey."

"Thank you, Mae." Russ grinned again as Steve leaned over the bar.

"Break it up, you two. I'm a jealous man, Mae."

I untangled myself from Russ's embrace and leaned over the bar, pointing to my mouth. "Pucker up, baby. I got plenty to go around."

Steve rolled his eyes but gave me a quick kiss before winking at Russ and turning away to fill another drink order.

"You need help up the stairs?" Russ asked.

"Nope." I shook my head. "I've got this."

Five minutes later, I stood at the top of the staircase. A large, beefy man blocked my path. He looked me up and down carefully, studying my chubby body in its cheap dress.

"Invitation only, Miss," he said with a bored look.

I folded my arms at my torso, knowing it made my breasts push together, and smiled with satisfaction when his eyes dropped to my cleavage.

"I'm sure you can make an exception," I purred.

"No, Miss, I can't," he said.

I pouted and tried to peer around his broad body. My feet hurt, and my ass hurt, and I wanted to sit on that oversized couch I knew was behind him.

"Are you sure?" I asked huskily, leaning forward a little so more of my tits were on display.

A small smile broke across his face. "Quite sure."

"Dammit," I muttered.

I watched hopefully when Dick suddenly appeared next to the burly man. "Let her in, Teddy."

Teddy shrugged and stepped aside as Dick held his arm out to me. "Come in please, Miss…?"

"Temple," I said.

"Miss Temple. What can I get you to drink?"

"Whiskey, neat." I licked my lips and thanked God for my flat shoes. I was tipsier than I thought. The last thing I wanted to do was trip and land flat on my face in front of all the beautiful people staring at me.

"Of course." Dick snapped his fingers, and a blonde woman in a short skirt, five-inch heels and carrying a tray nodded and tottered her way down the stairs.

I stared around the room. It was much busier than it was two hours ago. Dick had decided to let more people schmooze with the rich and powerful Mr. Knight, and all of the couches I yearned for were full.

Half the people in the room were making out like teenagers, their bodies smashed up against each other on the couches and armchairs scattered around the room. One couple leaned against the balcony railing as they kissed passionately. The knot of tension in my stomach eased when I realized it was Allie. She was kissing a tall and very blond man, and as I watched his hand cup her ass, I smiled a little. Apparently, she had grown tired of Mr. Knight. Of course, as Dick put one plump hand on my elbow and urged me forward, I realized Liam was probably making out with some other woman.

Nausea surged in my stomach. Why had I come up here? Did I want to watch Liam making out with some random gorgeous woman? No, I decided, I did not. I tugged my arm free of Dick's sweaty grip and gave him a weak smile.

"I'm sorry. I think I'll go back to my friends at the bar."

He frowned at me. "But you only just got here."

"Yes, I know, but all the seats are full, and I'd like to get off my feet. I have a sore ankle," I fibbed brightly.

"Here, Mae. Take my seat."

My stomach dropped at the sound of Liam's voice. I turned to see him standing up from an oversized dark blue armchair.

"No, no, that's fine," I said. "I don't want to take your seat."

"I insist," he said politely.

I crossed my arms over my torso again, this time out of nervousness. There was a slow beat of desire in my stomach when Liam's gaze dropped to my breasts. Later, when I was sober and thinking straight, I would blame what I did next on the booze, but at that moment, it was the hard rush of need that made me do what I did.

"We can share," I said cheerily. I stepped away from Dick and put my hand on Liam's chest. I pushed hard. Surprised by my action, he stumbled back and collapsed into the armchair. Immediately I sat down next to him, half of my considerable ass on his lap and the other half wedged between his body and the armchair.

I felt his sharp intake of breath as I wiggled against him and reclined against his hard chest. The waitress appeared with my drink, and I took it from her with a nod of thanks before reaching into my cleavage and pulling out a twenty. The waitress took it and gave me a few bills back in change. I stuffed them back into the bottom of my bra and smiled at Liam before taking a sip of the whiskey.

"Comfy?" I asked.

"Uh, yes," he said before reaching for his glass of booze on the small table beside us. He drained it in one healthy gulp and nodded to the waitress for another. She took his glass and disappeared as Dick melted into the crowd of people milling about the room.

I looked around. We were at the back of the room, and it

was dark and warm and as private as it could be in a room full of people. I smiled at my boss again.

"Did you ask old Dick over there to let me in?"

"Yes."

"How nice of you. Are you enjoying the club, Mr. Knight?"

"It's Liam, and yes, I am."

"Have you been here before?" I took another sip of whiskey, barely feeling the burn of the alcohol underneath the hot burn of my desire.

"No."

"Me either," I said.

"Russ hasn't brought you here before?"

It almost sounded like jealousy in his voice. I gave him a slow smile and traced my finger along the stubble on his jaw.

"You sound jealous. Are you?" I said.

He didn't reply, and my hand squeezed his hard jaw. "Answer me, Liam."

"No," he said.

I stared into his grey eyes for a moment. "Liar."

I squirmed around until my back leaned against the arm of the chair, and my legs draped across his hard thighs. Usually, there would be a small part of me worried about being too heavy, but Liam was a big man and had already carried me around numerous times. He could hold my weight.

I studied him carefully. His tie was still cinched tightly around his neck, and I reached for it. "You need to loosen up a bit, Mr. Knight."

I tugged on his tie until it was loose and unbuttoned the first two buttons of his shirt. "There, isn't that better?"

He nodded as our waitress reappeared. She handed him a glass, and he took it with another nod of thanks. He didn't give her any cash, and as she disappeared down the stairs, I said, "Let me guess – drinks are on the house for Mr. Knight."

A small smile played on his full lips. "Perhaps."

Dick appeared in front of us. "How is everything going, Mr. Knight? Everything to your liking? Do you need anything? Another drink? Some food, perhaps?"

I rolled my eyes as I watched the man fawn over Liam.

"I'm fine, thank you. Just some privacy, please," Liam said.

"Of course." Dick gave an almost formal nod of his head and walked away. I snorted loudly.

"What?" Liam asked.

"I have a feeling that man would have dropped to his knees and sucked your dick if you asked him to," I said.

He blinked in surprise, and I laughed. "I'm not saying you would ask him, but knowing it's an available option must feel good."

"I don't swing that way, Mae," he said.

"Oh, I know you don't." I widened my eyes and gave him an innocent look. "At least all the women you parade around would suggest you don't."

"Now who's jealous?" He grinned at me.

"Not me," I said blithely. "I'm perfectly aware I'm not your type."

"Not my type?" He arched his eyebrow at me. "Tell me – what exactly is my type, Ms. Temple?"

I swept my arm around the room. "Pretty much any woman in this room is your type, Mr. Knight. Except for me, of course."

"Of course," he agreed, and I felt a sharp pang of disappointment in my belly. I tipped my head back and swallowed the rest of my whiskey in one large gulp. The alcohol quickly turned my disappointment into anger. I leaned across him and put my glass on the table with a loud thump.

He was watching me closely, and I licked my lips for his

benefit, the anger turning into lust when he dropped his gaze to my mouth. I took a deep breath. The roller coaster of emotions made my stomach nauseous. Or maybe that was the whiskey.

"How's your ankle, Mae?"

"Why?"

"You said it was sore. Is it?" His hand dropped to my ankle and massaged it gently.

I shrugged and ignored the tremor of desire I felt at the touch of his strong fingers. "It's fine. My feet hurt from walking back and forth to the train station."

I suddenly glared at him. "I'm mad at you for that, by the way."

"What did I do?" His hand moved to my shoe, slipping it off my foot and letting it fall to the floor.

"You got my car junked!" I sat up straight in his lap and scowled at him. "Good old Dale fed me some bullshit about his starving children. He said if I drove the car off the property, you'd pull your fancy-schmancy cars from his garage, and he'd lose his business and be homeless."

He grinned. "Really? My understanding was that your duct tape finally failed, and your front bumper fell off."

I scowled again at him. "That car was just fine, and you – ohhh…"

My protest turned into a low groan of pleasure when his fingers massaged the bottom of my foot.

"God, that feels good," I groaned.

"Does it?"

His voice was suddenly lower and huskier, and I unconsciously mimicked him. "Yes, definitely."

"Good. I like making you feel good, Mae," he said as his fingers continued to massage my foot.

I squirmed a little on his lap, and he inhaled sharply. It took me about four seconds to recognize the hardness under my ass. I bit my lip and tightened my hand around his tie.

"Mae..."

His face was flushed, and with a wicked grin, I tugged him forward by his tie and placed a soft kiss on his mouth.

"Yes, Mr. Knight?"

"Nothing." He tried to angle his mouth over mine, and I slid my hands into his hair and tugged firmly.

"No. Hold still," I demanded.

He consented immediately. I nodded my approval before pressing my mouth against his. I traced my tongue along his lips, and when he opened them, I slipped my tongue deep into his mouth. I felt his low groan against my lips as I swirled my tongue around his and then sucked hard on it. His hand tightened on my foot, and the bulge under my ass grew until it pressed firmly against me.

"You seem to like that, Mr. Knight," I whispered into his ear before sucking lightly on the lobe.

"Yes. Kiss me again," he said.

I pulled his hair sharply, another one of those beats of pleasure coursing through my belly when he gasped.

"Say, please."

"Please," he groaned.

"Please, what?" I dipped my tongue into his ear, and his hips bucked against me.

"Please kiss me, Mae."

I kissed him again, this time letting him suck on my tongue. The wet heat of his mouth felt good, and I moaned softly. He tasted like bourbon and mint, an odd combination that I found highly arousing. Of course, I supposed I would find everything about him arousing at this moment. Especially his hard cock rubbing desperately against my ass.

He flicked his tongue lightly in my mouth, exploring and tasting. Wetness surged between my thighs when I imagined his tongue flicking along my clit. My hands tightened in his hair, and I pulled him back, staring at him. His nostrils flared, and his grey eyes turned dark with need.

"Do you like kissing me, Mr. Knight?"

"Yes," he said.

I leaned forward and rubbed my breasts against his chest, wanting to see what he would do. He groaned again and stared down at my cleavage.

"I want to touch your tits, Mae."

I reached between us, quickly unbuttoned another two buttons on his shirt and slipped my hand inside. I ran my hand across his chest, feeling the rasp of his hair against my fingertips as I found his flat nipple. I rubbed my thumb over it and then pinched it hard. He grunted and growled deep in his throat but made no move to stop me.

"You want to touch my tits in a room full of people, Mr. Knight?" I raised my eyebrow at him and pinched his nipple again. "What kind of girl do you think I am?"

"No one is looking at us." He was staring at my cleavage with bright desperation. I took a quick look around. He was right. The closest people to us were a young man and woman on the couch a few feet away, and they were completely ignoring us. His hand was up her skirt, and her hand was on the crotch of his pants, massaging firmly. I watched them kiss for a few minutes, a little turned on by the enthusiastic way they were going at each other's mouths before I turned back to Liam.

"Ask me nicely," I said.

"Please, Mae. Will you let me touch your tits?" he said.

I shook my head. "No. But you can look at them." I twisted until my back was to the others in the room. I let my ass rub against his erection before reaching up and tugging the low neckline of my dress downwards. My breasts, clad in the thin satin of my push-up bra, popped free, and he stared hungrily at them.

"Would you like to see more?" I asked.

"Yes, please, mistr – Mae," he murmured.

I used both hands to pop my breasts free of the bra. It didn't take much – they were already overflowing out of it, to begin with – and his eyes darkened to a stormy grey. My nipples were a dark rose colour, and they were stiff and tight, practically begging for his mouth.

"Oh Jesus," he whispered. He started to dip his head, and I quickly threaded my hand in his hair and pulled sharply.

"No touching," I reminded him.

He groaned softly. "Please."

"No." I leaned a little closer. "Do you like them, Liam? Do you think they're pretty?"

"Yes," he said.

"Do you want to have my nipples in your mouth?"

"God, yes." He gave me a hopeful look, and I shook my head.

"Not here. It's too bad, you know. They're so sensitive. I love having my nipples sucked on."

"Jesus Christ, Mae. Please," he pleaded.

I shook my head again and then gasped with surprise and pleasure when he bent his head and sucked one hard nipple into his mouth anyway. My hands tightened around his head as his tongue curved around my throbbing nipple, and he sucked aggressively.

Before the combination of booze and pleasure could completely overtake me, I grabbed his ear and yanked hard. He cursed and released my nipple with a soft pop, glaring up at me.

I returned his glare. "I said no."

Quickly, before I could change my mind, I tucked my breasts back into my bra and then pulled up my dress. I was so hot for Liam I could hardly think straight. The way he had begged and how his mouth felt on my nipple had me ready to fuck him right there in the chair.

He made a soft noise of disappointment as I relaxed against his chest. His shoulder was digging into my back, and I smiled when he moved his body so that it was a better cushion for mine.

I stared unseeingly at the people in the room. I liked the way he moved to accommodate me, the way he continued to massage my foot as I settled my body against him. He was much more submissive than I could ever have imagined, even with his uninvited sucking of my nipple. I wouldn't mind his occasional bad behaviour. It sounded strange, but I liked submissive alpha males. They made me work for their submissiveness. I knew from experience that I rapidly lost interest in the men who rolled over and showed me their bellies too quickly.

My stomach made another funny lurch, the liquid in it sloshing unpleasantly. I ignored it and reached between our bodies. I wanted to touch Liam's cock, wanted to feel its velvet skin in my hand. I slipped my hand inside his pants and his underwear.

He made a gasping moan as my fingers wrapped around his hard cock. A soft noise of surprise escaped my mouth. "My goodness, Mr. Knight. You're nice and thick, aren't you?"

He panted harshly in my ear, and his hands reached for my hips. I gave his cock a firm squeeze. "No. Keep your hands on the arms of the chair. We wouldn't want anyone to know what we're doing, would we?"

He made a croaking noise and squeezed the arms of the chair so tightly that his knuckles turned white. I moved my hand slowly up and down his thick, hard shaft.

"Good boy," I said sweetly. "Do what I tell you, and you'll be rewarded. Do you understand?"

"Yes," he said through gritted teeth. A fine sheen of sweat covered his forehead, and my entire body moved as he thrust his hips against me.

"Try not to move," I said. "You don't want people knowing what I'm doing, do you?"

He shook his head no and bit down on his bottom lip when I rubbed my thumb over the tip of his cock. I moved my hand slowly. I didn't want to draw attention to the fact that I was wanking him off in the middle of a busy club. I listened with delight to the delicious sound of his soft groans and loud panting.

"Do you know how wet you make me, Liam?" I whispered into his ear.

He took a shuddering breath. "I want to taste you, Mae. I want to bury my face between your legs and lick every part of your pussy until you're shuddering under me. Please, will you let me do that for you?"

Before I could answer, I saw Dick heading towards us. "Uh-oh," I whispered. "Here comes Dick."

"Let me go." He wiggled his hips against me, and I tightened my hand around his cock.

"No. I'm going to touch you the entire time he's here, and if you do something to make him realize it, I'll punish you. Do you understand me?" I whispered as Dick drew closer.

"Yes," he groaned.

"How are things, Mr. Knight? Still satisfactory?" Dick gave him an eager grin as I settled my body firmly against Liam, keeping my arm tucked behind my back. I slowly moved my hand up and down his cock. My arm barely moved as I stroked, and I could feel Liam's heart pounding against my back.

"It's fine," he croaked out, clearing his throat roughly. "I'm having a – a wonderful time."

"Oh good, good. You're welcome at the club anytime, Mr. Knight." Dick's eyes wandered over me for a moment. The look in his eyes was unmistakable. He couldn't figure out why Liam had a chubby, plain brunette sitting on his lap when there were more than a few gorgeous blondes and redheads to choose from.

"Thank you. I appreciate that." Liam cleared his throat again, and I smiled at Dick.

"This is my first time at the club as well. It's quite lovely."

"I'm glad you're enjoying it, Miss…"

"Temple," I reminded him.

"Right, right," Dick said. I smiled broadly at him as I continued to stroke Liam's cock with agonizingly slow strokes.

Liam panted loudly in my ear, his heart thudding like a runaway freight train against my back. I knew instinctively he was close to coming. I squeezed his cock in silent warning as Dick smiled again at us.

"Well, I'll leave you two alone. Just let me know if I can get you anything."

When he was gone, I turned my head until my mouth was at Liam's ear. "Don't you dare come, Liam."

"Mae, please," he moaned. My stomach clenched with delicious desire at the desperation in his voice.

"Don't." I squeezed his dick again, and he made a strangled noise of need.

I stroked his cock, ignoring the growing queasiness in my stomach. I rarely drank, and the alcohol sloshing around in my belly was starting to get to me.

"Oh God, Mae. I'm so close, please," he groaned when I circled the head of his cock with my thumb.

The room suddenly seemed too warm, and I took in a

large gulp of air. It did nothing to help my nausea, and I flinched at a sudden burst of loud laughter. I recognized that laughter as Allie's laughter. I realized with horror that she was walking toward us, her hand firmly wrapped around the blonde's bicep.

I didn't want her to see me sitting on my boss's lap. Why, I wasn't sure, but my drunk haze of desire lifted, and I was suddenly horrified by my behaviour. I would be fired for sure after tonight.

I yanked my hand from Liam's pants and stood as Allie and her new date weaved closer.

"Mae?" Liam stared at me with concern, and I smiled feebly.

"I'm sorry. I'm not feeling very well. Please excuse me."

I brushed by Allie with my hand over my mouth and staggered down the stairs. The need to vomit was powerful now. I barely made it to the bathroom before the alcohol came up. Thanking God there was an empty stall, I stumbled into it and knelt before the toilet, throwing up wretchedly.

After a few minutes, my stomach was empty, and I straightened, wiping my hand across my mouth. I flushed the toilet and weaved out of the stall, staring with dismay at my reflection in the bathroom mirror. My face was pale, but my cheeks were flushed bright red, and sweat dotted my forehead. Despite throwing up, I was still extremely nauseous, and my head was beginning to throb.

What had I done? I washed my hands and rinsed my mouth before staggering to the door. I had to get out of here. I had to go home before Mr. Knight found me. I pushed open the door and walked straight into my boss.

He held my shoe in one hand and had a worried look. "Mae? Are you okay?"

"Just fine," I groaned. I put a hand on my stomach and

took another deep breath. "I'm sorry. I've had too much to drink, and I need to go home. I'm not feeling very well."

"Here, let me help you." He reached for my arm, and I yanked it out of his grip before stumbling back and leaning against the wall.

"I'm fine." My legs shook, and I wanted to sink to the floor and curl into a ball. Maybe that would help the nausea. The music in the club was suddenly too loud, every beat reverberating through my aching skull.

He frowned. "You're not fine. You're about to pass out."

"I'm not. I'm just tired," I whispered.

"No, you're not."

The room was starting to spin. I closed my eyes, not protesting when Liam picked me up. I let my head fall on his broad shoulder and kept my eyes closed as he carried me through the club.

He carried me outside, and I could have wept with joy at the quietness and the cool, fresh air on my face. I breathed deeply as Liam carried me across the parking lot. He set me on my feet, and I heard the sound of a car door opening before he slid me into the leather seat.

"Wait," I protested. "Are you drunk?"

He snorted softly. "No. I've had two drinks, Mae."

"Don't put me in your car," I warned. "I might throw up again."

"It's fine," he said. "Just let me know if you feel sick, and I'll pull the car over."

The last thing I remembered before passing out was Liam's hands clicking the seatbelt around me.

CHAPTER 7

I woke with a bad taste in my mouth and a throbbing headache. I sat up with a soft groan and squinted blearily at my surroundings. The bright sunlight flooding through the window was hell on my headache. The bedroom was decorated in greys and blues, and I was pretty sure the large artwork on the wall to my left was worth more than an entire year of my salary. The room was dominated by the king-size bed I was currently lying in, and there was a sitting area with two wing chairs in front of a gas fireplace.

I turned my head, groaning at the pain, and stared at the alarm clock. It was just after nine, and I had a bad feeling in the pit of my stomach. I was almost certain I was in Liam Knight's bedroom. A glass of water and a bottle of Advil sat on the nightstand, and I shook out four of them, gulping them down with the glass of water before collapsing on the bed again. I threw my arm over my eyes to block out the relentless light and tried to collect my thoughts.

I had drunk way too much last night. I couldn't even remember the last time I was that drunk. I was never going out with Allie and Russ again. They were too much of a bad influence on me. I would never have done what I –

I sat up straight in the bed and stared out the window at the bright blue lake beyond it.

"Fuck me," I whispered as the night came flooding back to me. The things I said and did to my goddamn boss! What the hell was I thinking?

I wasn't thinking. That was the problem. I had gotten drunk and made a fool of myself in front of my boss. Or, more accurately, on my boss. I stared down at myself and breathed a sigh of relief. Although I was shoeless, I was at least still wearing my dress.

I threw back the covers and staggered to the door, praying it was a bathroom. It was, quite frankly, a spectacular bathroom. A shower with multiple shower heads loomed to my left, and the most enormous bathtub I had ever seen was at the room's far end. The sky light above it let in direct beams of warm sunlight. I stumbled to the double-sink vanity and stared at myself in the mirror.

Sweet Jesus. My hair was a tangled mess around my face, and my eye makeup had smudged and smeared. I looked like a chubby raccoon. A considerable pillow crease crossed my left cheek, and the flecks of white dotted across my chin clearly indicated I was drooling in my sleep.

"Sexy," I muttered. I hung my head and rubbed my aching forehead. A toothbrush, still in its plastic wrapping, sat on the counter. I opened it and quickly brushed my teeth.

I shut the bathroom door and looked longingly at the tub before starting the shower. I stripped and climbed into the shower, dipping my head directly under the hot water. It felt amazing, and I let it bead down my naked body for nearly ten minutes before I grabbed the soap.

Half an hour later, squeaky clean and wrapped in the

bathrobe I found hanging on the back of the bathroom door, I went searching for my boss. I peeked into the open door next to Liam's bedroom and discovered a guest room. The bed was rumpled with the covers thrown back, and I guessed he had slept there last night.

I wandered down the hallway, trailing my hand along the railing until I reached the staircase. I leaned over the railing and peered down. The house had an open concept, and from my vantage point, I could see into the living room and the large kitchen. The walls were made of logs, and there were so many windows a warm, bright glow lit the entire house. The large floor-to-ceiling windows in the living room revealed Liam's car parked on a long, winding driveway. Beyond the driveway was nothing but trees.

I was in the mother of all log cabins. Rich, dark colours dominated the decor without a hint of a woman's touch. Still, it had a decidedly cozy feel to it. I imagined it would be amazing in the winter to curl up on the couch in front of the fireplace with a glass of wine and a good book. I glanced at the gleaming, modern kitchen before continuing down the hallway.

A third door revealed another smaller bathroom with a shower only, and I continued to the last door. It was slightly ajar, and I could hear soft grunts from within the room. I cocked my head, listening intently. What was he doing in there?

I pushed the door open. Wearing just a pair of shorts, Liam was rhythmically lifting a bar full of weights over his head. His eyes were closed, and I stared unabashedly at his half-naked body. My suspicions about his body were one hundred percent correct. The man looked like he was carved out of stone. The muscles in his arms bulged as he lifted the weights over his head. His chest rippled, and I studied his six-pack with more than a little passing interest. He had a light dusting of hair covering his upper body, and I licked my lips as I stared at his treasure trail.

I took a moment to cool my lust and collect my thoughts and then cleared my throat loudly. His eyes popped open, and the bar of weights paused mid-thrust.

"Hi." I smiled half-heartedly.

"Good morning, Ms. Temple. How are you feeling?" He dropped the weights and grabbed a towel hanging off a rack of hand weights. He wiped the sweat from his face and chest as I looked away nervously.

"Um, fine. I have a headache."

"Yes, I imagine you do," he said.

"Okay, well, I should get going. I just wanted to say thank you for, um, for everything."

He picked up a smaller weight and lifted it, curling his right arm up and down. "I'll give you a ride home."

"Oh no, that's fine. I can take a cab."

He continued to lift the weight. "I live a lengthy distance from the city, Ms. Temple. Do you have enough money for a cab?"

I flushed. "How far exactly?"

"Far enough," he said. "Just let me finish my workout, and then I'll drive you home. Make yourself comfortable downstairs."

I nodded and left the room. Feeling sick to my stomach and my head throbbing, I walked downstairs and sat on the couch. Last night, the alcohol had filled me with confidence and a sexiness that I didn't feel now. I closed my eyes and rubbed my forehead. I needed to figure out what I was going to do after Mr. Knight drove me home and then fired my ass. I curled up on the couch and buried my face in one of the pillows. I was a complete moron.

When I woke up the second time, I was still lying on the couch and covered by a thick quilt. I sat up and rubbed my face. My headache had disappeared, and I thought my stomach might not be as queasy.

"Feeling better?"

I screamed breathlessly and nearly fell off the couch. Liam, wearing a tight blue t-shirt and worn jeans, sat at a small desk in the corner of the room. A laptop sat on it, and I could see a few files from the office spread over the top of the mahogany desk.

"Uh, yes. I'm sorry," I mumbled, pushing the quilt down my lap.

"Sorry for what?"

"Falling asleep. I – what time is it?"

"Just after twelve. I was about to make some lunch." He swiveled in his chair and studied me carefully. "Do you remember what happened last night, Ms. Temple?"

I hesitated and then shook my head. "No, not really."

I hated lying and wasn't very good at it, but if it came down to keeping my job or being fired, I was determined to make an Oscar-worthy performance.

I wondered if I was imagining the relief that crossed his face. "You did have quite a bit to drink."

"Yeah, I don't normally drink that much," I said.

"What do you remember?"

"Um…" My face flushed as I thought quickly. "I remember doing shots at the bar with Russ. I remember talking to you and Dick in the VIP room. After that, it's pretty much a blur."

I wondered if he could tell I was lying through my teeth. I took a deep breath and smiled widely at him. "I hope I didn't do anything too embarrassing."

"You didn't. We talked, and then you excused yourself to

the bathroom to throw up. You nearly passed out in the bar, and I brought you back here and put you to bed."

He hesitated. "I would have taken you back to your place, but it was quite late and considering your neighbourhood, I didn't want to risk my car being stolen."

"It's not that bad of a neighbourhood," I protested weakly.

"Yes, so you keep saying."

"You, uh, have a lovely home, Mr. Knight."

He sighed irritably. "Liam. How many times must I tell you to call me Liam?"

"Sorry." I gave him another wide, nervous smile. "It was nice of you to let me use your room. You should have dumped me on the couch or the guest room."

He shrugged. "My bed is more comfortable, and I thought having you near a bathroom might be a good idea. In case you needed to vomit again."

"Yeah." I tugged self-consciously at the collar of the bathrobe. "I had a shower and borrowed your bathrobe. I hope you don't mind. I'll take it with me and have it cleaned."

He shrugged. "There's no need for that. Are you hungry?"

"Not really. I am thirsty, though. Could I trouble you for a glass of water?"

"Of course." He stood, and I followed him into the kitchen, trying not to drool at the sight of his ass in those tight jeans. He indicated for me to sit on a bar stool, and I climbed up on it, cursing my short legs and trying to keep the robe closed as I sat on the padded seat.

I leaned against the island as he poured me a glass of water. I took it with a grateful smile and drank it in four giant gulps. He refilled the glass and set it down in front of me.

I studied the kitchen as he took eggs and vegetables from the fridge. It was very modern looking, with stainless steel appliances and granite countertops. The cupboards were smooth, dark grey, and the floor tile was gleaming white.

"Your home is lovely," I said tentatively. "I had no idea you lived in a log cabin in the middle of nowhere. I assumed you lived in, I don't know, a penthouse downtown."

He laughed. "Up until a few years ago, I did have a penthouse downtown. I hated it. I used to rent a cabin a few miles from here, and when this plot of land came up for sale, I bought it. I built the house as close to the lake as possible, and I've been here ever since."

"It's very peaceful," I said.

"It is," he agreed. "And private. I value my privacy."

That didn't surprise me. He was a bit of a mini-celebrity in our city, and the long hours he spent at the office and the numerous events he went to undoubtedly left him very little time to himself.

"Do you like omelettes?"

"Yes, but you don't have to cook for me," I said.

"I don't mind."

We sat silently as he cooked, adding cheese and vegetables to the eggs before expertly flipping the omelettes. He slid them onto two plates, grabbed some silverware, and indicated for me to follow him.

I hopped off the barstool and followed him through the living room to a set of French doors I hadn't noticed earlier.

"Oh my God," I breathed as I opened the doors.

"Do you like it?" He stepped onto the patio and set our plates on the glass table.

"It's so beautiful," I said.

"It is a nice view," he agreed.

I sank into the luxuriously soft patio chair. It was more comfortable than the furniture in my living room, and I stared with delight at the lake. Liam had left just enough room for a patio. After that, it was nothing but sandy beach. The beach was only about twenty feet wide, and I listened to the soft lapping of the lake before us. I breathed deeply of the clean air as Liam handed me my knife and fork.

I dug into the omelette as Liam did the same. It tasted delicious, and I was suddenly ravenously hungry. I ate it quickly and then sat back with a small sigh, curling my legs underneath me.

"Thank you. That was delicious." I smiled at him.

"You're welcome."

We sat in silence for a few minutes. "So, do you ever worry about flooding?"

He laughed. "Only you would wonder about that, Mae."

"What? You're pretty close to the water. If we get a lot of rain and the lake rises enough – you'll be knee-deep in lake water."

He shrugged. "I suppose it could happen. If it does, I'll tear it down and rebuild. Perhaps a little further back, though."

I shook my head, and he frowned at me.

"What?"

"Nothing."

"Tell me," he insisted.

I shrugged. "I find it amusing that you would just tear it down and rebuild. You don't even think about the cost."

"No, I don't," he agreed.

He disappeared into the house and returned with coffee for us five minutes later. "Two sugars, one cream, right?"

"That's right. Thank you." I sipped at the coffee. It tasted a hell of a lot better than the swill at work, and I sighed happily. "This coffee is amazing."

"It should be. I pay enough for it," Liam said.

I took another sip of coffee as he stared at me.

"How did you become a PA?"

I shrugged. "I was looking for a job, saw the ad online, and applied. Ida hired me, and the rest is history."

"No, I meant, why did you become a PA?"

"Why not?" I took another sip of the hot coffee. I was starting to feel uncomfortable. I hated talking about my life. It hadn't exactly turned out as I had planned, and frankly, I was embarrassed by the debt, my less-than-impressive job, and my shit apartment. If Neil hadn't broken up with me, I'd probably live in a nicer place, and my student loans would be paid off. Of course, I had long decided I was better off without that loser. No matter how broke I was.

He sighed impatiently. "Did you always want to be a PA?"

I laughed. "No, definitely not."

"What did you want to do?"

"I wanted to be a nurse."

"So why didn't you go into nursing?"

"I'd rather not talk about it."

"Why not?" he said.

"Because it's embarrassing."

When he stared at me expectantly, I curled deeper into the chair and tugged at the bathrobe collar. "I went to nursing school. My parents had very little money, so I took out student loans. I went through the schooling, graduated, and got lucky with finding a job right away. I wasn't working at a hospital but a senior's home."

I stared moodily at the lake. "The first six months were fine. I liked the residents of the home, and I enjoyed my job - even the gross parts. And let me tell you – there were some really gross parts."

"I can imagine," he said dryly. "Go on."

"There was a resident there. His name was Frank, and he was such a sweet old man. He didn't have any family, at least, I never saw anyone visiting him, but it didn't seem to bother him much. I really liked him."

I smiled. "He was such a flirt. I used to tell him I'd date him if he were only a few years younger, and it would make him giggle like a girl. Anyway, I was working the night shift. It was so damn cold that night. My car wouldn't start, and I almost didn't make my shift. They were ready to call in a replacement when I finally arrived. It was a quiet night, and I was doing my rounds when there was a code blue. It was coming from Frank's room. I ran down there, and Marcy, the other nurse that night, was already in his room."

I shivered a little. "Frank was thrashing on the bed. He was having a seizure. We called for the doctor even though Frank was already coming out of it. He…"

I swallowed and heard the dry click of my throat. "He seemed okay at first. He smiled at me, told me I was so pretty, and he loved me. I laughed and called him a flirt. He laughed, and then he just – just grabbed at my arm, his entire body arching off the bed, and then he was dead. Just like that. He'd had a massive stroke and died instantly."

"I'm sorry," Liam said quietly.

I blinked back the tears. "I couldn't go back after that. All that money spent, all the schooling, and one old man's death finished me. Isn't that the most ridiculous thing you've ever heard?"

"No."

"I tried a few times to go back to work. I even quit that job and tried working in a doctor's office, but I couldn't handle that either. I had this stupid, irrational fear that the patients would die on me."

I sighed heavily. "Like I said - ridiculous."

"It isn't."

"I worked at a coffee shop for a while and loved it, but Neil -"

"Neil?"

"My ex-fiancé."

He blinked at me in surprise but motioned for me to go on.

"Neil thought I should do something more with my life, and he was tired of shouldering the financial burden of my student loans. So, I applied for the job at Knight and Associates, and two days after I started, Neil called off our engagement."

"You're kidding me."

"No," I said. "Neil said I was dragging him down. He was making a name for himself as a lawyer, and I didn't fit his idea of a perfect wife."

"Asshole," he grunted.

I shrugged. "I don't blame him. I'd gained some weight, drowning in debt, and working as a secretary. I was different from when we first started dating, and besides, shame on me for not realizing how superficial he was."

"That explains all the random bursts of crying," he said.

I laughed. "Yeah, I was a wreck when I started working for you. Sorry about that. Thanks for not firing me."

"You're welcome. You're much different than I thought you were."

"How so?" I asked.

"I thought you were timid and a bit of a crybaby," he said.

"You should talk to my mother. She would love to hear me referred to as timid."

He gave me a wry smile. "I realized my mistake the first day you started as my PA. You do have a certain..."

"Strong but loveable personality?" I suggested.

"I was going to say 'bossiness'."

I laughed, and we sat in silence for a few minutes before I shifted awkwardly in my seat. "I probably should get going. It looks like you have quite a bit of work to do."

He nodded. "I do. If you want to grab your things, I'll give you a ride home."

I bit back my disappointment. What was I expecting him to say? No, Mae, stay the day with me. You can take a swim in my giant tub while I work, and then I'll cook you dinner and afterward take you to my bed so you can fuck the bejesus out of me.

I snorted softly, and Liam raised his eyebrows at me.

"Nothing." I stood and gathered up my plate and silverware. "I'll be ready to go in ten."

CHAPTER 8

"Hello, Mae."

I looked up from my computer, a large smile crossing my face. "Hey, Russ! How are you?"

"I'm okay," he said.

Russ' usually tanned face was pale, and he looked sick to his stomach. I hadn't seen him since our evening at Night Play last week and wondered if he was angry with me.

"Russ? What's wrong?"

He shook his head. "Nothing. I'm here to pick up Mr. Knight for his business dinner tonight, but he's not in his office."

I stood and walked toward him. "He's not back from his meeting with Ida yet. He shouldn't be long."

"Okay, thanks."

He turned to go, and I reached out and snagged his arm. "Russ, please tell me what's wrong."

He sighed, and I could hear the tears in his voice. "My cousin died yesterday. He was only twenty-nine."

"Oh, honey," I whispered. "I'm so sorry."

I turned him around and cupped his pale face. "I'm really sorry."

He closed his eyes, and I stood on my tiptoes and put my arms around him. He tucked his face into my neck, and I rubbed his back soothingly. "I'm so sorry for your loss, honey."

We stood in my office, and I continued to hug him tightly. After a few minutes, he stepped back and sighed deeply. I wiped the tears from his face with the heel of my hand.

"Where's Steve, honey?"

"He's at home. He told me not to go to work tonight, but I didn't want to sit there and think about it, you know?"

"I do." I wiped away another stray tear with my thumb.

"The funeral is tomorrow. I'm dreading going. My entire family will be there, and they disapprove of my lifestyle choice. They're always rude to Steve, and he's so good about putting up with it, but I told him he didn't have to go with me. My family will just be a bunch of little bitches to him. Steve says he doesn't care, but it makes it worse for me, you know?"

"Yes," I said sympathetically.

"So now I have to go to the funeral alone. My mom will use the opportunity to lecture me about not finding a nice, sweet girl and giving her grandchildren. My grandmother will try to pray the gay out of me, and they won't even care that my cousin is lying there dead."

He drew another deep, hitching breath, and I squeezed his arms. "Honey, I'll go to the funeral with you if you want."

"Really?"

"Of course I will. We're friends, aren't we? That's what friends do."

"I – are you sure, Mae? It's a lot to ask."

"I'm positive," I said. "Let me just check with Liam that I can take the afternoon off, and I'll text you tonight, okay?"

"Thanks, Mae." He hugged me tightly, lifting me off my feet for a minute before setting me down gently.

"You're welcome," I said.

"I can't tell you how much I appreciate this." He bent and kissed me quickly on the mouth.

"Am I interrupting something?"

We both turned at the sound of Liam's voice, and I watched Russ wither under the fury of Liam's gaze.

I stepped protectively in front of Russ. "No."

Liam stared at us like an angry bull, and I squeezed Russ' hand before smiling at him. "I'll text you tonight, okay?"

He nodded and gave Liam a faint smile. "I'll wait in the car for you, Mr. Knight."

"Yes, please do," Liam said icily without looking at him.

Russ left, and Liam and I stared silently at each other for a few minutes before Liam said, "Do you have the file ready for my business meeting, Ms. Temple? Or were you too busy kissing my driver to finish it?"

"It's on your desk," I said.

"Excellent. Have a pleasant evening." He turned to leave.

"Mr. Knight?"

"Yes, Ms. Temple?" He refused to turn around.

"I know this is short notice, but could I have tomorrow afternoon off?"

He stiffened. "For what reason?"

"Russ's cousin died. I want to go to the funeral with him."

He looked over his shoulder, his face still angry. "That's fine."

I sighed as he stalked out of my office. This last week had been almost pleasant. My lie about forgetting what had happened at the bar had prevented me from being fired, and Liam had been busy and out of the office for most of the week. I had a feeling that the pleasantness was over.

* * *

"Ms. Temple!" Liam's angry bark echoed through his office. I squared my shoulders before leaving my office.

"Yes, Mr. Knight?"

"Where the hell is the Wenton file? Jesus Christ, the deposition is next week, and the goddamn file has gone missing!"

"It hasn't gone missing," I said calmly. I crossed the room, pulled open the filing cabinet behind his desk and plucked the file out. I placed it on the desk and crossed my arms over my chest.

"Anything else?"

"No," he snapped. He ran his hand through his hair and started flipping through the file. I eyed him carefully. He had a charity event this evening and had already changed into his tux. He looked sinful in it. It wasn't fair that one man could look so good in everything. Suits, jeans and a t-shirt, a tuxedo – it didn't matter. The man really *was* a walking sex god.

I snorted to myself as he studied the file on his desk. It didn't matter how good looking he was, how tasty his lips were, or how thick his cock had felt in my hand, the guy had been a complete and utter asshole to me since the day he saw Russ kissing me.

Frankly, I was surprised that he hadn't ordered Ida to move me out of the pool and give him another PA. I'd considered telling him that Russ was gay in hopes it might change his attitude, but it wasn't my information to share. Besides, it's not like Liam and I had a relationship. He hadn't brought up what had happened in the club, so he obviously wanted to forget it happened, too. So, what the hell was his problem with Russ kissing me?

I was still standing in his office and turned to head back to my office. Allie's voice stopped me in my tracks.

"Hi, Mae."

She stood in the doorway of Liam's office, looking stunning in a strapless red gown. Her hair and make-up were impeccable, as usual, and she smiled cheerfully at me.

I cleared my throat, shooting Liam a nervous look. "Hi, Allie. Did we – did we have plans this evening, and I forgot?"

She giggled. "No, silly. I'm Liam's date tonight."

My mouth dropped open, and I turned to stare at Liam. He was putting the Wenton file back in the drawer. He locked it and dropped the key into the top drawer of his desk before smiling at Allie.

"Good evening, Allie."

"Hello, Liam." Allie crossed the room and rested her hand on Liam's arm. "You're looking very handsome tonight."

He smiled at her, and I think I saw Allie's thighs loosen. I couldn't blame her.

"You're looking lovely as well," Liam said.

"Thank you."

I bit my lip as jealousy shot through me. I pasted a smile onto my face just as Liam turned toward me. "Make sure you finish the Harrison file before you leave, Ms. Temple."

"Of course, Mr. Knight. Have a nice evening."

"Oh, we will." Allie winked at me before sliding her hand into the crook of Liam's arm. As he led her toward the door, she turned her head and gave me a wide-eyed look of pure delight.

I forced myself to smile and give her the thumbs up as they disappeared into the hallway.

* * *

"What's wrong, Mae?" Russ asked as I sipped my glass of wine.

We were sitting in their small backyard, and I shook my head. "Nothing."

Steve sat beside me on the swing and started it rocking. "You're lying. Tell us what's wrong."

I sighed and tipped my head back to stare at the stars. "I'm sorry. You guys were kind enough to invite me over on the one weekend Steve gets off a month, and I'm being a total downer."

"We don't mind," Steve said before patting my knee. "Just tell us what's wrong."

"Mr. Knight's been a real dick at work lately, and then tonight he took Allie to the charity event, and I'm green with jealousy. Which is incredibly stupid because what the hell do I care if Allie is banging my boss?"

Russ gave Steve an 'I told you so' look. "It's because you like him, Mae."

"No, I don't," I said grumpily.

"Yes, you do, and he likes you too."

"No, he definitely does not." I glared at him. "Did you forget the part where I mentioned he's been a complete dick all week?"

Russ shrugged. "He's being a dick because he saw me kissing you in your office."

"Whoa, whoa, whoa." Steve held up his hand. "What's this about kissing?"

Russ grinned at him. "It was completely innocent, baby. You know you're the only one for me."

I took another sip of wine as Russ said, "Just tell him I'm gay, for Christ's sake, Mae. I guarantee you he'll stop being a dick once you do."

"Your sexual preference is none of his business, Russ," I said. "Besides, it doesn't matter now. Allie is gorgeous, funny, and kind. No man can resist her. I guarantee she'll be flat on her back in Mr. Knight's king-sized bed by the night's end with her legs up in the air."

Russ snorted. "I doubt it. I've been Mr. Knight's driver for two years, and I can count on one hand the number of times he hasn't just dropped one of his dates off at her door at the end of the night. And he's never once taken a woman to his house."

I frowned. "You're joking, right?"

"I'm not," Russ said solemnly before sipping his water.

"Forget about that," Steve said suddenly. "I want to know how you know that your hot boss has a king-sized bed."

I turned red as Russ grinned delightedly at me. "Hell yeah. How do you know that, Mae?"

"Uh..." My cheeks flushed even brighter as Steve squeezed my leg.

"Spill your guts, honey."

"That night at the club when I drank too much - which I'm blaming entirely on the two of you, by the way - Mr. Knight drove me to his house after I passed out."

"Holy shit! He did not!" Russ said.

"He did. In the morning, he made me an omelette," I added.

Russ laughed. "I told you, Mae."

"It doesn't mean anything," I protested. "Liam was worried about his car being stolen if he drove it to my place."

Russ laughed again. "Whatever, girl. That man has it bad for you. We all saw how he carried you out of the club like a white knight."

He snorted and glanced at Steve. "See what I did there, baby?"

"I saw." Steve tipped his beer to him.

"How come you've never carried me out of the club all romantic-like? I've been drunk plenty of times," Russ pointed out.

Steve rolled his eyes. "You weigh 210 pounds."

"Yeah, 210 pounds of pure muscle." Russ lifted his shirt and rubbed his admittedly impressive six-pack.

I snickered as Russ's cell phone rang. He glanced at the number and grinned. "Speak of the devil."

"Hello, sir." He paused. "Yes, sir. I'm on my way."

He winked at me and then said, "Mr. Knight, I wanted to ask you if I could have the weekend of the twenty-third off. My boyfriend Steve has the entire weekend off for a change, and we were thinking of getting out of the city."

I slapped my forehead as Russ grinned like a lunatic at me. "Yes, sir, that's right. My boyfriend - Steve."

Steve snorted laughter and took a drink of beer as Russ grinned again. "I can? Thank you, sir. I appreciate that. See you soon."

He ended the call, and I threw the pillow from the swing at him. "Russ! What the hell?"

"Shall we make a bet, Mae? I'll bet you a dinner at that swanky restaurant, Darnell's, that our Mr. Knight is much more pleasant to you this week."

I shook my head. "Nope."

"Chicken," Russ said.

"No, I'm not. Knowing my luck, Mr. Knight will get lucky with Allie tonight and be a pleasant human at work tomorrow. I can't afford to buy you dinner at Darnell's."

Russ laughed and stood, holding his hand out to me. "Come on, Mae. I'll drop you off at home before I pick up Mr. Knight."

CHAPTER 9

"Hello, Mae. I need a favour," Liam said.

"What kind of favour?" I asked.

It was Friday, just before lunch, and I was surprised Liam had called. He was at meetings all afternoon, and I knew he was going directly to another charity event after that.

I closed the document I was working on and swiveled in my chair to stare out the window, nervously pulling at the phone cord. It was a damn good job that I hadn't made a bet with Russ. I would have been taking him out for dinner at Darnell's tonight if I had. Liam was perfectly pleasant Monday morning and even apologized for his behaviour the week before.

He had said something about not sleeping well and having a large caseload before giving me a faint smile and returning to his office. I'd quickly checked my cell phone, half-expecting that Russ had texted me to ask if Liam was nicer to me this morning. There was nothing, and I'd re-read the text he sent me late Friday night.

Just dropped Allie off at home. Your white knight

walked her to the door, gave her a polite peck on the cheek and is headed back to the car alone. Told u so.

"You know I have the charity event tonight." Liam's voice was warm and silky smooth.

"Yes," I said, wondering where he was going with this.

"My date has cancelled for the event. I know its short notice, but could you step in for her?"

"I – what?"

He sighed audibly. "I need a date for tonight. Could you help me out? I'll pay you overtime for your trouble."

The extra money would come in handy. Still, I hesitated and said, "Couldn't you just go alone?"

"No, I can't." He didn't bother explaining why. "I won't lie – it'll be boring, and the people there are dull, but the food's excellent, and the night shouldn't go that late."

"Mr. Knight, I don't think I should go. It doesn't seem appropriate."

"It's not an actual date, Ms. Temple. There's nothing inappropriate about it," he said dryly.

I flushed. "Why don't you call Allie? I'm sure she can go with you on short notice."

He sighed. "I know Allie's your friend, so please don't take offense to this, but she talks way too much."

I snickered a little. I couldn't help it. "Yeah, I know."

"Can you help me out or not?" he said impatiently.

"Um, yeah, I guess. It's not a date, though, right?"

"That's what I said. Russ is on his way to pick you up."

"What? Why?"

"Because the event is quite formal and based on the state of your office wardrobe, I'm quite sure you don't have anything formal enough for tonight. He'll take you shopping."

Whatever I bought would be way out of my budget.

Maybe I could leave the tags on and return it the following day.

"Ms. Temple?"

"Yes?"

"Russ will be there in about twenty minutes."

"Okay. I'll meet him downstairs."

"Good. And thank you. I appreciate this."

He ended the call, and I rubbed my forehead. What the hell was I doing?

"RUSS, WHERE ARE WE?" I STARED UP AT THE BUILDING IN confusion. 'Sunlight Day Spa' was written across it in bold font, and I frowned as Russ took my arm and led me into the building.

"We're getting you ready for your date tonight, Cinderella."

"It's not a date!" I said. "You're supposed to be taking me dress shopping."

"I know, and I will. But first – you need to be beautified."

"I can't afford this," I muttered as he dragged me toward the pretty redhead at reception.

"It's all on Mr. Knight," Russ said cheerfully.

"What? What do you mean?"

"Mr. Knight told me to charge it all to his card."

"He told you to take me to a spa?" I blinked at him.

He shook his head. "Nope, that was strictly my idea. Hey, Judy!"

"Hi, Russ!" The redhead gave him a warm smile. "How's Steve?"

"He's great. Listen, I have a bit of an emergency." He pulled me in front of him. "This little lady here has a date with the most powerful lawyer in the city tonight. I need you to work your magic."

Judy walked around the desk and stared down at me. I suddenly felt like a bug pinned to a board as she reached out and gripped my chin. She lifted my face and cocked her head.

"She's got potential. We'll need to do something about those eyebrows, and the mustache has to go."

I felt the top of my upper lip. "Mustache?"

She grinned. "Don't worry, honey. It happens to us all."

She turned to Russ. "How long have I got?"

Russ glanced at his watch. "I'd say about three hours."

She sighed deeply. "It'll be close." She ripped the elastic out of my hair, and I winced as it pulled more than a few strands of my dark hair with it.

"Ooh, this is good. I can do something with this." She smiled delightedly as she touched my thick hair.

She stepped back and clapped her hands. Two women appeared beside her. "Sandra, Alice – time to work our magic."

I gave Russ a desperate look as I was dragged into the depths of the salon.

* * *

"AHHH! SWEET BABY JESUS!" I SCREAMED AGAIN AS SANDRA, the mistress of torture, ripped another swatch of leg hair off my upper thigh.

Russ winced as my hand tightened onto his. "Christ, Mae. Ease up a bit."

"Shut up!" I snarled at him. "You're not the one having all of your hair ripped from your body, strip by strip.

Sandra made a clucking noise under her breath. "It's not that bad, dear."

I glared at her. "Not that bad? I've had nearly every hair

on my body ripped out. How about you hop on the table, and I'll start ripping out your body hair!"

She laughed. "Try going to esthetician school and having newbies waxing you. Then you'll know my pain."

She slathered on another layer of wax. "One last strip. Ready?"

"Yes," I gritted out.

I was lying on my back on a table in one of the spa rooms. I had spent the last two hours plucked, waxed, pedicured and manicured. I had to admit the facial was lovely, and my feet and hands felt like heaven after the paraffin treatments, but the waxing was pure torture. I rubbed my finger along my now hairless upper lip.

"How attractive will I be when my face is bright red from having all the hair ripped off?" I grumbled to Russ.

He laughed. "It's called make-up, Mae."

I winced as Sandra ripped the fabric strip off my leg. "Christ, that hurts!"

"It's about to get a lot worse, sweetie," Sandra said.

"What do you mean? You said it was the last strip."

"The last strip on your leg. There's still the girlie bits to do."

"Oh, hell no!" I snapped. "You are not going anywhere near my hooch with that hot wax!"

Before Sandra could reply, Judy entered the room. "How are we doing in here?"

"Just fine," Russ said. "Mae's about to get her first Brazilian."

"Oh no, I am most certainly not!" I said hotly.

"Come on, Mae. Just try it once. You'll love it and never go back. Trust me," Russ coaxed.

"How the hell would you know?" I glared at him.

Judy laughed. "It's true, honey."

97

She lifted the bottom of my bathrobe and stared at my naked crotch. "Have you ever waxed here before, Mae?"

"No," I said, blushing furiously as I pushed down the bathrobe.

"I don't think we should go completely bare, Sandra. Let's leave a landing strip for her lover," Judy said.

"He is not my lover!" I gritted out.

Russ laughed. "He will be after tonight."

"Shut up, Russ!"

"Spread your legs, please, Mae." Sandra was pushing on my thighs. I sighed and spread my legs as she lifted the bathrobe.

"Stop looking, Russ!" I snapped.

"Oh, please. Seen one, you've seen them all. Besides, you're the one who dragged me in here to hold your hand," Russ said airily.

"Exactly how many vaginas have you seen?" I asked.

He shrugged. "I've seen enough." He glanced again at my crotch. "I've never seen one that hairy, though. You're rocking a serious seventies vibe, Mae."

"Not for long," Sandra announced.

I smacked him on the chest. "I am going to kill you."

He laughed again. "Speaking of underwear..."

"We aren't speaking about underwear!" I grabbed his hand again as Sandra climbed onto the table between my legs and spread warm wax on my crotch.

He pointed to my bra and underwear piled neatly on the chair. "You need to get some new underwear. That looks like something my grandma would wear."

"It keeps everything tucked in," I informed him as Sandra smoothed the fabric strip over my flesh.

"Yeah, well, they're granny panties, and I'm not letting you wear them on your date tonight."

"Ooh, you should take her over to Esteem's. They've got the best lingerie in the city," Judy said.

"I don't need new underwear! My underwear is just – AAAHHH!" I shrieked again as Sandra ripped away the strip.

"Oh my God!" I grabbed Russ by the shirt and dragged him down to my face. "She took skin with that one, Russ! I swear to God!"

"She didn't take skin, Mae. Stop overreacting."

"Go and look! I guarantee you I'm bleeding!" I said.

When he didn't move, I shook him lightly. "What are you waiting for?"

"You told me not to look," he said.

"Now I'm telling you to look!" I pleaded hysterically. "Please, Russ. I think I need to go to the hospital."

He pulled away from my grip and studied my crotch. "Nope, everything's normal."

"You're lying!" I moaned as Sandra grinned and slathered more wax onto my throbbing crotch.

"I'm not. It looks like a perfectly normal and disturbingly hairy vagina," Russ said.

He took my hand again as Sandra popped up from between my thighs and glanced at Judy.

"We're gonna need more wax."

"Okay, dollface. Open your eyes," Alice said.

I took a deep breath and opened my eyes. My mouth dropped open as I stared at the woman in the mirror. The sleek-haired, smooth-skinned goddess couldn't possibly be me.

"Wow." Russ whistled.

I turned my head. The woman in the mirror turned her

head. I widened my eyes. The woman in the mirror widened her eyes.

"Now remember," Alice said as she brushed another coat of lip gloss across my full lips, "try not to touch your eyelashes too much. They're only temporary, and the more you touch them, the quicker they'll fall out."

I leaned forward and stared at the long, sweeping lashes. "I can't believe it," I said.

The false eyelashes and eye makeup Alice had carefully applied made my dark eyes look impossibly large. "Alice, I – I..."

I trailed off and stared at the plump, grey-haired woman. She grinned delightedly. "I know right? I'm so awesome at what I do."

"You really are," I breathed as Judy stepped forward and sprayed something sweet smelling on my hair.

She had given my hair a quick trim, cutting off the split ends, before she blow-dried and straightened it. I couldn't get over how shiny and sleek it looked. I continued to stare at myself as Russ handed over a credit card to Judy.

She quickly ran it through, and Russ held his hand out to me. "Let's go, Mae. We still need to get you a dress, and the dinner starts in less than two hours."

I slipped out of the chair and then hugged the three women impulsively. "Thank you so much, ladies. I appreciate everything you've done. And Sandra, I'm sorry I called you a merciless spawn of Satan."

Sandra grinned. "Come back and see me anytime, dear."

CHAPTER 10

"You okay, Mae?" Russ stared at me in the rear-view window.

"What was that? I can't hear you." I cupped my ear, and he rolled his eyes.

"The limo isn't that big."

"I still don't understand why we had to arrive in a limo anyway."

Russ shrugged. "Mr. Knight said he wanted a limo tonight. I'm not going to argue."

"Seriously, speak up, man. You're like eighty feet away from me," I shouted.

He laughed. "Yeah, yeah. Listen – are you okay? You seem quiet."

"My hoochie hurts."

"Ask Mr. Knight to kiss it better."

"Shut up, Russ."

"Are you nervous?" Russ asked.

"A little. I feel like I'm playing dress-up, and everyone there will figure out I'm a loser PA who's drowning in debt. I don't get why Liam asked me for this favour. There must be a hundred other women who could step in at a moment's notice."

"Christ, Mae. How often do I have to tell you that Mr. Knight has it bad for you?"

"He told me himself that this wasn't a date. I'm being paid overtime for it," I said.

"So, you're Julia Roberts from Pretty Woman instead of Cinderella. You still look stunning," Russ said dismissively.

"I am not sleeping with our boss tonight, Russell!"

"Why not? He's attracted to you, and you're attracted to him. Plus, I wasn't kidding when I said you look stunning tonight, Mae. Hell, you're even giving me a bit of a stiffy."

"How sweet," I said. "Do me a favour and stop talking, Russ."

"Sure. We're here anyway."

Anxiety trickled into my belly. Russ stopped the car and gave me one last grin.

"You really do look great, Mae."

"Thank you, Russ."

I smoothed my hand over my dress as Russ parked and climbed out of the car. He opened my door. I took his hand and, surprisingly, exited the car without revealing the shockingly tiny red thong that covered my new and improved hairless crotch.

"Are you sure I look okay, Russ?" I asked in a small voice.

He nodded and brushed back a stray strand of my hair. "You're going to knock his eyeballs right out of his head, Mae."

I smiled and walked toward the lobby of the building, willing myself not to wobble in my new heels. Behind me, Russ yelled, "Have fun, Cinderella."

I put my hand behind my back and gave Russ the finger as I smiled at the doorman. He returned my smile and opened the door. I took a deep breath and walked into a lobby filled with people. I stopped, searching the crowd hesitantly for Liam. He was nowhere to be seen, and I felt a little anxious. Although, in reality, only a few people looked at me, the longer I stood there, the more I felt like the entire room stared at me.

I breathed a sigh of relief when I saw Liam. He looked my way, and his eyes slid over me without a hint of recognition. I watched in amusement as his body twitched, his eyes widened, and his gaze returned to me.

I smiled and waved, but he just stood there staring at me with a slight frown. I looked down at my new dress and cursed Russ in my head. I had told him it was too much, but he and the saleslady had shot down my protests.

I smoothed the blue silk with hands that trembled slightly. What was it that Liam didn't like, I wondered. Was it the way the silk clung tightly to every curve? I thought it made my ass look even bigger than usual, but Russ had assured me it didn't.

Maybe it was the fact that it was strapless. I had protested the dress primarily because of that. I didn't wear anything strapless. My large breasts and chubby arms had me convinced it was a bad idea.

"They're your best asset," Russ said patiently when I snapped at him that I wasn't wearing the dress the saleslady held out. "Besides, your boobs aren't going anywhere in that corset."

I hitched up the fire-engine red corset impatiently. "It's too small. It barely contains my tits."

Russ rolled his eyes. "Jesus, Mae. Are you a woman or not? The corset is meant to push them up like that."

"I do like the way it keeps my stomach sucked in," I mused while staring into the full-length mirror. "The stockings are a bit much. Don't you think?"

"No, they're not," Russ said. "When Mr. Knight sees you

in this, he'll throw you over his shoulder and carry you to his bed. I guarantee it."

"Mr. Knight is not going to see me in my underwear, thank you very much," I said.

The saleslady finished zipping me into the dress. She glared at me and slapped my hands away from the top of it when I tried to pull it up to cover more of my breasts.

"It is meant to enhance the cleavage," she said testily. I squeaked when she grabbed my tits and gave them a firm shake. "Stop hiding these glorious gifts from God behind baggy t-shirts."

"You heard the lady." Russ grinned. "They're glorious gifts from God."

Now, I forced myself not to pull at the neckline. I had finally agreed to wear the dress only on the condition that we taped my boobs to the fabric of the dress. The sales clerk had brought out tape specifically for that, but I had taken one look at the thin, white tape and snorted disdainfully.

A quick stop at the hardware store, a few strips of duct tape later, and I could take a deep breath without worrying that my tits would fall out of my dress. I took a final look to ensure the duct tape wasn't showing, and then Liam stood in front of me and gripped my arm tightly.

"Hi." I smiled tentatively at him. His eyes were dark with anger, and I could feel the nerves in my stomach rising to a fevered pitch.

"Mae, you – you look amazing," he said hoarsely.

I took a deep breath, and his eyes dropped to my tits, his hand tightening on my arm. "Thank you, Liam."

He raised his face to mine, and the crotch of my panties was instantly and embarrassingly wet. What I had mistaken for anger in his eyes was actually a lust so intense that my body responded helplessly to it.

Dimly, I was aware of his arm circling my waist as his

head dipped to mine. He brushed his mouth against my cheek and whispered, "Let's get out of here."

"I just got here," I said breathlessly. "Aren't you making a speech after dinner?"

"I don't care," he growled. "Come back to my place and -"

"Liam, good to see you!"

A loud voice broke through my haze of desire. Liam cursed lightly under his breath, stepped away, and turned me so I stood directly before him. I was puzzled by it until he leaned forward to shake the man's hand, and I felt the hard outline of his thick cock against the small of my back.

"Hello, Dallas," Liam said. "How are you this evening?"

"Just wonderful, just wonderful." Dallas was only a few inches taller than me and had a ruddy complexion. Broken veins in his nose suggested he liked his liquor.

"And who is this marvelous creature?" Dallas licked his thick lips and stared at my cleavage before holding out his hand.

I shook it quickly as Liam slipped his hand under my hair and gripped the back of my neck possessively.

"Dallas, this is Mae Temple, a good friend of mine. Mae, this is Dallas Todd. He works for a rival firm."

Dallas laughed. "Now, now, Liam. You don't have to put it that way. I wouldn't want to give this gorgeous young thing the wrong idea about me."

He leaned a little closer. "I'd be happy to buy you a drink later if Liam here doesn't mind me squirreling you away."

I smiled but didn't say anything as Dallas' gaze dropped to my chest again. Liam's hand tightened on the back of my neck.

"Liam does mind," he said.

Dallas laughed again and gave him a quick salute. "Message received, loud and clear."

"Dallas! Over here, please!" A thin woman wearing a

yellow dress and carrying a clipboard waved at him. Dallas took one final look at my cleavage before scurrying off toward her.

We stood in silence for a few minutes. Liam's hand was still on my neck, and his cock was still hard against my back.

"What are you doing?" I said when I could no longer stand the silence.

"Thinking about baseball," he said through gritted teeth.

I peered up at him. "What?"

"Cold showers, uh, really fucking cold showers..."

I could see tiny drops of sweat on his forehead, and I said helpfully, "Margaret Thatcher naked on a cold day?"

"Christ, Mae. Stop taking such deep breaths," he said. "That dress is barely covering your breasts as it is."

"It'll be fine." I brushed aside his concerns, secure in my knowledge that if duct tape could hold on the front bumper of my car, it could keep my tits in my dress.

His cock was still hard against me, and I smiled prettily at him. "Will I have to walk in front of you for the entire evening, Mr. Knight? Or are you going to get your dick under control?"

"Give me a minute, for God's sake," he muttered. His eyes remain glued to my cleavage.

"It'll probably work better if you stop looking down my damn dress," I said.

"Mae, please," he suddenly pleaded. "Leave with me. We can go back to my place and -"

"No." I shook my head. "You have a speech to make after dinner, remember? Besides, I'm starving and hear the food will be delicious."

He made a low groan of disappointment. "I can't stand up there with my dick hard as a rock, and if I have to watch you in that dress all night, it's not going to go down."

I laughed. "Let me tell you how much this dress cost you, Mr. Knight. That'll soften it."

He leaned down, and I whispered the amount in his ear. He stared at me, his eyes still hazy with desire. "It's worth every goddamn penny, Ms. Temple."

I flushed prettily, and he stared at my mouth, massaging my neck gently with his warm hand. "Can I kiss you, Mae? Please."

"No. It isn't appropriate," I admonished, even though every part of me wanted his kiss. "You're my boss."

"Right." He cleared his throat, dropped his hand from my neck, and stared across the lobby.

I TOOK ONE FINAL LOOK AT MYSELF IN THE BATHROOM MIRROR, turning a little to ensure the price tag was still tucked away inside the dress. The cost of the dress was outrageous. It was more money than I made in a month, and I had quietly hidden the price tag inside the dress. I would take it back tomorrow and return it. I couldn't justify the amount my boss had shelled out with the hair and makeup and ripping out of body hair, not to mention the lingerie. Terrified of spilling on the dress, I had eaten like a bird during dinner despite Liam's urging to eat more.

I left the bathroom and walked down the hallway. Liam would be making his speech soon, and I wanted to return to my seat in time to hear it. Lost in my thoughts, I didn't hear the man call my name until his hand fell on my arm.

"Mae?"

I turned to see Neil standing behind me, dressed in a dark charcoal suit. His hair was shorter than the last time I'd seen him, and he had grown a beard.

"Neil?"

"Oh my God. What – what are you doing here?"

"What are you doing here?" I countered.

"Marketing." His eyes travelled down my body, lingered on my chest, and then searched my face. "You look amazing."

"Thank you," I replied stiffly. He still held my arm, and I pulled, but he didn't let go.

"Seriously, you look so – so…"

"Mae? Are you ready to go back?"

Liam joined us in the hallway and tugged me away from Neil. He put his hand on the small of my back and held his other out to Neil.

"Liam Knight."

Neil shook his hand. "Neil Dorman. It's nice to meet you finally. I own Dorman's Law Corporation. Have you heard of it?"

"No, I'm afraid not." Liam gave him a thin smile and stepped closer until my hip brushed against him.

"Well, I'd love to talk business with you. Maybe we could meet for lunch sometime?"

Liam shook his head. "I don't think so."

Neil cleared his throat. "So, it's really good to see you again, Mae. Are you still working for Mr. Knight?"

"I am," I said.

"Oh good, good. How are your mom and dad doing?"

"They're fine."

"That's nice to hear. I've, uh, I've missed you."

I didn't say anything, and Neil gave Liam a broad smile. "Mae and I used to date."

"Did you?" Liam said with apparent disinterest.

"Yes. Letting her go was the biggest mistake of my life." Neil shoved his hands into his pockets. "I was thinking about giving you a call, Mae. I thought maybe we could go for coffee."

I laughed. "Oh yeah?"

Neil flushed. "Yes." He took a step closer. "I ran into Allie a couple of weeks ago. She said you haven't dated anyone since we broke up."

I smiled politely and made a mental note to punch Allie in her giant mouth the next time I saw her.

Neil glanced at Liam again. "Do you think we could speak alone for a minute?"

Liam's arm tightened around me. "We need to return to the room, Mae."

"I just need a minute. I'll be right there," I said.

"It was nice to meet you, Mr. Knight." Neil gave him a large shit-eating grin. I was reminded all over again why I was happy the loser had dumped me.

Liam didn't reply. He stared down at me, his gaze dropping to my mouth. I had a second to realize his intention before his mouth was on mine. His tongue pushed at my lips, and I opened them as he swept me against his body in a hard, possessive grip. He dipped his tongue into my mouth, stroked it along mine twice and released me.

"See you soon," he murmured.

I nodded, too breathless from the unexpected kiss to answer. Without speaking to Neil, he disappeared down the hallway.

Neil was staring at me with his mouth open, and I scowled at him. "What?"

"Dating your boss, Mae? I don't think that's a brilliant idea."

"Like I care what you think."

"Don't be like that, Mae. We had something good once, remember?"

"*Had* Neil. Then you decided to dump my ass," I said.

He sighed. "I meant it when I said it was the mistake of my life."

"Sure, you did," I snorted.

"No, really. I've been thinking a lot about you lately, and I was going to give you a call. I've been lonely."

"Oh, I'm sure you have been." I crossed my arms over my torso. "In between dating your model girlfriends."

"None of them meant anything to me, Mae. They're all just – just..."

"Stupid? Vapid? All boobs and no brains?" I supplied.

He flushed. "Just think about going for coffee with me, okay?" He pressed his business card into my hand. "Just coffee. We can talk about old times."

He hesitated and kissed my cheek lightly before squeezing my hand and walking away.

CHAPTER 11

I tugged nervously at the hem of my dress as I sat in the limo. Liam glanced over at me but didn't say anything, and I gave him a hesitant smile. He'd been distant and brooding since finding Neil and me in the hallway together.

I caught Russ' eye in the rear-view mirror, and he raised his eyebrows at me. I shrugged as Russ cleared his throat.

"Am I taking Ms. Temple home, sir?"

"Yes," Liam snapped. "Where else would you be taking her?"

"Sorry, sir," Russ replied.

"Raise the glass, please," Liam said.

There was a soft hum as the glass rose, separating us from Russ. The moment it was fully closed, I turned on Liam. "What the hell is your problem?"

"What do you mean?" He glared at me.

"I mean, you were rude to Russ and, frankly, you've been a bit of a dick to me ever since I ran into Neil in the hallway.

"That was quite the coincidence, wasn't it?" Liam scowled. "You just happened to run into your ex-fiancé at a charity event."

I gaped at him. "Are you kidding me? You were the one who forced me to go to the charity event with you. I wouldn't have even been there if you hadn't asked me to do you a damn favour."

He snorted and looked out the tinted window. I stared angrily out my window.

"Are you going to go out with him again?" he asked suddenly.

"What?"

"He wants to date you again. Are you going to?" He repeated himself slowly as if he were speaking to an idiot.

My temper flared, and I gripped my knees until my knuckles went white. "Maybe."

I had no intention of calling Neil again, but Liam didn't need to know that.

I squeaked in alarm when Liam suddenly slid across the seat and pressed his body against mine. With nostrils flaring, he cupped the back of my neck and said quietly, "I don't want you seeing him again, Mae."

"Since when did you become the boss of me?" I retorted without thinking.

He paused as a weird look crossed his face. I started giggling when I realized what I said. His face relaxed, and he smiled. God, he was fucking gorgeous when he smiled.

"Don't call him, Mae. He's an asshole."

"Are you jealous, Mr. Knight?"

"No."

"Liar," I said.

He bent his head and brushed his mouth against mine. I moaned and kissed him hard, grabbing his head and yanking it down. He groaned when I parted my lips and gave him access to the warm wetness. We kissed hungrily, our tongues battling for control before I pulled my head back.

Breathing heavily, he ran his hand over my arm. "Your skin is so soft, Mae."

"That's because earlier today, I had all of the hair ripped from my body by a sadistic woman named Sandra."

"I'm sorry?"

"Oh, and you paid for it."

He stared at me in confusion, and I laughed. "Russ took me to a spa before we went dress shopping."

"And I paid them to rip out all of your body hair?" He cocked his head at me.

I nodded. "Yep. Well, most of it."

"Have I mentioned how much I like this dress?" He dipped his head and kissed the top of my exposed breasts. "Because I really, really like it."

"That's so nice of you to say, Mr. Knight," I moaned.

He licked a gentle path from my cleavage to my throat. "You smell so good, Mae." He buried his face in my throat and trailed soft kisses to my earlobe. "I've been dying to peel that dress off you all goddamn night."

I pushed on his hard chest. "Sit back."

He sat back on the seat, and I threw my leg over his lap and straddled him. My dress rose to the top of my stockings, and another soft groan snuck past his lips. He reached down and traced the top of my stockings, his fingers lingering on the strap that held them up.

I slapped his hand away. "You're being awfully familiar with me, Mr. Knight."

He stared at my chest. "I was certain that most of the people at that charity event would be familiar with your breasts before the night was over."

I laughed. "Well, they are glorious gifts from God."

He blinked at me. "Are you drunk again?"

"Nope. I've only had one glass of wine. Why? Are you thinking you'll get to look at my tits again if I am?"

He arched his eyebrows at me. "I knew you remembered what happened that night in the club."

I blushed as I realized what I had done. "I don't know what you're talking about."

He gave me a predatory grin. "Now who's lying?"

He leaned forward and kissed the top of my breasts again. "I want to suck on your nipples, Mae."

I shuddered and looked behind me at the glass partition. "Russ is right there."

"The glass is soundproof and tinted." His fingers reached for the zipper of my dress and tugged it down. He frowned when my dress stayed put. He tugged lightly on the sides of it, his frown deepening when it stuck fast to my skin.

"What the hell?"

I grinned. "I didn't want to be flashing my tits at a charity event."

He pulled the top of my dress down a little and stared in surprise at the thick grey tape. "Duct tape?"

"It's not just for taping bumpers back to cars, you know."

He burst out laughing, and I grinned at him. "Now you know why I wasn't worried."

"Indeed." He tugged on the tape. I hissed a little as it stuck tightly to my skin.

He frowned. "It's really stuck."

"Yeah, I'm starting to think this might not have been such a good idea," I said.

He pulled a little more and made a soft sound of distress at the red mark it left on my skin.

"Maybe you should rip it off quickly like a Band-Aid," I suggested.

He shook his head. "No. Just hold still."

I winced as he slowly peeled the strips of duct tape from my skin. He crumpled them into a ball and dropped them on the seat before running his fingers across the bright marks on my skin.

He bent his head and licked a slow path across each red stripe. "Poor, Mae."

I threaded my hands in his hair and tugged until he lifted his head. I kissed him hard on the mouth, my tongue thrusting between his lips as he groaned and gripped my waist.

"Please, Mae," he moaned against my mouth. "Let me see those magnificent breasts."

I nodded my permission, and he folded my dress down. "My God," he breathed as he stared at the bright red corset.

"What is this?" He pointed to the small white tag that lay against the inside of the dress.

I blushed and reached for it, but he held my hand away. "Why is the price tag still on the dress?"

My blush deepened. "The dress was super expensive. I know you weren't planning on spending a bunch of money on spa treatments, so I thought I could take the dress back tomorrow and get your money refunded."

He ripped off the tag, making me jerk in surprise. "Liam!"

"You're keeping the dress. It looks amazing on you, and you deserve it."

"Liam -"

"No arguments, Mae," he said.

I rolled my eyes before reaching between us and slowly unhooking the tiny silver hooks that held the corset together. His hands covered mine, and he pulled open the top of the corset. My breasts spilled free, and I moaned when he cupped them in his large hands. He rubbed his thumbs over my hard nipples and then pinched them lightly.

"You have the prettiest nipples, Mae," he murmured. He bent his head, and I pulled his hair again.

"Ask first," I demanded.

"Please, may I suck on your nipples?" he said.

"Yes." I released my grip on his head, and my back arched when he quickly sucked my right nipple into his mouth. He suckled greedily at it, rubbing the tip of it against the roof of his mouth until I moaned again.

He switched to the left one, giving it the same careful treatment until I was gasping and rubbing myself against his erection.

"You are so good at that," I said.

He grinned and cupped my breasts, pushing them together so he could lick from one nipple to the other. "I could suck on your nipples for hours, Mae."

I sighed and arched my back again. I untied his bowtie as he sucked and kissed and licked my throbbing nipples. He shrugged out of his jacket, and I quickly unbuttoned his shirt before pulling it open so I could stare at his naked chest.

I touched his stomach muscles. He sucked in his breath when I traced the waistband of his pants. Smiling, I leaned forward and brushed my wet nipples against his hard chest. We both moaned at the contact, and he slid his hands around me to grip my ample ass. He kneaded it firmly and then pushed me against his erection.

"I want to fuck you. Come back to my house." He kissed me lightly.

"That's not a good idea, Liam."

"It's an excellent idea. You have no idea how badly I want to make you come," he said.

I shuddered all over. "Liam, I can't."

"Yes, you can." He dipped his head and kissed the warm crevice between my breasts. I could feel my resolve weakening, and I took a deep breath.

"Think about how good it will feel to have my fingers in your pussy," he whispered into my ear. "How nice it would be to have my cock sliding into you. Come home with me right now."

I suddenly yanked his head back and bit his bottom lip. He grunted in surprise as I said, "Are you telling me what to do, Liam?"

He shook his head. "No."

"I think you are." I grinned at him as a wicked idea entered my head. I knew that Liam was submissive, but I was curious about how submissive he was.

I lowered my head and sucked on his earlobe. "I'm not going to fuck you, Liam. Not tonight."

"Mae, please just -"

"Quiet, Liam." I nipped his ear hard, making him jerk. His hands squeezed my aching breasts. "We don't have much time left before we're at my apartment. I'll be nice and give you a choice. Only one of us gets to come tonight. I'll let you decide who it is."

"You," he said immediately.

I smiled my approval and rewarded him by reaching into his pants and stroking his thick cock. "Are you sure? If you decide I'm the one who comes tonight, you don't get to come at all. No going home and masturbating in that big, comfortable bed of yours. Do you understand?"

"Yes," he rasped out as his hips rose and fell with the motion of my hand. "I want to make you come, Mae."

"Such a good boy," I whispered. I licked his mouth, and he parted his lips eagerly so I could slide my tongue into his mouth. He sucked hard on it, and I moaned when he traced my thigh with one big hand.

"I want to use my mouth to make you come," he said.

"No, not this time. Just use your hand, Liam."

He slid his hand up and under my skirt as I pulled my hand from his pants and gripped his shoulders. He traced the top of my stockings again and then abruptly cupped my mound. I moaned when he rubbed me through my panties.

"Your panties are so wet," he rasped.

"They've been wet all night." I smiled. "Since the moment you touched me in the lobby."

He made a low noise of need and worked his fingers under my panties. He touched my freshly waxed skin and made another husky groan. "God, you're so soft, so smooth."

"Do you like it?" I asked.

"Yes. Very much."

I said a silent thank you to Sandra as he slid his hand upwards. He made a soft grunt of surprise when he felt the strip of hair. I shivered when he tugged lightly on it.

"I like this too," he whispered.

"Make me come, Liam. Right now," I suddenly demanded.

"Yes, Mae." He moved his fingers to my swollen, throbbing clit and rubbed it with a firm, circular motion. I arched my hips into his hand, and he slid his middle finger deep into my tight opening.

"Oh God," I whimpered as he thrust his finger back and forth in my quivering pussy.

"Christ, you're tight," he muttered.

He curled his finger and rubbed the rough patch of skin on the front inside wall of my pussy. I buried my face in his neck to muffle my sudden scream of delight.

"Does it feel good, Mae?" His left hand cupped my breast, and he pulled on my swollen nipple as he used the thumb of his right hand to rub my clit.

"Yes," I moaned. My fingers dug into Liam's shoulders, and I couldn't stop from thrusting against him wildly.

He bent his head and sucked my nipple into his mouth, biting it lightly as he pressed firmly on my clit with his thumb and rubbed at my G-spot with his middle finger. My entire body quivered and shook, and I could feel my orgasm starting in the pit of my stomach. Waves of pleasure radiated down my lower body, and I rode his hand like a madwoman as my orgasm crashed through me.

"Oh God, oh God, Liam!" I moaned as I shook and shuddered against his hard body. I collapsed against him, panting harshly as he stroked my pussy and kissed the top of my bare shoulder.

I could feel his erection against my belly. "Regretting your choice yet?"

He shook his head. "No. Watching you come all over my hand was amazing."

I flushed, suddenly feeling embarrassed by my actions, and sat up. I tugged his arm out from under my skirt and quickly did up the corset before pulling up my dress.

"Can you zip me up?"

He nodded and reached around me to pull up the zipper. I gave him a nervous smile of thanks and slid off his lap and onto the seat beside him. With a slight grimace, he adjusted the crotch of his pants before buttoning his shirt.

"Are you okay?" he asked.

I nodded. "Yeah, I just, um – I've never seduced my boss before."

He smiled a little. "That's good to know."

The car stopped, and Russ's voice came over the intercom. "We're at Ms. Temple's apartment, sir."

I reached for the door handle, and Liam grabbed my hand. "Mae -"

I shook my head and leaned toward him. I gave him a quick kiss on the cheek and whispered. "Remember, Liam, no coming tonight. Don't touch that magnificent cock of yours until I say you can."

"I won't," he groaned.

"Good boy." I kissed his cheek again and slipped out of the limo and into the cool night air before he could say anything else.

CHAPTER 12

The loud knocking woke me. I sat up in bed and squinted at the alarm clock. It was just after eight, and I blinked in confusion when the knocking sounded again.

"Who is it?" I shouted irritably.

"Mae, it's Russ. Let me in."

I crawled out of bed, threw my bathrobe over my t-shirt, and stumbled to the door. I yanked the door open.

"How did you get into the lobby?" I yawned as he and Steve pushed their way into my apartment.

"Oh, please." Russ handed me a coffee in a paper cup. "The door was wide open. We just walked right in."

They sat down at the table as I opened the coffee lid and took a sip. "What's going on? Why are you two here?"

Russ gave Steve a nervous look. "Hey, uh, have you happened to be online yet this morning?"

"No, you guys just woke me up." I glanced at the clock on the wall. "Seriously, it's Saturday morning. Why are you guys here so early?"

Steve crossed his leg over his knee and picked at the

bottom of his jeans. "So, Mae, don't freak out, but there's something you should read."

"What?" I stared at his and Russ's solemn faces, and anxiety nipped at my insides. "What's wrong?"

"Nothing serious," Russ assured me. "It's just... well, you know who Gloria Franklin is, right?"

I nodded. Who didn't know her? She was a journalist who made her living writing a salacious and juicy gossip column for our local online newspaper.

Russ glanced at Steve. "Okay, and again - I can't stress this enough - don't freak out, honey. She was at last night's charity event and wrote in her column about you and Mr. Knight."

I blinked at him. "You're kidding me."

"I'm not," Russ replied. Steve pulled his phone from his pocket and scrolled across the screen.

"What did she say?" The anxiety in my stomach was growing by the minute.

"I just think you should remember that she's a gossipy old bitch, and no one takes her columns seriously, okay?" Russ said.

"Oh God." I stared wide-eyed at him. "How bad is it?"

"It's not great." Steve handed his phone to me, and I stared at the small screen.

Last night at the Hope for Children's charity event, the city's most influential and notorious bachelor - the to-die-for Liam Knight - supported a brand new charity. Although Mr. Knight typically prefers beautiful blondes with bodies as smoking hot as his own, last night marked a first for him. The handsome and dashing Mr. Knight escorted a short brunette, who obviously had never met a donut she didn't like, to the event. The mystery woman was seen canoodling with Mr. Knight throughout the night, and it was evident to all who attended that she had the sinfully sexy lawyer wrapped around her chubby little finger. Although there is the slim

*possibility that Mr. Knight has become a chubby chaser, one
burning question remains – will this pretty but chunky woman be
the one to melt his cold exterior, or was he throwing the poor
woman a pity date?*

My cheeks felt like they were on fire as, with a shaking
finger, I scrolled down. A groan of dismay escaped my lips.
The stupid woman had taken a picture of us, and she
couldn't have taken it at the worst possible time. His body
pressed against mine and arm wrapped around my waist,
Liam whispered into my ear. Based on the flushed and
excited look on my face, it had been the exact moment he
was asking me to go home with him.

"Oh, fuck me." I handed Steve his phone and dropped my
head to the kitchen table. I banged my forehead against the
hard surface until Russ reached out and pushed me back.

"It's no big deal, Mae."

"No big deal? No big deal?" I stared at him. "She makes it
sound like I'm a pathetic, fat loser on a pity date with the
hottest man in the city."

Russ shook his head as I groaned again. "Fuck – that's
exactly what it was!"

"It was not, Mae," Russ scolded as Steve grabbed my hand
and massaged it gently. "Mr. Knight asked you out on a date,
and you accepted. And you looked fucking hot last night.
Besides, it's not all bad. It's a great picture of you."

"I told you last night, Russ – it wasn't a date," I said. "His
actual date, probably a tall, blonde supermodel, cancelled on
him. He's paying me overtime for last night."

"See," Steve soothed, "you weren't on a pity date. It was a
work function."

"Thanks, Steve." I sighed and went back to hitting my
head on the table.

"Stop." Russ slid into the chair beside me and pulled me
back by my shoulders again. "I think you're making too

123

much out of this, Mae. No one reads that damn gossip column anyway. Right, honey?" He stared pointedly at Steve.

"Yeah, that's right," Steve said hastily. "That gossipy bitch is way past her expiry date."

"Oh really? If it's no big deal and no one reads it, why the hell did you two come storming over here first thing this morning to warn me about it? Hmm?"

"Uh..." Russ looked at Steve, who shrugged.

"We were in the neighbourhood? It's, like, a really great neighbourhood, Mae. We're thinking of buying something here."

I laughed despite my anxiety. "Yeah, sure you are. Well, what's done is done, right? I'm sure by Monday, it'll have all blown over. Besides, no one at work reads that gossip shit anyway. Right?"

"Yeah, right. I mean, probably," Russ said without much conviction.

"Oh God." I groaned again and smacked myself in the forehead. "I am so screwed."

Russ brightened. "See, I knew that underwear would get you laid!"

I slapped him lightly on the arm. "I did not fuck Liam last night, Russ."

"What? You mean nothing happened at all? When he asked me to put the glass up, I figured you two were getting down and dirty."

"Nothing happened!" I lied hotly.

Russ looked at me carefully and then grinned at Steve. "See what I mean when I said she was a terrible liar."

Steve nodded, and I sighed loudly. "Fine, we might have made out a little."

"Nice. Give us the details," Russ said.

"No. He's my boss, and I shouldn't have done anything

with him," I said. "Although, after that goddamn article, I'll be lucky if I still have my job Monday morning."

I glanced around my apartment. "I'll miss this rathole when I'm homeless and sleeping in a box in an alley."

"It'll be fine, Mae. Don't worry," Russ soothed. "Now," he eyed my smeared makeup and ratty bathrobe, "go and shower, Cinderella. You've got two Prince Charmings ready to take you out for breakfast."

* * *

"Good morning, Christine." I smiled at her as I walked past her desk toward my office.

"Oh, uh, hey, Mae," she said. "How, uh, was your weekend?"

I stopped, my spidey senses tingling at the weird tone in her voice. "Just fine, thanks. How was yours?"

"Fine, fine." She wouldn't meet my eyes as Roxie sidled up to the desk.

"Hi, Mae."

"Hello, Roxie."

"Ida's looking for you."

My stomach dropped to my ankles. Based on the way Christine and Roxie were looking at me, or rather not looking at me, the article about Liam and me had already spread like wildfire through the office. I glanced at my watch. It was just after eight on Monday morning.

"Okay, thanks. I'll stop in and see her." I forced myself to smile at them and walked away. They whispered behind me, and I knew they were talking about me. I straightened my back and headed toward Ida's office.

I knocked on her open door and stuck my head in her office. "Hey, Ida. You were looking for me?"

Her face grave, she nodded. "Yes, come in and shut the door, Mae."

My knees shaking and my stomach rolling with nausea, I shut the door and crossed the room to sit in the chair across from her desk.

She stared silently at me, and I crossed my arms nervously across my torso.

"Mae, did you attend a charity event with Liam on Friday night?"

I nodded. "Yes. His date cancelled on him, and Liam asked me to fill in."

She raised her eyebrows, and I added hastily. "It was a work thing. Liam said he would pay me overtime."

She picked up a pen from her gleaming desk and tapped the end of it against her teeth. "Are you aware of the article written by Gloria Franklin?"

I nodded. "Yeah, I saw it."

"Are you sleeping with Liam?" she said.

"I'm not."

"Are you aware we have stringent rules about inter-office dating?"

"I read the employee manual when I was hired," I said.

"Mae, I don't think I have to tell you that the picture accompanying that horrid woman's article has the potential to be very damaging to your future here at Knight and Associates," Ida said.

I didn't reply, and she sighed. "I like you, Mae. You know I do. I think you're smart, and I believe you have a bright future here. But if I find out you're dating Liam, I'll have no choice but to fire you. Do you understand?"

"Yes. I'm not dating him, Ida. I swear."

"I believe you. Still, I think it would be a good idea if I do a shuffle of the PAs again. Effective immediately, you're no longer Mr. Knight's PA."

My heart sank, but I forced myself to smile at her. "That's fine."

"I'll assign you back to Kevin. He's been grumbling for the past month about how much he misses you anyway."

I took a deep breath. "Thanks, Ida."

"You're welcome. Move your stuff out of the office and back to the desk outside Kevin's office this morning, okay?"

"I will." I stood and hesitated. "Should I, uh, let Mr. Knight know?"

She shook her head. "No, I'll inform him. He's not in yet, but I'll text and ask him to come see me as soon as he gets to the office."

I left Ida's office. Twenty minutes later, I was packed up and back at my old desk outside Kevin's office.

"Mae, you have no idea how glad I am that you're back." Kevin smiled at me as I plugged in my laptop.

"I'm glad too, Kevin. I've missed you." I returned his smile and sank into the chair. "What do you need me to do first?"

Kevin laughed. "Yeah, I've definitely missed you. Can you pull the Jackson file and go through their personal account information? I need you to circle all the purchases made from the seventeenth to the twenty-fifth.

"You bet," I said. Kevin disappeared into his office, and I stared miserably at my desk. I liked Kevin, but I was already missing the sound of Liam's deep voice.

CHAPTER 13

"Mae? What are you doing?" I looked up from the Jackson file to see Liam beside my desk. I smiled nervously at him.

"Um, have you not spoken with Ida?"

"No. I just got in. Why are you sitting here?"

"I think you should talk to Ida."

"Just tell me what's going on, Mae," Liam demanded as Kevin left his office.

"Hey, Liam."

"Hello, Kevin. How are you?"

"Good. Great, in fact, now that I have my girl back." Kevin squeezed my shoulder in a friendly way, and I bit my lip as Liam's face darkened alarmingly.

"What the hell do you mean?" he snapped.

Kevin blinked and took a step back. "Mae's back as my PA."

Liam's nostrils flared, and his lips pressed together into a thin line. Without a word, he turned and stormed off toward Ida's office.

Kevin stared curiously at me. "What's gotten into him this morning?"

"I don't know."

"Weird." Shaking his head, Kevin disappeared back into his office. The moment he was gone, I stood and bolted down the hallway.

"Bailey!" I skidded to a stop in front of the chubby PA's desk. "Is Doreen in her office?"

"No, why?" she said.

"I need to borrow her office for a minute. I, uh, have a personal call to make."

"Sure." She shrugged, and I slipped past her into Doreen's office. I closed the door behind me and ran to the far wall. I hesitated and then pressed my ear firmly against the wall.

Doreen's office was next to Ida's. I plugged my other ear and strained to hear the voices drifting through the wall.

"Ida, what the hell is going on? Why is Mae no longer my PA?" Liam's voice was low and angry.

"Liam, did you ask Mae to be your date to the charity event on Friday night?" Ida said.

"She wasn't my date. It was a work thing. I needed someone to accompany me, and she agreed to help me. I'm paying her overtime for it," he snapped.

Ida sighed. "There was an article -"

"I saw it," he said. "It doesn't mean anything. I'm not dating Ms. Temple."

"Yes, well, the picture certainly made it look like you were," Ida said.

Liam didn't reply. Ida's chair squeaked as she pushed it back and stood up. "Liam, people are already talking about you and Mae in the office. Everyone's read the article, and it's not reflecting very well on Mae."

"Nothing is going on between us, Ida," Liam said.

"I believe you. I spoke with Mae this morning, and she said the same thing."

"Good. I'll let you tell Kevin that Mae is coming back as my PA," Liam said.

"That isn't a good idea, and you know it. You made the rules about inter-office dating."

"I'm not dating Ms. Temple," Liam gritted out.

"Yes, you keep saying that. But it's still not a good idea for you to work so closely with her. I think it's best if you keep your distance."

"Well, lucky for me, you don't have the final say in who I employ as my PA."

"Liam -"

"Enough, Ida!" Liam suddenly shouted. "Mae's the best damn PA I've ever had, and I'm not giving her up. I know the goddamn rules of the office, and I don't need you to remind me of them. You'll inform Mae and Kevin that she's back as my PA, and I don't want to hear another word about it. Do I make myself clear?"

"Perfectly," Ida said.

I heard the heavy thud of Liam's footsteps and then the door to Ida's office slamming shut as he strode down the hallway to his office. I waited a few minutes and then slipped out of Doreen's office.

Bailey stared wide-eyed at me. "Did you hear Mr. Knight yelling at Ida?"

I shrugged. "No, I was making a phone call. Talk to you later, Bailey. I need to get back to my desk and work on that file for Kevin before he discovers I'm missing."

"You won't be working for Kevin for long," I heard Bailey mutter as I hurried down the hall to my desk.

* * *

"Mae?"

I looked up from the small table in Liam's office. It was covered in piles of paper that I had painstakingly sorted through for the last three hours.

"Hi, Ida."

"Hey. You're working late again?"

"Yeah, such is the glamorous life of Mr. Knight's PA, right?" I said.

She smiled before glancing around the office. "I'm about to head out. Is Liam still here?"

"Nope, he left a few hours ago, and I'm not expecting him back tonight. Do you want me to leave him a message for you?"

"No, that's fine. It's just you left in the office. Don't forget to set the alarm when you leave, okay?"

"You bet. Have a nice night, Ida."

"You too, Mae."

She left the office, and I sighed to myself. It had been four days since Liam insisted I return as his PA. There was a small part of me that really wished Ida had won the argument. He'd been in a ferocious mood since his fight with Ida, and most people in the office were avoiding him. We hadn't discussed what happened in the limo or the article and picture. Hell, he barely spoke to me and had me working twelve-hour days all week.

Despite his coldness and near-hostility toward me, Ida had been careful to stay late each night that I did. I knew she was doing it to help me. It wasn't wise for Liam and me to be alone in the office, at least if my co-workers' muttering and side glances were any indication, but it bugged me that she was babysitting me.

I stacked the papers neatly on the table. I just wanted to go home and sleep for a hundred hours. I hadn't slept well at all. I dreamt nightly of Liam and all the things I wanted to do to his naked body. Even my nightly quality time with "Paul" barely helped to ease my need. It was Liam's cock I wanted, not my vibrator.

I turned to grab a file folder, and my meaty hip bumped the table. "Goddammit!" I shouted when a stack of papers slid off the back and landed under the table.

Grumbling to myself, I dropped to my hands and knees and crawled under the table. I was reaching for the paper when my phone rang. Startled, I reared up and hit my head on the bottom of the table so hard I saw stars.

"Fuck!" I shouted again and collapsed under the table. I snagged my phone out of my pocket with one hand while I rubbed the top of my head with the other. "Hello?"

"Mae? What's wrong?" Russ asked.

"Nothing," I said grumpily. "I'm on my hands and knees under a table, and I just smacked the top of my head, and I've got seventy-two paper cuts. Also, I'm tired and hungry, and my underwear is too tight."

Russ laughed. "So, you're having a bad day?"

I sighed as I collected the papers from under the table and crawled out from under it. "More like a bad week."

"Are you and Mr. Knight not playing nice with each other?"

"He'd have to be talking to me for us not to play nice." I walked into his private bathroom and peered at the top of my skull. There was a slight bump, but it wasn't bleeding.

"So, I take it you haven't had sex yet?"

"No, Russ, we haven't. Thanks to that goddamn article, Monday morning, the HR manager threatened to fire my ass if I slept with him."

"Ouch. That's not good."

"No, it isn't. A girl has needs. Do you get what I'm saying?" I asked.

"Yep, I do," Russ said. "You're a healthy girl, Mae. Are you trying to tell me you don't have any battery-operated toys?"

I wiped at the dust on my shirt, closed my eyes, and rubbed my forehead. "Trust me. I've had nightly visits with good old Paul. It's not helping."

"You named your vibrator?" Russ laughed.

"Doesn't everyone?"

"Why don't you come over tonight, and I'll make you dinner. Steve's at the club, and we can hang out and watch bad TV together."

I smiled. "Thanks, but I'm going to pass. I've got a hot date with Paul, remember?"

He laughed, and we quickly said goodbye. I ended the call and rubbed at my aching skull again.

"Who's Paul?"

I jumped and twisted around. Liam stood in the bathroom doorway, a scowl on his face.

"You scared the hell out of me!" I scolded. "What are you doing here?"

He raised his eyebrow. "I work here, remember?"

"How could I forget?"

"What's that supposed to mean?" he asked.

"It means you've been kind of a jerk to everyone this week. Trust me – everyone knows you work here."

He snorted. "It's not my fault if people take it personally."

"Whatever, Mr. Knight," I said. I needed to get away from him. Being trapped in the small bathroom with his hard body only inches from mine made me antsy. When he left three hours earlier, he wore his usual dark suit. Now, he was dressed in a dark green t-shirt and the same faded jeans he'd been wearing at his house.

He looked decidedly lickable this evening.

"Excuse me," I said pointedly. He took my arm and

pushed me gently against the wall as I tried to squeeze by him.

He pressed his body against mine and stared down at me. "Who's Paul?" he repeated.

"Why do you care?" I squirmed against him and gasped when I felt the hardness of his cock brushing against my belly.

He groaned, and his pelvis thrust against me almost helplessly. He had a strange look of anger combined with lust and pain on his face.

"Liam, are you okay?"

"Fine," he grunted. His breath hissed out between his teeth when I wiggled against him again.

"Christ, Mae! Stop doing that! Do you think it's made of stone?"

He turned away from me with his entire body trembling. I stared curiously at him before understanding flooded through me.

"Liam?"

"What?" He didn't turn around.

"Have you touched yourself since the night in the limo?"

His body jerked, and I had my answer.

"Not even once?" I asked.

"You told me not to," he said.

My eyes widened in surprise. The man had willpower. I had to give him that. If he wanted me even half as badly as I wanted him – well, I was surprised he hadn't exploded.

"No wonder you've been Mr. Cranky Pants for the last few days," I said.

He didn't answer, and I touched his back lightly. He jerked again, and I made a soothing noise in the back of my throat.

"Look at me, Liam." I closed the bathroom door as he turned to face me.

"I want you to touch yourself right now."

A muscle in his jaw flickered, and he shook his head. "I can't."

I arched my eyebrow at him, and he looked away from me. "You'll be fired, Mae."

"For what?" I asked. "I'm not doing anything. Where does the rule book say I can't stand in your bathroom? Besides, there's no one left in the office but us. My boss has been a real asshole and making me work late all week."

"Mae," he groaned, "please. You have no idea how much I want to touch myself, but just let me go home and do it, okay?"

"No," I said. "I want to watch you touch yourself, Liam. Take off your shirt and unzip your jeans."

"Mae..." he whispered, but his hands were already reaching for the bottom of his t-shirt. As he pulled it off his muscular torso, I felt a ripple of lust and power go through me. I wondered if this was how a Dominatrix felt. Wondered if this addictive, heady rush of power would eventually wane or if watching Liam do everything I told him to would forever make me this goddamn horny.

I took a deep breath. Maybe it was time I ditched the PA thing and looked into a career as a Dominatrix. I could specialize in alpha males who needed a little extra convincing to be submissive.

Speaking of which... Liam watched me carefully, and his jeans were still firmly buttoned around his narrow waist. The bulge of his cock was unmistakeable against the fabric.

"What are you waiting for?" I asked.

"This isn't a good idea," he said. "It's not that I don't -"

"Stop arguing with me," I said sharply. I stepped forward and ran one finger over his broad chest. He groaned loudly.

"After today, we won't do this again. We'll be strictly

professional. You've been such a good boy, Liam." I smiled at him. "Don't you think I should reward you?"

He panted harshly as I stepped even closer. When he reached for my waist, I shook my head. "No. No touching me, Liam. Do you understand?"

He nodded, and I traced his abs. "If you touch yourself and let me watch while you come, I'll tell you who Paul is."

His hands reached for the button on his jeans, and he hurriedly unbuttoned and unzipped. He reached in and tugged his hard cock free.

He wrapped his hand around it almost immediately, and I shook my head again. "No, let me look at it."

With a soft groan, he dropped his hand. I studied his beautiful cock, and he groaned again when I licked my lips. I was tempted to drop to my knees and take his very erect, very thick shaft into my mouth, but the urge to dominate Liam was powerful now.

"Goodness, Mr. Knight," I said, "your cock is deliciously thick."

I reached for the buttons on my shirt and undid the top four. I wore the black push-up bra, and Liam stared hungrily at my exposed cleavage. I stepped forward until his cock almost brushed against my stomach and smiled at him. He reached out and slipped his hand neatly into my bra. He rolled my nipple between his fingers, and I arched my back in unexpected pleasure before pushing him back.

"Mr. Knight! Do that again, and I won't let you come for a month. Do you understand?" I said sternly.

He swallowed and nodded. "Yes."

I put my hands on my hips. "Yes, what?"

"Yes, Mae. I'm sorry."

"Good." I walked around him, my fingertips trailing across the exposed flesh of his torso. His hands clenched into tight fists, and his breath puffed out in harsh pants. His cock

- his gloriously thick cock – wept copious amounts of pre-cum.

"I want you to touch yourself now, Liam. But I want you to rub yourself slowly. Do you understand? Very, very slowly. If you go too fast, I'll make you stop, and we won't finish what we've started. Do you understand?"

"Yes," he moaned.

"Do you masturbate with your left hand or your right?"

"Right," he muttered.

I stood behind him and slightly to his right so I could watch. "Start with your left hand, please."

His hand trembling, he gripped his cock in his left hand and stroked himself slowly. I watched silently, then traced his spine with my finger.

"Very good, Mr. Knight. Keep going – a little faster, please."

He groaned and moved his hand faster. Already he was panting with his hips thrusting against the motion of his hand, and I knew he wouldn't last long.

"Stop," I demanded.

He made a soft, pleading noise but stopped obediently, his hand gripping his cock tightly.

"Your right hand now, Liam. Nice and slow, please." I plucked the hand towel from the rack on the wall and held it. The man was so worked up he'd be a goddamn fountain when I finally let him come.

He switched hands, and I murmured once again for him to go slowly as he moved his hard palm back and forth over his swollen cock.

I leaned closer, letting my breasts rest against his arm. He twitched, and I smiled up at him. "Does it feel good, Liam?"

"Yes, Mae. So good," he moaned.

"Rub faster," I instructed.

His hand sped up, and his hips thrust helplessly as his left hand reached out and gripped the sink.

"Do you wish it was my hand touching you?" I whispered as I lazily rubbed his naked back.

"Yes, mistress," he gasped out.

A bolt of pure pleasure shot from my pelvis to my toes. I bit my lip and squeezed my thighs together. Hearing Liam call me mistress had nearly made me come right there. My pussy quivering, and my nipples so hard they felt like glass, I took a deep breath.

"Do you want to come, Liam?"

"Yes! Please, mistress. Please let me come," he begged.

My pussy quivered again. Christ, I could listen to Liam's deep voice calling me mistress all goddamn night.

The man's entire body shook now, his hand stroking and squeezing as he fought not to come. Again, I was impressed by his self-control as I stretched up and whispered in his ear. "Come for me, Liam. Right now."

His hand clenched down on his cock. His back arched, and he shouted, the sound echoing in the small bathroom as he climaxed. I covered his cock with the hand towel and held it there with one hand to catch the warm liquid that was pouring out of him. He shook with the force of his climax. His eyes squeezed shut, and his jaw clenched as his hips thrust forward repeatedly.

After a few minutes, his body relaxed, and he bowed his head. His eyes were still closed, and his chest was heaving for air. I stepped in front of him, and he jerked in surprise when I gripped him through the towel.

"Shh," I whispered, carefully wiping him clean before dropping the towel in the sink. He opened his eyes and stared at me, his body trembling lightly.

"Do you feel better?" I smiled at him.

"Yes. Thank you," he said.

"You're welcome," I said.

He smiled, and I stood on my tiptoes and pressed my mouth against his. I kissed him gently, but he deepened it almost immediately. I moaned into his mouth and then quickly pulled away. If I let him kiss me that way for much longer, I would push him to the floor and fuck him.

His hands were reaching for my breasts, and I pushed them away lightly. "No," I whispered, "you know we can't."

He sighed and gave me a look of frustration. "Mae -"

"Goodnight, Liam." I stood on my tiptoes again and kissed his cheek before moving my mouth to his ear. "Paul is my vibrator."

He stared at me, a small smile turning up his lips as I left the bathroom.

CHAPTER 14

I sighed and swivelled in my office chair to stare out the window behind me. The view was stunning, but I barely noticed it. My mind, like it had been for the last two months, was too preoccupied with thoughts of my boss even to notice the gorgeous summer day.

For two months, Liam Knight was nothing but professional. There were no accidental touches or lust-filled looks. There was no mention of anything that had happened between us, and he treated me exactly like he treated the rest of the PAs in the office. He spent more time out of the office than usual, and I tried not to take it personally.

I sighed again. I should have been happy about his professionalism and detached attitude. I had come dangerously close to losing my job, and I'd told him myself that things needed to be strictly professional between us.

So why was I constantly searching for hidden meaning when he did look at me? Why couldn't I stop imagining how it would feel to climb on top of him and whisper in his ear that I didn't care about my job? That if he didn't fuck me and fuck me hard, I would go mad.

I was being ridiculous. He had already been photographed with his usual model-type dates at several business functions. His infatuation with me had faded, and it wasn't hard to figure out that Liam was over me. I, on the other hand, was still hopelessly lusting after him.

You need to find a new job, Mae.

Yeah, I did. But I couldn't do it, and not just because jobs were few and far between. At some point in the last two months, the thought of not seeing Liam every day filled me with a weird anxiety. In the last two months, his behaviour made me positive that quitting my job would only mean I'd never see him again. It wouldn't turn the possibility of dating him into reality. So, I came to work every day just to see his face. Just to stand near him and inhale his familiar scent while I tried to erase from my brain the memory of his voice moaning my name.

"Mae?"

I swung around and smiled at Kevin. "Hey, Kevin. How are you?"

"Can't complain. How about you?"

I shrugged. "The same. What's up?"

"I wanted to confirm that you gave the Richardson file to Liam before he left. He's meeting with them Sunday afternoon."

My stomach dropped, and I glanced at the manila file folder on my desk. "Oh shit."

"Tell me you didn't forget, Mae." Kevin had a decidedly panicked note in his voice, and I gave him a cheerful smile.

"Of course I didn't."

"Are you lying to me, Mae?"

"I might be."

"Shit! Mae, he needs that file. There's information in it that isn't in our computer system.

"I know, I know. I'm sorry, Kevin. I'll drive it out to his

house right now." I grabbed the file and my purse and stood up.

Kevin glanced at his watch. "I'd take it myself, but I'm supposed to meet my wife in ten minutes."

"Don't be silly. I created the problem, and I'll fix it. I'll use the company car to drive the file to his house," I said.

Kevin nodded distractedly as he glanced at his watch again. "Okay. Thanks, Mae."

He left my office. I waited a few minutes before I headed toward reception to grab the keys to the company car. I was ridiculously excited to go to Liam's house again and snorted impatiently. Maybe it would eventually sink in if I told myself enough times how ridiculous I was.

* * *

I KNOCKED AGAIN ON THE WIDE FRONT DOOR TO LIAM'S HOUSE and waited. I frowned a little. His car was in the driveway, but I'd been standing on the front step for nearly five minutes. He told me earlier that he would be working from home this afternoon.

I stared again at his car, tapping my foot anxiously. Would he have gone for a walk?

Maybe he's driving one of the twenty other cars he owns, you idiot. Or maybe Russ drove him somewhere.

Probably, I decided. I looked at the thick folder in my hand, trying to decide what to do. I was hit with sudden inspiration. Maybe he was on the patio at the back. There was no harm in checking.

Holding the folder, I walked around the side of the house. If he weren't there, I would leave the folder on the patio table and text Liam to tell him it was there. It was supposed to be sunny all day today, so there was no fear that rain would ruin the file.

I rounded the corner of the house and came to an abrupt stop. My mouth dropped open, and a small squeak of surprise escaped from my throat.

Liam, naked with his hands bound behind his back and a leather collar around his neck, knelt on the hard stones of the patio. His erect cock jutted out proudly from his body, and his eyes widened with shock as he caught sight of me standing frozen at the edge of the patio. The woman standing in front of him turned around.

She blinked in surprise and then smiled. "Hello there."

I stared at her. She wore tight leather pants and a bright red bustier. Her large breasts were nearly spilling out of it. Black silk gloves covered her hands and arms up to her elbows. Her dark hair was pulled back in a high ponytail, dark shadow outlined her brown eyes, and she wore bright red lipstick. I stared at her short and chubby body before my eyes were drawn to the leather crop she carried in one gloved hand.

I stood motionless as she glanced at Liam before she walked toward me. She stopped before me and studied me carefully, a small smile on her lips. We would have been the same height if it weren't for her four-inch heels.

She reached out and traced my cheek with one finger. "We could be twins, could we not?"

I nodded dumbly as she looked me up and down and said softly, "The resemblance is quite remarkable."

I swallowed and licked my lips nervously. The woman was right. With her dark hair and dark eyes, the extra pounds she carried on her small frame - even the shape of her mouth – she was a dead ringer for me.

"Are you friends with Liam?" Her tone demanded an answer.

"I, um, I work for him."

"Do you? How interesting. Are you a lawyer as well?"

I shook my head. "No, I'm his PA."

Her grin widened and became distinctively shark-like, and my stomach churned with nervousness as she turned to Liam.

"My, you are a naughty boy, aren't you, Liam? I'm beginning to understand why you specifically requested me."

His face pale and his eyes dark and unreadable, Liam struggled to his feet.

"No!" the woman said sharply. "Stay right where you are."

He hesitated and sank back to his knees as she faced me again. "What's your name, my love?" She walked around me, her hand ran feather-soft down my arm, and I twitched nervously when she used the crop to stroke my long hair.

I stared at Liam and said, "My name is Mae."

"Mae. A pretty name for a pretty girl. My name is Mistress Chelsea."

"It's, uh – it's nice to meet you."

She laughed. "It's nice to meet you as well, Mae. Why are you here?"

I looked at the file folder in my hand. "I – I have a work file for Mr. Knight."

"You may put it on the table." She indicated for me to move forward. I stumbled toward the table and set the file down with a trembling hand.

I couldn't tear my gaze from Liam. Although his cock had softened, the look of lust on his face as he stared at me was unmistakeable.

I took a deep breath and turned to go, but Mistress Chelsea stood directly behind me. She smiled and moved to my side as my gaze returned to Liam. She gently turned my head until I looked at her. "Do you find your boss attractive, Mae?"

I hesitated, and she grinned at me. "Don't be shy. Obviously, your boss finds you attractive, or I wouldn't be here, would I?"

"Yes," I said hoarsely. "I find him attractive."

"Excellent," she purred. She put her arm around me and rested her head against mine. When she slipped her hand under my arm and let it press against the side of my breast, neither of us failed to notice the way Liam's cock immediately hardened.

"He has a beautiful cock, does he not, Mae?" Mistress Chelsea said.

I swallowed and nodded as she stroked the side of my breast gently. She kissed my cheek softly, then crossed the short distance to Liam and ran her gloved hand through his short hair.

"Would you like her to stay, Liam? I have no objections to another if that's what you desire."

Liam inhaled sharply, and a thick drop of pre-cum dripped from his cock. My pussy dampened in response, and I could feel my nipples hardening against my bra.

My twin yanked hard on Liam's hair, and I winced as he made a hoarse cry of surprise. He stared up at her as she traced her finger across his cheek. "Answer me."

"No, Mistress Chelsea. I don't want her to stay," Liam said.

Stupidly, I could feel hurt rippling through me. My face flushed with embarrassment.

Mistress Chelsea frowned at him. "Your cock would suggest otherwise."

She traced the crop along his bare chest when he didn't reply. "Would you care to change your answer? You know you'll be punished for lying to me, Liam."

"I don't want her to stay," he repeated.

"Very well." She smiled at me. "It was nice to meet you, Mae.

"Nice to meet you as well." Without looking at Liam, I turned and hurried away.

* * *

HE SHOWED UP AT MY APARTMENT SATURDAY AFTERNOON. I let him in and stood nervously in the kitchen as he stared silently at me. He had two envelopes in his hand and handed one to me after a moment.

"What is this?" I asked.

"Read it." He sat at the table and folded his hands neatly in his lap.

I sat down across from him and slid the document out. It was four pages long, and I scanned the first few paragraphs. My jaw dropped, and I sat at the table and stared at him.

"You'll pay me fifty thousand dollars to keep quiet about what I saw yesterday."

"Yes," he said.

"Do you really think I would tell anyone, Liam? Do you honestly believe you need to bribe me into keeping quiet?" My shock was turning into anger.

He flushed. "You know if this got out, it would ruin me. Don't pretend you don't. Everything I've worked so hard for would be destroyed. You can't blame me for wanting to do whatever I had to to protect myself. Besides, there's more, Mae. Please, keep reading and you'll -"

I shook my head. "I've never been more insulted in my life. I think you should leave."

"Please, just keep reading," he pleaded.

I stared silently at him, took a deep breath, and picked up the document again. He waited patiently as I read through it. I put the last page down nearly ten minutes later and stared at the table.

"Mae?" he said.

"Yeah?"

"Are you okay?"

I laughed. "Am I okay? Well, let's see. Yesterday, I walked in on my boss naked and tied up while a woman who looked exactly like me threatened him with a leather crop."

"Mae -"

I held my hand up. "Then – *then* – today, my boss offered me fifty thousand to not only keep my mouth shut about what I saw but also to spend the next thirty days dominating him and having sex with him."

"It's not -"

"Are you secretly insane, Liam? Do you hide it really, really well?"

"I'm not insane, Mae. I happen to like pleasing women. I like to submit to them and -"

"I don't mean that," I said. "I mean this… this contract. Do you expect me to whore myself out to you for fifty grand? I'm not a sex worker, and I don't have sex with men for money."

"I'm not asking you to have sex with me," he said quietly. "There's nowhere in that contract where I ask for sex. If we have sex, it violates Knight and Associate's rules about coworkers having a sexual relationship. We won't have sex, and your job at the firm will be safe."

"That's bullshit, and you know it, Liam," I scoffed. "Just because we don't engage in sex doesn't mean I won't be fired. The employee handbook talks about relationships of a sexual *nature*."

He shrugged. "I could argue it and win."

"Of course you could," I said.

He leaned forward. "Mae, think of this as a business contract and nothing more. It's not prostitution. I'm asking you to provide me with a service, one for which you'll be paid, for one month. And it's not even the entire month."

I gaped at him. "You're forgetting one thing - I'm not qualified for this job."

"I think you are," he replied.

"How long have you been involved with Mistress Chelsea?" I asked.

"I'm not *involved* with her. She provides me with a certain service that I pay for. The same one I'm asking you to provide."

"Yeah, yeah. I read the contract. How long?"

He regarded me carefully. "I've seen her three times now."

"Where did you find her?"

He hesitated, and I shook my head. "Never mind. I don't need to know."

I bit at my bottom lip for a moment. "Is this the first time you've hired someone to..."

"No. When I was younger, I went to several agencies that catered to men specifically looking for this type of thing. Once my firm became larger and I started attracting more media attention, I quit going. I didn't want to risk being caught."

"So, none of those blonde models you're always going out with, have any idea?" I asked.

"No. I date these women because it's what the media and my clients expect to see me with. I rarely sleep with them, and if I do, it's strictly vanilla sex."

"So why the sudden change? Why did you hire Mistress Chelsea and risk exposing your dirty little secret?"

He frowned. "It's not a dirty little secret. I'm not ashamed of who I am, Mae, or what my sexual preferences are. But I employ a lot of people at the law firm, and if my reputation is ruined and the firm starts to do poorly, many of those people would be out of a job."

I hadn't thought of that. I stared at the contract in front of me. "Why are you asking me to do this? Why not just continue with Mistress Chelsea?"

He leaned back in his chair. "Mistress Chelsea enjoys inflicting pain and, I suspect, humiliation on occasion. I don't enjoy that."

I frowned. "Then why did you choose her? You said you've seen her three times now."

"She looks like you."

I could feel my cheeks heating up at his directness. I looked away and took several deep breaths. "Have you had sex with her?"

"No."

I ignored the trickle of relief that went through me. "Have you ever slept with a – a mistress?"

He nodded. "Again, when I was younger. Occasionally, the service provided would end with sex."

"Why didn't you sleep with Mistress Chelsea?" I asked.

"I didn't want to."

"What's in the second envelope?"

"Results of my tests for STIs. If you agree to this, I wanted you to have a copy. I'd prefer not to wear condoms, and I wanted you to be assured that you would be safe with me."

"And you want me to provide you with STI results as well," I said.

He nodded. "It says so on page three of the contract."

"Yeah, I saw it. Do you want proof that I'm on the pill as well? Should I give you a copy of my prescription?" I said sarcastically.

He shook his head. "We won't be having sex, remember? There's no concern about pregnancy."

"Right," I muttered.

Liam leaned forward again. "Mae, I know you're struggling financially. This contract will benefit both of us. You'll be able to pay off your student loans, and I'll be given the chance to do what I've wanted to do since the first day I saw you."

"What's that?" I asked.

"Make you come until you scream. Bring you pleasure until you're weak and trembling, and you're begging me to stop."

I swallowed thickly. My crotch was suddenly wet, and my heart thudded in my ears.

"Just one thing, Mae. I only like to be dominated sexually. None of this will overflow into my personal life or work life. At the office, I'm still your boss."

"I read that in the contract as well. I'm not stupid," I said.

"I know. I thought it would be best to clarify that point." He hesitated. "Do you have any questions?"

"Actually, I do. Page two says additional funds will be provided for any props or costumes. What kind of props? Handcuffs and whipped cream? Whips and chains?"

"Whatever props you want to buy."

"You'd let me whip you?" I raised my eyebrows at him. He had explicitly said he wasn't into pain. I wondered how deeply he wanted to submit to me.

He cleared his throat. "I'm not into pain, but if that's something you believe you'd enjoy, I'd be willing to try it."

I shook my head quickly. "I'm not going to ask you to do that. I don't want you doing anything you won't enjoy, and besides, I'm not into pain or humiliation either."

I didn't think I imagined his brief look of relief. He took a deep breath. "As the contract states, I'll provide you with a rental car to drive to my house on the weekends. You can also use it for the month to drive back and forth to the office if you'd like."

I scanned the second page of the contract again. "Why only the weekends?"

"Having you at my house every day would increase the

chance of us being discovered. I have a busy schedule during the week, and I know you also have your own life. I've cleared my schedule for the next month, so my weekends are free. As I noted in the contract, I'd like you to come directly to my house after work on Friday and stay until Sunday evening."

When I didn't reply, he cleared his throat again. "You don't have to sleep with me in my bed. I can move to the guest room once we're … finished if you prefer your space."

"What's your preference?" I asked.

"I want you in my bed with me," he said.

"All right." I stared down at the contract again.

"Does this mean you're accepting the offer?"

"Can I think about it?"

"Of course." He stood and glanced around my dismal apartment before walking toward the door. "Thank you for considering it, Mae."

"What if I say no?" I asked before he could open the door. "Will you offer me a second contract for fifty grand to keep my mouth shut about your...preferences?"

He shook his head. "No. I was wrong to include that in the contract. I trust you, Mae."

CHAPTER 15

When he knocked on my door Monday night, I straightened my t-shirt, took a deep, fortifying breath, and opened it.

"Hello, Mae."

"Hi, Liam. Thanks for coming by." I had sent him a text just before I left the office, asking him to stop by my apartment.

I spent the rest of Saturday and Sunday thinking about Liam's offer. I read and re-read the contract until I thought my eyeballs would start bleeding. Lying sleepless in my bed on Sunday night, I made a mental list of pros and cons.

Pro – you want your boss. He's offering you the chance to have him.

Con – you could lose your job.

Pro – you'll be fifty grand richer.

Con – no actual sex with Liam.

Pro – I apparently had a much stronger urge to dominate than I ever suspected, and Liam was giving me the opportunity to explore that.

Con – he's my goddamn boss.

Pro – I'll have my goddamn boss on his knees in front of me, ready and willing to do all sorts of delicious, naughty things to me.

Con – it's only for a month.

I weighed the options back and forth until I finally got up and went to the bathroom. I stared at myself in the mirror and sighed deeply. I was going to do it. I had known that as soon as Liam admitted he wanted me.

Now, I sat on the small couch and smiled nervously when Liam joined me, his large bulk taking up most of the space.

"You were quiet today." His smile was tinged with anxiety as well.

"I had a lot on my mind."

"Have you decided on my offer?"

"Yes."

He stared expectantly at me. I reached for the envelope on the coffee table and handed it to him. "I'll do it. I've signed the contract and provided you with a copy of my most recent blood tests."

His hand gripped the envelope, and warmth flooded me when he smiled at me. "Thank you, Mae."

I nodded. "When, uh, when do we start?"

"This weekend, if that works for you?"

"It does." I took another deep breath as he relaxed on the couch.

"There's something else, Mae."

"What?" I gave him a wary look.

"We need to talk about hard and soft limits."

"Meaning what's acceptable and what isn't?"

'Yes. How much do you know about this lifestyle?"

I shrugged. "I know a bit."

"Have you done this before?"

"No, not really. I mean, I've always been kind of bossy in bed…"

He smiled at me. "I like bossy."

"Obviously," I said.

He smiled again. "We can talk about our limits now, or I can give you my personal email address. You can think about it, and then we can email each other and discuss it Friday."

"I'll have to think on it for a bit, but could you give me some of your list now?"

"Sure." He sat back and put his arm along the back of the couch. I wondered if it would be too weird of me to curl into the circle of his arm when his hand dropped to my shoulder, and he tugged me closer.

I leaned into him, and he stroked my arm gently. "Before we start on limits, there's one other thing I wanted to bring up. I know this is a business arrangement, but when you're at my house, I'd like it if you'd allow me to touch you for reasons other than sex. Part of my enjoyment in submitting to a woman comes from doing things like foot rubs and non-sexual touching. Does that make sense?"

I nodded. "You like to cuddle."

He laughed. "Yes, I guess I do."

"What are your hard limits?"

"Blood, any tearing of the skin, that sort of thing. As I mentioned before, I'm not really into pain. I don't mind hair pulling or, as an example of a soft limit, spanking. If spanking me is something that will please you, I'm willing to consider it."

I thought about that for a moment. "I don't think I'm into spanking, and I'm definitely not into causing any type of pain that draws blood."

"Okay."

"What else?" I tucked my feet under me and sighed with pleasure when Liam moved his hand to the back of my neck and rubbed gently.

"Anal insertion is a hard limit."

"Nothing up your butt - got it," I said.

He laughed. "Is that a hard limit for you?"

"I don't know. I've never had anyone offer to stick something up my butt before. Do you want to do that to me?"

"Only if it's something you want."

"We only have four weekends together. We might not even get to that," I pointed out.

"True," he agreed.

"What else?" I repeated.

"No third-party involvement. I'm not sharing you with anyone else."

I glanced up at him. "Is that why you didn't want me to stay the other day?"

He nodded. "Yes."

"But it turned you on when she touched me. We both saw it."

"It did," he acknowledged. "But not enough for me to be willing to share. I want to be the only one who pleases you, Mae."

He hesitated. "Are you – do you want a threesome?"

"No. I don't like the idea of someone else touching you either," I said honestly.

"Good. Then a third party is a hard limit for the both of us." He smiled at me.

"Is that it for your hard limits?"

He shook his head. "No. Animals, children, incest play, and humiliation or degradation are all hard limits for me."

I could feel the blood draining from my face. Liam squeezed my neck lightly. "Are you okay?"

"I'm beginning to think I'm not the right person for this. I don't know very much about this lifestyle. Being bossy in bed is one thing, but I'm not an actual Dominatrix."

"I know that, Mae. I'm not expecting you to be one."

"Are you sure?" I asked.

"Positive," he said. "And you are the right person for this. I like what you say and do to me when we're together. If that's all it ever is, I'll be perfectly happy. I just thought it would be best to have a clear understanding of what our hard and soft limits are."

I was still staring at him doubtfully, and he smiled reassuringly. "Mae, please trust me on this. Over the next four weeks, you might find that you want to try different things. Your natural bossiness might lead to stronger dominant behaviour. If it does – great. If it doesn't – I'll be happy with whatever you're willing to give me. Okay?"

"Okay." I stared at my hands for a moment. "In your office, you called me mistress. I liked that. I want you to call me that again. Will you?"

"Yes. What you need to understand about me is that pleasing you is what turns me on most. I have a natural urge to submit in bed, and you have a natural urge to dominate. It makes our... business arrangement ideal," Liam said.

"Yes, I guess it does," I said.

"I know it's a lot to take in. I'll leave and give you some time to think about it. If this conversation changes your mind, I'll rip up the contract. Okay?"

"I won't change my mind. I'm just worried that I won't be as good at this as you think or want me to be."

"You are. You have no idea how badly I want you, Mae. I can hardly think straight. I'm sleeping like hell. I've spent the last six months dying to touch you, to know how you look and taste when you're coming on my mouth."

I blushed, and he grinned at me. "Friday can't come soon enough."

"What happens after the month is up?" I asked.

He hesitated. "We go back to the way things were. It's too dangerous to continue long-term. Eventually, we'd be discovered. I don't want to risk getting you fired."

When I didn't reply, he rubbed my back gently. "This is why this business arrangement is good. You can pay down some of your debt, and we can get this need for each other out of our systems. Then things can return to normal."

I stared at my hands. I knew Liam was only being honest and trying to make me feel better, but I felt more like a whore now than before.

"Are you okay?" he said.

"Yeah."

"I'm not asking you to have sex with me. This isn't prostitution," he said as if he had read my mind. "Even if we did have sex, it still wouldn't be prostitution. Do you consider what Mistress Chelsea does as prostitution?"

I thought silently for a few minutes. "No, I guess I don't."

"This isn't anything different from what she does," he said

That's where he was wrong, I thought. I highly doubted Mistress Chelsea had any interest in a relationship with Liam. I wasn't foolish enough to believe I didn't want more from him than a one-month business contract.

I rubbed my forehead. There was no point in thinking that way. By offering me this contract, Liam had made it clear what he wanted from me, and it wasn't a relationship. I couldn't blame him. He said he dated the blonde models because that was expected of him. The one time he deviated from that caused a minor scandal. No one wanted to see the most eligible bachelor in the city shacking up with a short, fat girl. Talk about ruining the fairy tale.

"I know you've already signed the contract, but, Mae, if you're having second thoughts, you can back out," he said. "It's not a legally binding contract by any means."

"It isn't?"

"No, a contract between a Dom and a Sub is only a personal agreement. It wouldn't hold up in any court of law."

"I'm not having second thoughts. Text me your email, and I'll send you my hard and soft limits list," I said.

"Okay. I should go. I have a lot of work to do this week." He hesitated and then kissed me softly on the lips. "I'll see you tomorrow, okay?"

I nodded and walked him to the door. He paused with the door open. "Remember, if you change your mind before Friday, just tell me. It won't affect our working relationship."

"I won't change my mind," I said. "Good night, Liam."

"Good night, Mae."

* * *

I CLIMBED OUT OF THE RENTAL CAR AND STARED apprehensively at Liam's house. I opened the trunk, pulled out the small suitcase, and walked slowly toward the front door. Before I was halfway there, it opened, and Liam stepped out.

He smiled and took the suitcase before ushering me into the house. I slipped out of my shoes, and he took my jacket and hung it up neatly on the coat hook on the wall. The house smelled delicious, a tantalizing combination of cheese, tomato, and spices.

"How was your afternoon?" he said.

"Good. I finished the correspondence for the Richardson file." Liam had left just after lunch for a meeting and had not returned to the office.

"That's good. Thank you." He smiled again at me, and I cleared my throat nervously.

"So, um, what do we do first?"

"Have you eaten dinner?"

I shook my head. He took my hand and led me to the kitchen. "Then we start with dinner."

The narrow island was set with plates, cutlery, and a

bottle of wine chilled in an ice bucket. A cluster of candles on the island's far end gave the kitchen a warm glow. I climbed onto the stool as Liam opened the wine.

"Do you like lasagna?" He poured me a glass of wine.

"Yes." I took a sip of wine, hoping to soothe my nerves. I'd been too anxious to eat anything today, and I felt a thin thread of hunger when Liam opened the oven door. He pulled the lasagna out of the oven and sat it on the top of the stove.

"It looks delicious." I took another sip of wine.

"Thanks. It's my mom's recipe."

"You made that?" I could hear the surprise in my voice. Evidently, he could, too, because he laughed.

"I did. I like to cook. My mom started teaching me at an early age."

"Do your parents live here?"

"No. They retired to Arizona. Of course, Dad stayed retired for about a month before he took on consulting work for a law firm there."

"So, your dad is a lawyer, too?"

"He is. How about your parents? Do they live here?" He pulled a large wooden bowl from the fridge and used salad tongs to toss the salad in it.

"Yes. My dad owns a cleaning company, and my mom is a librarian."

He set the bowl of salad on the island in front of me. "You must like to read then?"

I grinned. "As a matter of fact, I do."

"Do you have any siblings?"

"Yes, I have a younger brother, Toby. He just became a pilot for a commercial airline."

"Wow." Liam took my plate and scooped some lasagna onto it before setting it before me.

"He's the youngest pilot in the airline's history. He's very mature for his age." I watched as Liam took a piece of lasagna and sat beside me.

I placed my napkin on my lap and ate a bite of lasagna. "This is delicious."

"I'm glad you like it." Liam smiled and put some salad on my plate. "Eat up. There's lots."

He poured some more wine. "Are you close to your family?"

I ate some salad to give myself time to think. I wasn't sure that now was the time to discuss my family issues.

"Mae?" he prompted.

I smiled at him. "Do you want the version I usually share with people or the truth?"

"The truth."

"I had a great relationship with my parents until I stopped being a nurse. My dad values hard work, and although he's never come right out and said this, he thinks I'm a quitter for walking away from nursing. Honestly, he's got a point. Just because people are too polite to say it doesn't make it untrue. You know?"

"You're not a quitter, Mae."

I shrugged. "Anyway, he and my mom always struggled to provide for us, and it's hard for them to see me struggling now. Especially since I have no one to blame but myself. They were so proud when I graduated from nursing school."

"And now?" Liam said.

"Now they're proud of my brother." I took another bite of lasagna. "This really is delicious. If you ever stop being a lawyer, you could have a career as a chef."

"Thanks."

"Do you have any siblings?" I drank a sip of wine as he finished the lasagna on his plate.

"Yes. I have an adopted older sister, Eileen."

"Why did your parents adopt?" I asked.

"They didn't think they could have kids. They adopted Eileen when she was two. Two months after they brought her home, my mom found out she was pregnant with me."

I smiled. "That must have been quite the surprise."

"It was." He laughed.

"Are you close to her?"

He nodded. "She lives here in the city. We usually have dinner once or twice a month and talk or text weekly. She's married to an accountant, and they have a three-year-old boy named Dean."

I finished off my salad and washed it down with more wine. The conversation and the wine helped me relax, and I enjoyed hearing about Liam's personal life.

"Do you still talk to your parents?" he asked.

"Not as much as I used to, but we usually have dinner once a month. I'm going there on Thursday for dinner. Toby has a new girlfriend, and he's introducing her to us."

"That sounds nice."

I ate the last bit of lasagna on my plate. "It's usually nice when Toby is there. His many accomplishments help distract my parents from their disappointment in me."

He gave me a sympathetic look, and I grinned at him. "I sound like a jealous cow, don't I?"

He shook his head. I pushed my plate away before reaching for my wine glass. "I love Toby very much and am just as proud of him as my parents. It's just – you know…"

"Yeah, I think I do." He gathered up our plates and gave them a quick rinse.

"Can I help you clean up?"

"Nope. Sit and relax. It'll only take a minute."

When he was finished, he took my hand and led me into the living room. We stood silently for a moment, and I gave him a small smile. "So, now what?"

"We can sit and relax for a bit if you'd like. I'm sure there's a bad TV movie playing."

I took a deep breath. "Liam, I think – I think I'd just like to go to your bedroom if that's okay with you?"

His eyes darkened, and he nodded. "Yes, I'd like that, Mae."

He took my hand, picked up my suitcase, and led me up the stairs.

CHAPTER 16

I studied myself in the bathroom mirror. Once we were in Liam's bedroom, I took my suitcase and excused myself to the bathroom. I'd quickly brushed my teeth and smoothed on some body lotion. Not sure what Liam wanted or was expecting, I hadn't purchased any props or costumes. I had, however, brought the red corset and matching panties with me. I took another deep breath and smoothed my hands nervously over my corset. I'd been in here long enough.

When I opened the door, Liam stood up from the bed and moved to the middle of the room. I stood nervously before him, my hands folded behind my back as Liam looked me up and down. When he turned his gaze to mine, the look of dark lust on his face was enough to make my knees weak.

"You're so beautiful, Mae," he said.

"Thank you."

He reached out with a hand that trembled slightly and traced the curve of my bottom lip before running his finger down my throat and stroking the top of my exposed breasts.

I shivered and gave him another nervous smile. "So, um, do I just start barking orders or…"

He grinned at me and put his arms around my waist, tugging me towards him. "How about we start with kissing?"

He bent his head and kissed me softly. I made a low noise of need and returned his kiss as he stroked my bare back above the corset. When his hands slid down and cupped my ass, kneading the flesh roughly, I gasped and pushed my pelvis against his. I could feel his erection pressing against me, and I rubbed my pelvis back and forth against it. He groaned and kissed me more deeply, his tongue thrusting into my mouth to stroke urgently at mine.

"I want you so much, Mae," he muttered against my mouth. "You have no idea."

"Take off your shirt," I whispered.

He pulled his t-shirt over his head and dropped it to the floor. I stared at his broad chest and stroked the granite muscles of his abdomen. He shuddered under my touch, and I pressed my mouth against the bare flesh of his chest. I licked lightly as my hands traced the waistband of his jeans. He groaned, and his hands squeezed my ass as I placed soft, wet kisses across his chest before nipping his shoulder.

He kissed me again, his tongue hot and wet in my mouth as his hands reached for the hooks on the corset. I bit his bottom lip, holding it firmly in my teeth, and he paused. I released his mouth and soothed the bite with my tongue before smiling at him.

"Ask first."

"May I, mistress?"

My heart thudded in my chest. It was almost embarrassing how much I enjoyed Liam calling me mistress. I rubbed my pelvis against the bulge in his jeans. "You may."

He quickly unhooked the corset and eased it from my body before tossing it to the floor. He stared appreciatively at my breasts, then gently cupped them. I sighed and arched my back as he squeezed them lightly and ran the tips of his fingers over my nipples.

"Suck on them, Liam," I demanded.

He bent his head and took my right nipple deep into his mouth. He sucked hard and tugged with his teeth before sliding his tongue across it. The warm wetness of his mouth was making me shudder uncontrollably. He wrapped one arm around my waist, holding me steady as he switched to the other nipple. He ravished my tight nipple with his lips and tongue until my fingers were digging into his hard biceps.

I pulled lightly on his hair, and he looked up at me, his mouth hovering over my swollen, throbbing nipple. "Yes, mistress?"

I swallowed thickly, and he gave me a boyish grin before sucking on my nipple again.

"Oh God," I muttered, my pelvis arching against his hard cock. The aching between my legs, the wetness that was soaking through the thong, made me pull his hair again.

"On your knees, Liam." I tried to sound firm, but my voice was shaky and husky with need.

Liam dropped to his knees immediately and stared up at me. I felt another rolling wave of pleasure rush through my pelvis. My fantasy had come to life, and for a moment, I was so overcome with lust I couldn't say or do a damn thing other than stare at his perfect face.

"Tell me what you want, mistress," he said.

I closed my eyes. My entire body shook, and I took a deep breath. I felt Liam's hand on my thigh, the fingers stroking lightly and soothingly. His voice full of concern, he said, "Mae? Are you okay?"

I nodded without opening my eyes, and he placed a gentle kiss on my stomach just above my panties. "Do you want me to stop?"

I opened my eyes and stared down at him. "Christ, no."

He visibly relaxed and ran a lazy hand up and down my leg. "Good."

"Take off my panties," I said.

He hooked his fingers in the sides of my panties and pulled them down my legs. I stepped out of them, and he surprised me by grabbing my ass with strong fingers and brushing his face across the strip of hair on my pussy. He kissed it lightly, and I made a shuddering moan.

"Tell me, mistress," he whispered.

He looked up at me, his eyes dark with lust, and I ran my fingers through his hair.

"Lick me."

He immediately buried his face in my pussy, his tongue slicking between my wet and swollen lips to find my hard clit. He sucked greedily at it, and I shrieked with pleasure. My legs were starting to give out, and I clutched at his shoulders, trying to keep myself upright.

He stood, and I cried out at the loss of his warm tongue. He scooped me up easily and carried me to the bed. He placed me sideways on it so that my legs hung over the edge and dropped to his knees on the floor beside me. He draped my legs over his shoulders and slid his hands under my ass, gripping it firmly and lifting me to his mouth.

He winked at me, his grin flashing in the soft light of the bedside lamp before his dark head dipped between my thighs. I moaned his name at the first touch of his wet tongue, and my thighs dropped open.

He made a low hum of approval and washed his tongue over me. I rose on my elbows and watched as he kissed and licked my throbbing pussy. The lack of hair made everything deliciously sensitive, and when he rubbed the rough shadow of his chin across my swollen lips, I nearly slid off the bed.

"Oh my God, Liam," I moaned. My hands clenched in the

bed sheets, and my heels dug into his back as he grinned at me.

"You taste delicious, Mae. I could eat your pussy all night."

My hips thrust upward in helpless response, and he grinned again before burying his face back between my thighs. I groaned and whimpered and twisted weakly under his tongue. I tried to hold back and tried to stop from giving in to the need to come, but his tongue and lips were relentless. Within minutes, I was arching off the bed and having an earth-shattering orgasm. Liam held my hips and continued to lick my swollen clit until I squirmed and pushed frantically at the top of his head.

"Stop!"

He stopped immediately and stripped off the rest of his clothing before he climbed onto the bed beside me. "Did I hurt you?"

I shook my head. "Hell, no. But I was afraid I might black out if you didn't stop."

He laughed and stretched out beside me, his hand cupping my breast as my chest heaved for air. I glanced down at his cock. It was standing straight up with the tip brushing against his stomach, and it was slick and shiny with his precum. I reached down and wrapped my fingers around it. He groaned, and his hips bucked once before he reached down and tugged my hand away. I frowned at him.

"What are you doing?"

He gave me a faint smile. "This is about pleasing you, Mae."

"So, because we're not having sex, you don't get to come?" I asked. "I don't remember reading anything about that in the contract."

He shook his head. "No, it's not that. I want this first night to be about you. I want to please my mistress."

I reached down and took his cock in my hand again,

squeezing firmly and smiling a little when he inhaled sharply, and his hand tightened on my breast.

I leaned over him and nuzzled his ear before whispering, "What if I told you that what would please your mistress is having you come in her mouth?"

"Fuck!" He muttered in a harsh pant, his eyes dropping to my mouth. I licked my lips and then bit gently on the bottom one.

"Would you like that, Liam? Would you like to come in my mouth?"

"Yes."

I gave him an impatient look and pinched his nipple hard. "Yes, what?"

He winced a little, and I dipped my head, licking at his flat nipple until his hand was cupping the back of my head. "Yes, mistress. I want to come in your mouth."

"Yes, I imagine you would." I smiled at him and slid off the bed before walking towards the bathroom.

He sat up, blinking in surprise. "Mae, where the hell are you going?"

I turned and arched my eyebrow at his demanding tone. He flushed and cleared his throat, "Mistress, will you please tell me where you're going?"

"I'm going to do what I've been dying to do since I first saw it – have a swim in your giant tub. You," I pointed my finger at him, "are going to lie on the bed and touch yourself. Keep yourself hard, but don't come, do you understand?"

He nodded, and I stopped and stretched in the bathroom doorway. Liam's eyes dropped to my breasts, his cock bounced, and he moved his hand to stroke it rapidly.

I smiled to myself. Usually, I would have wrapped myself in a sheet before walking to the bathroom, anxious to hide my chunky thighs and round stomach. I had no inclination to hide this time. Something in the way Liam looked at me made me believe he thought I was beautiful. Or maybe it was just the fact that staring at me had made his cock so hard and swollen that the head of it was nearly purple.

He was still stroking rapidly, his hand tightening and loosening around his hard shaft. I gave him a warning look. "You might want to slow down. You'll be punished if you come before I say you can."

I smiled approvingly when he slowed the stroking of his hand. "I'll call you when I need you to wash my back."

* * *

I SANK BACK INTO THE WATER AND STARED UP AT THE CEILING. It had been nearly twenty minutes since I climbed into the tub. I cocked my head and listened closely. Faintly, I could hear Liam's soft moans, and I decided I had tortured him long enough.

I called his name, and he walked into the bathroom with one hand still clasped around his cock. It was apparent he hadn't come, and I admired his willpower as he knelt next to the tub and kissed me softly on the mouth.

"Hi." He gave me a strained smile, and I ran my fingers over the stubble on his cheek.

"Hi, yourself. How are you?"

"Fine." He shifted a little, grimacing when his dick pushed against the side of the tub.

"Good. Wash my back, please." I sat forward and then handed him the soap. He lathered the soap between his hands and washed my back, kneading and pressing with his strong fingers until I was moaning with pleasure.

I scooted forward. "Get in behind me."

He climbed in and sat down. I leaned back against him, wiggling my wet ass against his rock-hard cock, and smiling at his groan of need.

He slipped his hands around to my breasts and rubbed and stroked them. Although I hadn't given him permission, the feel of his wet fingers pulling on my nipples had me forgetting about punishing him. Instead, I arched my back and moaned encouragingly when his right hand slid down my stomach and between my thighs.

He found my small, pink nub and went to work. His fingers stroked and petted and danced across my swollen flesh until I white knuckle gripped the tub and bucked my pelvis against him. When he gently pinched my clit and then tugged, my sudden orgasm took me completely by surprise. I thrashed against him, water surging over the tub to splash on the tile floor as he held me tightly.

Panting harshly with my legs shaking and my hair plastered wetly against my cheeks, I turned my head and kissed him deeply. He moaned and returned my kiss, our tongues tangling together as I rubbed my ass against his cock.

He tore his mouth from mine. "Please, mistress," he moaned.

He sounded nothing like the Liam Knight from the office, and despite my recent orgasm, my pussy pulsed at the pleading in his voice.

"Help me out of the tub," I said.

He stood and climbed out, dripping water everywhere but not seeming to care. I stood up, and he lifted me out of the tub and wrapped a towel around me. He dried me carefully, his hand lingering a little longer than necessary between my legs. I smiled at him and returned the favour, using a second towel to dry his body. I avoided touching his cock, even when he thrust it helplessly against me.

I stared silently at it for a moment. I had a powerful urge to simply push Liam to the floor, fill my throbbing pussy with every glorious inch of his thick cock and ride him like a horse. I took a deep breath.

No sex, remember, Mae? Keep it together, you silly tart.

I wiped away the water droplets on his chest and stared at Liam. He stood with his eyes closed and a look of pure pain on his face. His hands were clenched into tight fists, and he panted harshly.

"Liam?"

"Yes?"

"Do you still want my mouth on your cock?"

He jerked, and I rubbed his chest soothingly before walking behind him.

"Yes, mistress."

I kissed his bare back. It made him jerk again, and I slid my hands around his front to rest them against his flat stomach. "Not this time."

His groan of disappointment turned into a strangled noise of need when my hand gripped his cock firmly. I pumped him three times before his pelvis twitched, and he shouted and came explosively all over my hand.

I kissed him again on his back as he shuddered and panted in front of me. "Good boy. Now take me to bed and make me come again."

"Yes, mistress."

CHAPTER 17

"Mae?"

I looked up from my cell phone to see Liam standing in my office doorway.

"Am I paying you to text now?"

I tucked my phone into the desk drawer. Neil had texted me a record seven times in the last two days, asking me to meet him for coffee. I had so far resisted from responding, but I was remarkably close to sending him a very short text that consisted of two words – 'fuck' and 'off'.

"No, I'm sorry. What do you need?"

"I can't find the Word document for the Richardson file. Did you put it somewhere else on the system?"

I shook my head as he stood next to me. With a few clicks of the mouse, I located the file and opened it on my laptop. "Here it is."

He didn't reply, and I glanced up at him. He stared down my shirt, and I nudged his leg with my foot.

"Stop staring at my tits, Liam," I murmured.

"Stop wearing such low-cut shirts then," he said.

I snorted and started to push back my chair. He glanced

at the open door of my office and then put his hand on my wrist, holding me in my spot.

"I have to work late tonight," he said. "I'm sorry. It can't be avoided."

"It's fine." I swallowed my disappointment.

"Will you still go to my house after work?"

I hesitated. I had spent the entire week thinking about nothing but being back in Liam's bed. "Do you want me to?"

"Yes. I shouldn't be any later than nine."

"Okay."

"There's an extra key in a key box under the patio table." His thumb stroked my wrist, rubbing my rapidly beating pulse. I pulled my hand free just as Kevin wandered into my office.

"Hello, Mae," he said.

"Hi, Kevin. How are you?"

"Good. Liam, can I borrow Mae for a few hours this afternoon?"

"For what?" Liam asked.

"I need her to show Roxie how to manage my calendar. She still hasn't figured it out."

Liam relaxed. "That's fine. I'm meeting with Doreen to review the Richardson file this afternoon anyway."

He glanced at me. "Do you have time to help Roxie?"

I nodded as the soft chime of my cell phone indicated yet another text message from Neil.

* * *

I sat on Liam's bed and stared idly around the bedroom. It was close to nine, and I hoped Liam would be home soon. After work, I stopped at the same lingerie store where I had picked out the red corset. I browsed through the selection, finally settling on a sheer pink baby doll nightie with matching panties. On Monday, after my first weekend with Liam, I found an envelope in the top drawer of my office desk. There was close to three grand in cash in the envelope and a short note that simply said, "For incidentals."

I slid off the bed and studied myself in the full-length mirror in the corner of the room. I smoothed my hand over the soft material of the lingerie before straightening my back and sucking in my belly. I hoped that Liam liked what I picked out. I had considered stopping at one of the sex shops on the east side but chickened out. We hadn't discussed what props Liam wanted, and I was nervous about picking out something he might consider too kinky.

My eyes fell on my suitcase, standing neatly next to the dresser. After hemming and hawing last night, I had tucked my vibrator into the suitcase. I knew that at some point this weekend, I would take it out and ask Liam to use it on me. Despite the multiple times Liam had made me come with his fingers and tongue last weekend, I was craving his cock. At one point, I was close to screaming at him to just fuck me, and I wasn't sure I could go another weekend of not having actual sex with him. I wanted Liam's cock, wanted it desperately, in fact, and even the thought that having sex with him meant I was being paid for sex was starting to lose some of its power.

I paced Liam's bedroom. I thought I would spend the week feeling ashamed of what I did with Liam. Instead, I spent every waking moment reliving the weekend and, if I were being truthful, coming up with new ideas of all the ways I could make Liam submit to me. I snorted and turned back to the bed. It took only one weekend of Liam calling me mistress to turn me into a goddamn wannabe Dominatrix. It was ridiculous how much I –

My baby toe hit the small wooden trunk tucked at the end of the bed. I muttered a curse and rubbed the throbbing toe as I studied the chest. It was too small to hold extra blankets. What was in it? I knelt in front of it and traced the top of it. After a moment, I shrugged and flipped up the lid.

I stared at the contents, my eyes widening in surprise and, I'll admit, lust. There were several collars as well as leather cuffs. A few heavy chains were coiled in the very bottom, and I pulled them out, touching the cold steel with the tip of my finger. I pulled out a collar, my pussy throbbing as I remembered the way Liam had looked on his knees on the patio with this very collar buckled around his neck.

Before I could change my mind, I quickly pulled the collar and cuffs out of the trunk and one of the chains. I set them on the bed and patiently waited for Liam to return.

I STOOD IN THE CORNER OF THE BEDROOM WHEN LIAM hurried into the room. It was closer to ten than nine, and he yanked off his tie and dropped his suit jacket to the floor as he entered the bedroom.

"Mae? I'm sorry I..." He stared at the collar and cuffs lying on the bed.

"Hello, Liam."

He turned, his eyes darkening when he saw my outfit. "Hello, mistress."

"You're late."

"I know. I'm sorry."

"Our agreement was Friday after work until Sunday evening, wasn't it?"

"Yes," he said, his eyes following the gentle sway of my breasts as I walked toward him.

"You've broken our agreement. Do you believe you should be punished?"

He stared thoughtfully at me. "I did tell you I would be late, mistress."

"You did. But you said nine, and it's almost ten."

He didn't reply, and I smiled at him. "Take off your clothes, Liam."

He stripped quickly. I admired the way his cock stood out proudly from his body before I picked up the collar from the bed. "Kneel, please."

He knelt beside the bed, and I buckled the heavy collar around his neck. My breathing was rapid, and just looking at him wearing the collar had made me wet.

"Give me your hands," I said hoarsely.

He held them out obediently, and I buckled the leather cuffs around them. My hands were trembling noticeably. When I finished buckling the cuffs, he took my hands and gently kissed each palm. "Okay?"

I nodded. "Yes. Get on the bed."

He lay on the bed, and I straddled him, rubbing my panty-covered crotch against his erection. He cupped my breasts, his fingers stroking my nipples through the soft material of the lingerie, and I smiled down at him before tugging his hands above his head.

I leaned over him, my breasts directly in front of his face, and he sucked on my nipple through the lingerie as I slid my hand under the pillow. I made a soft noise of pleasure and used my free hand to tug the neckline of my outfit down-ward. My breasts popped out, and Liam stared at them hungrily before latching onto one stiff nipple. His tongue grazed it lightly, and I arched my back, my hands tightening in the bed sheets as he sucked firmly and then gently.

I sat up with a low groan, pulling the chain from under the pillow. Liam stared at it momentarily, a small smile on his lips.

His arms were still above his head, and I latched one end

of the chain to the metal loop on the leather cuff around his left hand. I slid the chain around the metal headboard and clipped the other end to the cuff on his right wrist. I sat back and admired my handiwork for a moment. He tugged lightly. The chain clinked against the metal, and I grinned at him.

"Did you buy this headboard specifically so you could be chained to it?"

"No. My interior designer picked it out."

I stared suspiciously at him, and he laughed. "I swear, Mae. I've never brought a woman to my bedroom before you."

"What? Are you kidding me?"

He shook his head. "No. I told you – I value my privacy."

Unexpected warmth flowed through me at the thought that I was the first woman in his bedroom. Before I could stop myself, I blurted out, "Why did you bring me here then?"

He hesitated, and my stomach fluttered nervously.

"You live in a bad neighbourhood, remember?" he said finally.

Disappointment bit at my stomach, but I nodded and smiled. "Right. I really should teach you how to use mace."

He stared up at me. "Are you okay?"

I shook off my sudden melancholy. What was I expecting Liam to say? He brought me to his bedroom because he loved me? I needed to get my head out of the clouds and remember that the man was paying me to chain him to his headboard. I gave him a more natural smile. "I'm fine."

I traced the collar around his neck before tugging on the thick metal loop at the front of it. "I want you to wear this all weekend. You're not allowed to take it off without my permission. Do you understand?"

He hesitated, and I frowned at him. "Do you have a problem with that?"

"No, mistress."

"Good." I glanced at the leather cuffs around his wrists. "You're to keep those on as well."

He nodded, and I smiled my approval before sliding my fingers over his bare chest. "No shirt either."

He rolled his eyes, and I raised my eyebrows at him. "Keep that up, and you'll also find yourself without pants."

He grinned, and I leaned down and rubbed my breasts against his chest before kissing him. I traced his lips with my tongue, urging him to open them. He groaned with need before opening his mouth.

I kissed him lightly, pushing my tongue delicately in and out of his mouth until his hips were arching against me. I sat up and slowly pulled off my lingerie. I dropped it to the bed and cupped my breasts, rubbing my nipples with my thumbs.

He groaned and pulled at the cuffs. "Please, mistress. Uncuff me."

I laughed. "Begging already, Liam? I've only just started."

"I've spent all week dreaming about touching you, about making you come," he rasped out. "Let me make you come, and then you can cuff me again."

I shook my head and pinched my nipples lightly. "Were you a good boy this week, Liam? Did you do what I told you to?"

"Yes, mistress."

I studied him. "You didn't masturbate?"

"No."

"Good. That makes me very happy." I smiled and leaned down to kiss his chest. "I'll admit I'm torn about what to do."

"What do you mean?" he gasped when I sucked lightly on his flat nipple.

"Well, should I punish you for keeping me waiting or reward you for not masturbating?"

"Reward?" he said hopefully.

I laughed and bit his nipple. "I'll think about it a little longer."

I scooted down until I straddled his thighs and trailed soft kisses across his chest. I took my time tasting and licking every part of his warm skin until he was moaning and arching his back. The chain rattled loudly against the headboard as he pulled uselessly at the heavy chain.

I dipped my tongue into his navel, and he jerked wildly, nearly bucking me off his legs. I pressed my hands against his heavily muscled abdomen. "Hold still, please."

My breasts were rubbing against his cock, and I looked down to see moisture spread across them. I cupped my breasts and trapped his cock between them, rubbing up and down as he stared at me with lust burning in his eyes.

"Oh my God," he moaned. His hips thrust upward, and I sat up straight, frowning down at him.

"Please, mistress," he begged again.

I bent down until my mouth was hovering over his cock. I hadn't taken him in my mouth yet. I spent last weekend telling him repeatedly I would and then denying him.

Now, as I licked my lips and stared up at him, he yanked viciously at the chain holding him captive.

"Do you want me to suck your cock, Liam?" I asked.

"Yes! Please, mistress. Suck my cock," he pleaded.

I smiled at the desperation in his voice. "I'll suck your cock as a reward for your good behaviour this week. But if you move, if your hips rise even a little off the bed, I'll stop. Do you think you can keep yourself from moving?"

"Yes."

"Are you sure?"

He nodded frantically, and I licked my lips again. "One more thing, Liam. You're not to come until I tell you to. Do you understand?"

"Yes, mistress," he ground out.

"Good."

I ran my tongue over the head of his cock. His breath escaped in a long, drawn-out hiss, and I heard him moan as I slid his cock into my mouth. I sucked lightly on the head, running my tongue over it as I placed my hands on his hips. I pressed firmly, helping him to keep still as I sucked hard on just the head.

After a few moments, I released him and smiled up at him. "You're doing so well, Liam."

"Thank you, mistress," he panted. He stared at my hair piled on top of my head.

"What?" I asked.

"Will you take down your hair? Please?" he said.

I quickly pulled out the pins that held it up. I dropped them over the side of the bed and ran my fingers through my hair before leaning over him again. My hair tickled his thighs, and he jerked upward, his cock nearly brushing my mouth.

"Liam," I warned softly.

"I'm sorry, mistress," he groaned.

I ran my fingers over his thighs, feeling the muscles bunching and twitching under my hands. I squeezed his thighs before moving my hands back to his hips. I leaned down and took his cock in my mouth again. This time, I slid as much of his thick shaft into my mouth as I could. It brushed the back of my throat, and he moaned when I took the base in my hand and squeezed it lightly. I bobbed my head up and down his cock, my hair sweeping across his hips and thighs as my tongue stroked and licked his throbbing skin.

"Oh God!" he cried out, and I looked up as he yanked again at the chain around his wrists. "Please!"

"Please, what?" I smiled, my fingers tracing lazy circles over the head of his cock.

"I need to come, please," he moaned.

"I know you do," I said soothingly. "Not much longer now, I promise."

I bent my mouth to his cock. "You have my permission to move."

I took him into my mouth. He groaned and arched his pelvis upwards. My cheeks bulged as I took more of his cock deep into my mouth and sucked hard. He was panting harshly, his hips thrusting rapidly as I licked and sucked with wild abandonment. I could feel his cock swelling in my mouth, and I released it with a soft pop, ignoring his cry of disappointment.

"Do you want to come in my mouth?" I asked.

"Yes," he moaned.

I smiled at him. "You're allowed to come, Liam."

He cried out, his body twitching and shaking as I took him into my mouth a final time. I sucked him hard, and he arched his entire body upward, carrying me with him as he came into my mouth. I sucked and swallowed eagerly until he fell back against the bed, then released him and collapsed beside him.

His chest rose and fell rapidly, and his eyes were closed. I unclipped the chain from each cuff, pulling his arms down and rubbing them gently. He didn't move, and I squeezed his arm. "Liam? Are you okay?"

"I am fucking fantastic, Mae," he muttered.

I grinned and then twitched in surprise when he suddenly turned to face me. He kissed me hard on the mouth and slid his hand into my panties. He rubbed my clit with his rough fingers as he dipped his head and sucked on my nipple.

I cried out and came almost immediately, my hands

clamping down on his arms as my orgasm tore through me. I shuddered and shook before collapsing against him. He wrapped his arms around me and kissed me softly on the mouth before taking my thigh and hooking it around his hips. Warm and relaxed in his embrace, I drifted off to sleep.

CHAPTER 18

"You can't be serious."

"I am."

Liam stared at me in disbelief. It was late Saturday morning. He was in the kitchen wearing only the collar, cuffs, and jeans. He had given me three orgasms earlier this morning, but I was still throbbing for him. I was aching for his cock, and I squeezed my thighs together and sighed inwardly as he continued to stare at me.

"You don't like pancakes?"

"Nope. Find them disgusting."

He shook his head and opened the pantry cupboard. "I could make you French toast."

"Do you have any oatmeal?"

He nodded. "Yes."

He bent to pull the bag of oatmeal out of the cupboard, and I admired the way his jeans clung to his tight ass. He straightened and turned, grinning a little when he realized I was staring at his ass.

"What?"

"Nothing." He put a pot of water on the stove and leaned against the counter. I studied his six-pack until he cleared his throat, and I raised my gaze to his.

"You really do have an amazing body," I said.

He blushed a bit. "Thank you."

I stared down at my chubby self for a moment. "Can I ask you a question?"

"Sure." He poured some oatmeal into the water and stirred it.

"Have you always liked fat girls?"

He frowned at me. "I've always been attracted to women with curves."

"Well, I've certainly got the curves covered," I said.

"I like your body, Mae. I think you're beautiful."

I smiled at him. "Thank you."

He stirred the oatmeal again. "It's not just your body that I like. You know that, right?"

"Yup. You also like my bossiness and sass."

He laughed. "Yes, I certainly do."

There were a few moments of comfortable silence as he finished cooking the oatmeal, and I sipped at my coffee. The sun was shining through the large picture windows in the living room, and I could hear the faint sound of birds singing in the woods outside. I realized with a pang that I had fallen in love with Liam's home. It was so quiet and peaceful here. I had no trouble understanding why it was so appealing to Liam.

"What are you thinking about?" Liam had finished scooping the oatmeal into bowls and was loading a tray with milk and brown sugar. He set the bowls on the tray and then poured us each a glass of apple juice.

"Just that your home is gorgeous." I smiled at him and slid off the stool. I wore one of his t-shirts, and Liam stared unabashedly at my bare legs as I took the glasses of apple juice.

"Can we sit out on the patio?"

He nodded and picked up the tray before following me outside. We sat in the patio chairs, and I added a generous amount of milk and brown sugar to my oatmeal before tucking my feet under me and taking a bite.

"Have you ever thought about trying nursing again, Mae?" Liam said.

"No. I can't go back to it."

"Fair enough. Do you want to do something other than being a PA?"

"Maybe." I stared moodily at the lake. "Once he realized I wouldn't go back to nursing, Neil tried to pressure me into taking out more student loans and going back to school."

"You didn't want to?"

"I wanted to pay off my current student loans first, and back then, I wasn't sure what I wanted to do anyway."

"Do you know now?" he asked.

I hesitated, and he gave me an encouraging look.

"After quitting nursing, I worked at a coffee shop for nearly a year."

"I remember." He smiled at me and took a bite of oatmeal.

"Anyway," I stirred my oatmeal, feeling a blush rising on my cheeks, "I liked it. I mean, really liked it, you know? I was good at it, too. The owner made me manager after only four months, and I put in a lot of extra time learning the ins and outs of the business."

I stopped, and he looked at me expectantly.

"You're going to think it's silly."

"I won't," he promised. "Tell me."

"I'd like to open my own coffee shop."

He gave me a thoughtful look. "Have you ever run your own business before?"

"No, but I looked into business courses at the local

college. They're too expensive at the moment, but I plan on saving up and taking the courses first. Plus, I've been researching and reading about owning your own business, and I know I can do it."

He smiled at me. "I know you can, too."

We were quiet for a few minutes, and I looked at him shyly. "I already have my business plan written out."

"That's pretty impressive."

I shrugged. "I believe in being prepared."

"Do you have a name for your coffee shop?"

"Yup. The Bean Scene. What do you think?" I asked.

He grinned. "I think it's great."

"Thanks!" I ate the rest of my oatmeal before sipping my apple juice.

"Have you found a commercial property for your business?" he asked.

I laughed and shook my head. "God, no. I still need to take business courses and get the money for start-up costs. Once my student loans are paid off, I'll save up for the courses and start saving for the business."

"What about an investment partner?"

"I'm not comfortable with that idea. I don't think I could find anyone willing to invest in a business with someone without experience, and I would like to do it on my own. I want to prove to Neil and my parents that I'm not a quitter."

I took another sip of my apple juice. "Originally, I had worked out a ten-year plan. Five years to pay off my student loans at my current salary and another five years to take business courses and save for start-up costs. But now, with the fifty thousand, I'll be able to pay off my student loans, take the business courses, and put some money into savings. It's cut my plan in half."

There was a bit of an awkward silence between us, and I

wondered if it was rude of me to bring up the money that he was paying me. I risked a glance at him. He was staring silently at me, and I blushed. "I'm sorry."

"For what?"

"I've made it sound like I agreed to our contract just to get the money."

He shrugged. "There's nothing wrong with that."

My blush brightened. "That wasn't the only reason, Liam. I've wanted you for a long time."

Why was I so desperate to make him understand that I wasn't doing this just for the money?

"I've wanted you too, Mae." He smiled at me. "Speaking of the money…"

He reached into the back pocket of his jeans and pulled out an envelope. He handed it to me, and I opened it to find a money order for the fifty grand.

I frowned at him. "Why are you giving this to me now?"

He shrugged. "I didn't see any point in waiting."

"But the month isn't up yet."

"I know." He stood and stretched before piling our bowls on the tray. "I'm going to work out for a bit."

I stood and followed him into the kitchen. I tucked the envelope into my purse as he rinsed the dishes and put them in the dishwasher. He tugged lightly on the collar around his neck before pulling me into his arms and kissing me on the forehead.

"Will this bother you while you're working out?" I touched the leather collar.

"I sweat a lot when I work out. It might get uncomfortable."

I put my arms around his waist and squeezed him tightly. "You can take it and the cuffs off while working out. But they go back on when you're finished."

"Thank you, mistress." He winked at me and squeezed my ass briefly. "What are you going to do?"

"Go for another swim in that giant tub of yours."

He grinned. "Let me know if you need your back or anything else washed."

"Perv." I slapped him on the ass, and he grinned again before leading me up the stairs.

* * *

"YOU ARE SUSPICIOUSLY GOOD AT THIS."

"Thank you?"

I laughed. It was Saturday night, and I reclined on Liam's king-size bed, the pillows piled high behind my back. Liam, naked except for the collar and cuffs, sat at the end of the bed. I used my free foot to rub the inside of his thigh. His cock quivered, and he gave me a stern look.

"You're going to make me mess this up, and I'll have to start all over again." He bent back over my foot and quickly painted my toenail with the bright red polish. I giggled. The polish brush looked ridiculously tiny in his large hand, and his frown of concentration was way more adorable than it should have been.

"How are you so good at this? Do you secretly paint your toenails when no one is around?"

He applied another layer of polish to my next toe. "No. I have an older sister, remember? When we were kids, and she had her friends over for sleepovers, they used to drag me into her bedroom and make me paint their toenails for them."

I laughed. "That's adorable."

"Yeah, real adorable. Especially the part where they practiced their make-up techniques on me," he grumped. "Thank

God there was no Facebook back then. My ten-year-old face with blue eye shadow and pink glitter lipstick would have been plastered all over the damn thing."

I laughed so hard that Liam had to stop painting my toenails. When my laughter died down to the occasional giggle, he resumed his careful painting.

I watched him in silence for a while, admiring how the collar looked against his tanned skin. I decided I would be perfectly content spending every weekend at Liam's house, with him wearing nothing but a collar and giving me multiple orgasms.

I stared at his cock. That wasn't entirely true. I would be perfectly content if he fucked me. Every time he touched me, every time he used his fingers or his mouth to make me come, I had to fight the urge to simply push him on his back and impale myself on his thick cock. My pussy throbbed anew, and I shifted on the bed as Liam blew gently on my toes.

I continued to stare at his cock, imagining how good it would feel sliding into my oh-so-willing body. My fingers tightened on the rumpled bed sheets. He had the thickest cock I'd ever seen, and I was more than a little curious about whether I could take all of him or not. I was definitely willing to find out.

His cock hardened, and I dragged my gaze to his to see him staring at me. His hands tightened on my feet, and his eyes became silvery pools of liquid need. I shivered lightly. I loved seeing his need for me, loved the way I could make his cock harden with just a look, and I shivered again when he stroked my calf.

"Your toes are dry," he said softly. "What should we do next?"

I smiled at him. "Come up here and lie on your back."

* * *

"It feels so good when you suck on my nipples, Liam," I purred into his ear.

He kissed me on the throat. "I love making you feel good, mistress."

"I know." I bit his earlobe lightly, and he jerked beneath me. He was once again chained and cuffed to the headboard. I was naked and straddling his hips, and I sat up and ran my hands across his broad chest before I reached down and stroked his cock.

I rubbed the head with my thumb and then guided it to my clit. I rubbed his cock back and forth over the hard nub, grinding my hips against him as he moaned and twitched underneath me.

"I like having you at my mercy," I teased. I guided his dick up and down my slit before pausing at my tight opening and pushing his cock against it.

He sucked in his breath and tensed beneath me. I stared at him with my entire body trembling before I moved his dick back to my clit and rubbed again. He released his breath in a harsh rush, and I wondered if I imagined the look of disappointment on his face.

A strange kind of madness buzzed in my veins, and I pushed his cock back toward my opening. "I know we said no fucking, but I could fuck you right now if I wanted to. You wouldn't be able to stop me, would you?"

"No, mistress."

"Do you want me to fuck you?" I rested his cock against my opening.

"Yes!" he nearly snarled. "Fuck me!"

I shook my head. "You know I can't."

He glared at me and swore loudly. I leaned over him and scowled. "You're being disrespectful."

He continued to glare at me, and his entire body tensed when I bent my head to his nipple. Prepared for my bite, he cried out when he felt my warm tongue instead and bucked his hips upward. The head of his cock slid neatly into me, and I made my own cry of surprise and sat up.

Another inch of cock slid easily into my wetness, and we both moaned. I stared down at Liam with my fingers digging into his chest. I knew I should move off of him, but I couldn't force myself to do it.

"I'm sorry, mistress," he panted. "It was an accident."

"An accident," I repeated.

"Yes," he groaned.

I stared at him and relaxed my legs, slowly sinking onto his cock. It filled me and stretched me in a way that made me moan.

"Oops," I said.

"Oh my God, Mae," he moaned. "You're so fucking tight." His hips flexed under me, pushing his cock further into my body, and I pushed my weight against him.

"Don't move," I said.

"What? Please, I have to. I can't -"

I slapped him lightly on the chest. "Don't move, Liam. If you do, I'll stop. I swear to God."

I was lying. I couldn't have stopped if my life depended on it. Liam bit his bottom lip and gave a short nod.

I smiled and rubbed his hard chest. He was trembling under me, and I felt that addicting flood of power go through me again. I took a deep breath and squeezed my pussy around his cock. It wasn't easy. His cock was so thick I could barely squeeze it, but he immediately twitched beneath me and bit his lip again.

"Stop," I soothed. "Don't bite your lip like that. You'll make it bleed."

I leaned down and sucked on his bottom lip as I moved

my pelvis in a slow, rocking motion against him. He moaned into my mouth, and I slipped my tongue between his lips, urging him to kiss me. He stroked my tongue urgently. His hands were curled into tight fists, and he was yanking so hard on the chain that I was surprised it hadn't busted through the metal of the headboard.

"I'm going to fuck you now, Liam," I whispered against his mouth. "I'm going to use your cock to make myself come, and you're going to lie perfectly still and let me. Do you understand?"

"Yes, mistress," he moaned as I sat up and braced my hands against his chest. Every part of my body was screaming at me to fuck him hard, but I moved slowly. I slid up and down his hard cock as every thick inch rubbed my sensitive walls.

I tried to keep my movements slow, tried to tease and seduce, but I had waited months to have his cock. Within minutes, I was riding him wildly. Pleasure surged from my belly into my pelvis and down my legs.

Panting and moaning, I rode him hard. My fingernails dug into his chest as the pleasure grew until its white-hot fire consumed me. I threw my head back and screamed my release as my pussy tightened around his cock. Dimly, I was aware of Liam's hoarse shout as his hips bucked and warm wetness flooded through me. My pussy milked him hungrily, squeezing and shuddering around his hard shaft as he climaxed. He cried out again as I collapsed against his broad chest.

"Uncuff me," he said.

I reached up weakly, and my fingers fumbled at the clip on the chain before it finally released. Liam rolled to his side and drew me into his embrace. He pulled me close, stroking my hair and lifting my thigh around his hip. He kissed my throat and then my mouth.

My orgasm had made me sleepy, and I snuggled into his body. "Tired."

"Hmm," he agreed.

I tucked my face into the curve of his broad neck and drifted.

CHAPTER 19

I woke up in the dark. Liam's hands were on my breasts. His fingers gently teased my nipples, and I smiled and ran my hands over his broad chest.

"Liam?"

"Yeah?"

"Hi."

He leaned over and flicked on the bedside lamp. He stroked the hair back from my face and smiled at me. "Hi, beautiful."

He cupped my breast and then leaned down, sucking my nipple into his mouth. I moaned and ran my hands through his thick hair as he sucked and nibbled. My hands grazed the collar around his neck, and I reached for the buckle. I unbuckled it and tossed it to the floor before going for the cuffs.

"I want these off," I said.

He watched as I unbuckled them and threw them on the floor beside the collar. I traced the red marks on his wrists and frowned. "Why didn't you tell me they were too tight?"

"They weren't," he assured me before nuzzling my neck. "It's because I was pulling on them so hard earlier."

He ran his hand down my side and squeezed my hip. I could feel his cock pressing against my stomach, and I reached between us and stroked it lightly. His breath caught in his throat, and he closed his eyes as I squeezed and rubbed him.

"I'm sorry for earlier," he said.

My hand stilled on his cock, and he opened his eyes. I gave him a careful look. "Are you – do you regret it?"

"No. It was amazing. I'm sorry because I told you that we wouldn't have sex, and then I lost control."

I sighed. "It wasn't you. I was deliberately teasing you, hoping that I could get you to have sex with me. I should be the one apologizing."

He rubbed my lower back. "Honestly, it was ridiculous of me to think I could be with you and not have sex with you. I wanted to take you the very first night."

He kissed me gently. I returned his kiss, our tongues sliding against each other as his hand slid down and cupped my ass. I ran my thumb over the head of his cock, and he groaned loudly.

"You have a very thick cock. I like it. A lot," I informed him solemnly.

I watched in amusement as he blushed.

"It felt so good in my pussy," I whispered.

His eyes turned a dark and stormy grey. I shivered when he pushed me onto my back and pulled my thighs apart. He wedged his body between them and rubbed his cock against my pussy. "I want to be inside of you again, Mae."

"I want that, too," I said.

He stared at me. "Are you sure? I don't want to pressure you."

I grinned at him. "Don't make me chain you to the bed and have my way with you again, Mr. Knight."

He returned my grin and then thrust his hips in a smooth, downward motion. His cock pushed into my pussy, and I gasped and arched upward, sheathing him entirely inside of me. He propped himself on his elbows above me, and I reached up and cupped his face, rubbing my thumbs along his jaw. He moved in me with slow strokes that made me quiver with need.

I wrapped my legs around his waist, hooking my feet together at the small of his back. He was still moving with the same slow movements, and I slipped my arms around his shoulders. My fingers dug into his back as he stared down at me.

"Faster. Please, Liam."

He shook his head. "No, honey. Not yet."

I made a soft noise of frustration as he bent his head and licked my nipple. I gasped and arched my back before rocking my pelvis against him again.

"Liam, please," I moaned. "I want to come."

"Soon, honey," he promised.

We rocked against each other as Liam pressed light, fluttering kisses across my face. His gentleness, the way he touched me so sweetly as he moved within me, made my chest ache. I closed my eyes, feeling the burn of tears behind my eyelids.

"Mae?" he said.

I opened my eyes. Liam stared at me with concern on his face. He stopped moving. "Have I hurt you?"

"No, why?"

He wiped his thumb across my cheek and showed me the moisture on it. I kissed him. "Don't stop, Liam."

He kissed me again and continued to thrust. As his movements turned stronger and steadier, he reached between us and rubbed my clit. I moaned and rocked my pelvis against his as his fingers circled and pressed on my throbbing clit.

"Oh God," I whimpered. With a sudden, arching thrust, my orgasm tore through me, and I shook and quivered helplessly under him.

He groaned and propped his hands beside my head before plunging wildly within me. "Mae, oh, Mae," he whispered. "You feel so damn good. So warm, so wet…"

He stiffened, his back arching and the cords in his neck standing out in stark relief as he came deep inside of me. I held tightly to him with all of my limbs as he buried his face in my neck, panting harshly and shuddering wildly against my body.

He rested against me. I could feel his warm breath blowing against my throat, and I rubbed his back soothingly as I stared blankly at the ceiling. The tears rolled quietly down my face as a strange mixture of dismay and euphoria rushed through me.

I was in love with my goddamn boss.

* * *

"You're quiet today."

"Am I?"

"Yes. Will you tell me what's wrong?" Liam reached across the patio table and squeezed my hand.

I squeezed back. "There's nothing wrong. I'm just admiring the view." I pointed to the lake glimmering softly in the warm sun.

He set down his iPad and tugged me to my feet. "Come with me."

"Where are we going?"

"We'll dip our feet in the water. It's getting too hot sitting here in the sun."

Holding hands, we walked down to the lake. It was Sunday afternoon, and despite what I had told Liam, I was feeling depressed and blue. We had made love twice more this morning, each time what Liam referred to as 'vanilla sex', and it was incredible. In a few hours, I would be leaving to go back to my shitty apartment, and I was already moping about it. I wanted to stay at Liam's house. I wanted to sleep in his bed and wake up beside him each morning.

I had made a terrible mistake in accepting the contract with Liam. I thought about the envelope in my purse, and my stomach rolled with nausea. I was in love with Liam, and he had just paid me fifty thousand to have sex with him. We could both pretend it didn't make me a whore, but I knew the truth. I was just Liam's well-paid prostitute. For one horrible moment, I thought I might throw up. My hand tightened involuntarily on Liam's, and he looked over his shoulder.

He stopped and gripped my shoulders lightly. "Mae? What's wrong? You're very pale."

I cleared my throat. "I'm fine. Just a bit of a headache."

"Do you want to return to the house and lie down?"

"No. The fresh air is good, and I'd like to dip my toes in the lake," I said.

"We can do that later." He started back toward the house, and I dug my feet in.

"No, really. I want to stay here," I insisted. "C'mon, Liam."

"All right, honey."

My heart constricted painfully at the endearment, and my stomach gave another one of those nauseated lurches.

"Mae -"

"Come on, handsome. Let's cool our feet," I said.

He took my hand again before starting toward the lake.

I wouldn't take the money, I decided. I had two more weekends with Liam, and once they were done, I would give him back the fifty thousand. My dream of owning my own coffee shop wasn't worth feeling this way. Besides, it was only ten years and even less if I found a part-time job in the evenings and weekends. Which, considering how I felt about Liam, was probably a smart thing to do. I would need something to take my mind off of him.

The decision not to take Liam's money made me feel better. Standing beside the lake, I squeezed his hand and gave him a warm smile. "It's so pretty here."

"I'm glad you like it." The look of worry on his face disappeared, and his tense body relaxed. "You're sure you're okay, Mae?"

I nodded and slipped my arm around his waist. "I really am."

He bent and rolled up his jeans. I wore a tank top and shorts and waded into the water. I shivered delicately. "Cold!"

He laughed and waded in next to me. "It's not that cold."

"It's freezing. I can't feel my feet!" I started to head back to the beach, and he caught my hand.

"Walk with me. It'll warm up, I promise."

We walked down the beach, the water lapping at our feet. We were both barefoot, but the bottom of the lake was soft sand, not the rocks I had expected. After only a few minutes, the water felt refreshing rather than freezing, and I crinkled my nose at him.

"You were right."

"I know."

I poked him in the side. "No need to be smug."

He grinned. "I can't help it. I'm a lawyer, remember? We're naturally smug."

"Did you always want to be a lawyer?"

"Yes."

"Really? Even as a child?"

"Yes. When I was eight, I set up my first law firm. I charged neighbourhood kids a dollar to settle such disputes as – 'Who ate Jamie Davidson's bag of kettle corn?' and 'Did Joey Thompson deserve to be punched in the face by Kimmie Summers?'."

I laughed, and he gave me a mock glare. "Hey, I made fifteen dollars that summer."

"Nicely done." I laughed again, and he slapped me lightly on the ass.

"You did not just do that." I arched my eyebrow at him.

He gave me a wicked grin and then staggered back when I bent, scooped up water, and splashed him in the face.

"Why, you little minx," he growled.

I turned and ran, splashing through the water. He chased after me, and I ran faster, my heart pumping. I could see his house, and I was nearly to the beach when his arms snaked around my waist, and he lifted me out of the water.

I shrieked and struggled wildly. Not expecting it, Liam lost his balance, and we both tumbled into the calf-deep water. I gasped, and he bellowed a curse as the cold water soaked into our clothes and skin. I twisted in his grasp and quickly straddled him as he sat in the water.

"Jerk!" I laughed before kissing him hard on the mouth.

His hands dug into my hips, and I rubbed my pelvis against him as we kissed deeply. His hand cupped my breast, and he moaned his approval at the hardness of my nipple. I pulled my mouth away from his and stared down at him.

He ran his thumb over my mouth. "Your lips are blue."

"I told you the water was cold."

"Stand up, honey."

I climbed off of him, and he stood gracefully, his jeans

streaming water and his grey t-shirt sticking to his broad chest. He eyed me for a moment, his gaze lingering on my chest. I wasn't wearing a bra, and my nipples were poking against my wet and clinging tank top.

"Hey!" I prodded him in the chest, and he raised his gaze to mine. "Eyes up here, buddy."

He grinned cheekily, and I launched myself at him. His eyes widened with surprise, but he caught me neatly, lifting me as I wrapped my legs around his waist and rubbed my crotch against his. "Take me into the house and fuck me. Right now, Liam."

"Yes, mistress." He kissed me again, his hands squeezing and kneading my ass, and I moaned softly.

He carried me across the beach and into his backyard. I stroked his back and moved my mouth to his ear. "First, I'm going to make you lick my pussy until I come. Then you'll watch as I masturbate until I come again. Would you like that, Liam?"

"Yes, mistress," he groaned as he pulled open the French doors that led into the living room. He cupped my ass again, and I dipped my tongue into his ear.

"Even if I don't let you touch yourself?" I whispered. I could feel his hard cock against me, and neither of us cared about the water we dripped all over the floor.

"Maybe I won't let you come at all," I continued breathily. "As punishment for dunking me in the lake."

"Liam?"

I jerked in surprise at the soft voice, and Liam nearly dropped me to the floor. I stared over my shoulder at the slender Asian woman near the front door. She had a little boy in her arms, and he stared curiously at us as the woman gave us a weak smile.

"Eileen!" Liam set me down, and I self-consciously pulled my wet tank top away from my breasts.

"What – what are you doing here?" Liam asked.

"I'm so sorry." She was bright red and shifted the little boy in her arms, kissing him on the cheek before clearing her throat. "Dean wanted to see his Uncle Liam, and it's been so long since we've visited, I thought we would surprise you and drop by. I knocked, but when you didn't answer, I used my key … I'm sorry, I didn't realize you had a friend over."

Liam's cheeks were turning as red as his sister's.

I crossed the room with one arm covering my chest and held out a damp hand. "Hi, I'm Mae."

"Hi, Mae. I'm Eileen, and this is Dean," Liam's sister said as she shook my hand.

"It's very nice to meet you. I'm just going to change into some dry clothes. Please excuse me."

She nodded, and I quickly climbed the staircase. I could hear Liam murmuring, and then he climbed the stairs behind me. We entered his bedroom, and he shut the door. I gave him a wide-eyed look of dismay. "I'm so sorry."

He shrugged. His cheeks had already lost their redness, and he no longer seemed embarrassed. "It's no big deal."

I quickly stripped off my wet clothes and towelled dry before pulling on a fresh pair of panties and my bra. I slipped into jeans and a T-shirt as Liam stripped and dressed in dry clothes.

"I'll stay for fifteen minutes and then leave, okay?" I said as I hurriedly packed my suitcase.

He frowned. "The deal is until tonight, Mae."

"Yes, but your sister is here, and I'm sure you want to visit with her. I can – I dunno, maybe pop by Thursday night and make up the missing hours." I was babbling, I knew I was babbling, but I couldn't seem to stop.

He took me in his arms, his hand caressing my back. "It's fine. I want you to stay. If you're uncomfortable and don't want to, I understand. But I don't want you leaving because you think I want you to, okay?"

"Okay."

"Good." He kissed my forehead and took my hand. "Ready?"

"Ready." I gave him a shaky smile and let him lead me from the bedroom.

CHAPTER 20

"Dean, no! Honey, don't do that."

Dean smiled at me with his hands and face sticky with juice and cookie crumbs. He gripped my knees with his hands and rubbed his face across my thigh again.

"Oh, Dean," Eileen sighed.

I laughed. "I don't mind, really."

The little boy grinned at my laugh and held up his arms. I was sitting cross-legged on the couch and couldn't resist his silent request. I picked him up, setting him in my lap, and he hugged me enthusiastically. I could feel his hands patting my hair and knew he was leaving a trail of crumbs in it.

"He's adorable." I smiled at Eileen as Dean settled back against me.

We'd been visiting for close to an hour. I stayed quiet while Liam and Eileen got caught up, but now Liam had excused himself upstairs to answer a phone call.

I cleared my throat nervously before placing a gentle kiss on the top of Dean's head.

"So, what do you do for a living?" Eileen said.

"I'm a PA."

Please don't ask where, please don't ask where.

"Do you enjoy it?"

"I do. How about you? What do you do?" I was anxious to steer the conversation away from my career path.

"I'm an interior decorator." Eileen glanced around the room. "I helped Liam decorate this place."

"Really? You did a great job. It's so lovely," I said.

Dean made a squeal of delight, and I didn't need to turn to know that Liam was coming down the stairs behind me. He sat on the couch beside me, and Dean immediately crawled into his lap.

He planted a wet kiss on Liam's mouth. Liam laughed and wiped his mouth. "Mmm, apple juice."

"What are we talking about?" He tickled Dean, who giggled and shrieked.

"I was just telling your sister how much I liked the house and her design choices." An image of Liam chained to the headboard flickered through my head. I had to manufacture a coughing fit to hide my sudden spat of giggles. I doubted that was what Eileen had envisioned when she chose the headboard.

Liam thumped me firmly on the back as Dean crawled from his lap back into mine. He bestowed a sloppy kiss on my mouth, and I smiled at him. "Thanks, handsome."

He patted my face and then turned to wave at his mother. "Hi, Mama."

Eileen smiled affectionately at him. "Hi, honey. So, Mae, how did you two meet?"

"Um..." I stared at Liam, but the question had obviously stumped him as well.

"Wait. You're the girl from the gossip column, right?" Elaine said.

I flushed bright red. Elaine stared at me in embarrassment. "I'm so sorry. That was rude."

"It's fine," I said.

"I don't normally follow those gossip sites, but the girls at work are kind of obsessed with my brother. They were all over it when they saw him with a normal looking girl – I mean, not that you're not gorgeous because you are, but... oh my God, I am making a total fool of myself. I think it's time to go," Eileen said.

She stood and smiled at Dean. "Do you want to go potty before we drive home, honey?"

He nodded and looked at Liam. "Uncle Liam, you take me potty."

"Okay, buddy. Let's go." He scooped Dean out of my lap and flipped him upside down. Dean giggled and kicked his feet as Liam carried him up the stairs.

Eileen and I stood in awkward silence before she gave me a faint smile. "Mae, I'm very sorry. I'm acting like a complete idiot."

"Oh no, it's fine," I reassured her.

"Liam's so – well, he likes his privacy, I guess you could call it – and I don't think I've ever seen a girlfriend at the house before. I'm just surprised that he even let you into the house."

She coloured again before slapping herself on the forehead. "Jesus Christ, I need to shut my damn mouth."

I started to laugh. Eileen was so delightfully awkward that I couldn't help but like her. "It's fine, really and truly. Liam does like his privacy."

She gave me a grateful look. "It's nice to meet you, Mae. You're nothing like his previous girlfriends."

"Uh - thank you?" I said.

"Trust me – that's a very good thing. You don't seem nearly as high maintenance as the bottled blondes he normally sees."

I laughed, and she grinned. "Not that I've met many of

Liam's girlfriends. There was Kara a few years ago and Tylene last year, but they were both so stuck up. I couldn't imagine what they would have done if Dean had put his sticky little hands all over them. Dean wouldn't even go near Tylene. I don't blame him. Just between you and me – I'm pretty sure both her name and her boobs were fake."

I laughed again. "I don't look much like Liam's usual type, that's for sure."

"How did you two meet again?"

I was saved from answering by the return of Liam and Dean. Dean ran to his mother and hugged her leg. "Mama, I went pee!"

"Good job, little man." She took Dean's hand, and they walked to the front door. We trailed after them, and she paused as she opened the door.

Liam stood behind me and wrapped one arm around my waist, tugging me back until I was pressed against his broad chest.

Eileen smiled at us. "You two make a very cute couple. Liam, you should bring Mae by the house for dinner next weekend."

To my surprise, Liam nodded. "Maybe I will."

"Good." Eileen smiled at me. "It was nice to meet you, Mae. We'll see you soon."

"Nice to meet you as well," I replied.

She left, and I sagged against Liam with relief. He kissed the side of my head. "You okay?"

"That was too close." I turned to face him.

"It was fine," he said carelessly.

"Fine? She wanted to know how we met, Liam."

"We handled it. Don't worry about it, Mae."

"Don't worry about it? Don't worry about it? She invited us to dinner!" My voice was rising. I took a deep breath as he slid his arms around my waist.

"She's an even better cook than I am."

"This isn't funny."

He kissed me on the tip of the nose. "God, you're adorable when you're panicking."

"Dinner, Liam. Where she will ask us all sorts of questions we can't answer."

"Like what?"

"Like how we met." I wondered if he was being deliberately obtuse.

"She's too excited that I've finally got a girlfriend who, in her words, is 'normal'. She'll forget about asking how we met again."

I tensed against him. "Liam, I'm not your girlfriend. I can't afford to lose my job."

A strange look came over his face. His hands tightened momentarily around my waist before he let go and turned away from me.

"Yeah, I know," he said.

I cupped my elbows. Now that I had decided not to take the fifty grand, I needed my job more than ever. "I'm sorry."

He turned to face me, the expression on his face unreadable. "There's nothing to be sorry about, Mae."

"Are you sure?"

"Yes. Listen, I have a headache. I'm going to lie down for a while."

"Should I leave?" I asked.

He shook his head. "No, of course not."

He trudged up the stairs, and I sank onto the couch, burying my face in my hands. This whole thing was turning into a shit show. I was in love with my boss and was in danger of losing my job. Did he love me?

He was affectionate and warm enough when I was at his house, and it seemed to hurt his feelings when I said I wasn't his girlfriend. Of course, he treated me the same at the office, but here he –

I groaned and rubbed my forehead. Liam had told me himself that part of his enjoyment in submitting to a woman was touching and interacting in a non-sexual way. I was reading too much into his affection. It was just another way the man got his rocks off.

"You're such an idiot, Mae," I muttered. "You want him to be in love with you, so you're seeing things that aren't there."

I needed to stop imagining a life with Liam and start remembering that this was a contract. He wanted to give affection as part of that contract, and I agreed to it. If he wanted to rub my feet and hold my hand outside the bedroom, I would do it. Hell, if he wanted me to go to his sister's and pretend to be his girlfriend for a night, I'd do that too. He was paying me for a service. I would provide it, even if I weren't intending to keep the money.

As for the bedroom, well, it was time to make it more straightforward. Liam Knight wanted to be dominated - I'd dominate him. Simple, really. No more vanilla sex, no more pretending that he was doing this for more than the pleasure of me dominating him.

It was the only way to protect my heart.

* * *

HALF AN HOUR LATER, I CREPT SILENTLY INTO LIAM'S bedroom. He was stretched out on the bed and didn't move when I walked past him and into the bathroom. I shut the door and turned the shower on before stripping off my clothes. My hair and face were sticky from Dean's fingers. I ducked my head under one of the showerheads, letting the hot water run through my hair. I had just finished washing and rinsing my hair when the shower door opened, and Liam joined me.

"Hello, Mae." He reached for me, and I pushed his hands away roughly.

"Mistress," I said sharply.

"I'm sorry?"

I sighed impatiently. "You're to call me mistress. Not Mae."

His cock twitched, and he reached for my wet body. "I'm sorry, mistress."

I glared at him and shoved his hands away again. "Did I give you permission to touch me?"

"No, mistress."

"Turn around and put your hands on the showerhead. No speaking," I demanded.

He did as I asked. His cock was stiffening rapidly, and the water from the shower was splashing against his chest and dripping down his body. He gripped the showerhead as I slid my body between his and the shower wall. I rubbed my breasts against his body, my nipples hardening at the touch of his warm, wet skin. He inhaled sharply when I reached up and tugged on one of his flat nipples.

"You've been a very bad boy, Liam."

"Have I, mistress?"

My hand slid around his body, and I slapped him hard enough on the ass to make my hand sting. He jerked in surprise, and his hips bucked forward, pushing his cock against my stomach. I took his cock in my hand, squeezing firmly and not surprised to feel how hard it was.

"I thought you said you weren't into spanking, Liam."

He hesitated, and I smiled wickedly at him. "You may answer."

"I'm not, mistress," he said hoarsely.

I looked down at his cock. There was thick precum dripping from the tip of it, and I squeezed it again before rubbing my hand back and forth.

He moaned, and I raised my eyebrows at him. "Your cock seems to be into it."

"Mistress, I -"

I spanked him again. His breath hissed out between his teeth as his body swayed with the force of my slap.

"I've been much too nice to you, Liam. You know that, don't you?"

He nodded as I rubbed his ass, soothing away the sting of my slaps. I stroked his cock roughly as I ran my hand up his back. "I've been letting you come whenever you want. Letting you fuck me whenever you want."

I squeezed out from the wall and stood behind him. I admired how he looked with his hands wrapped around the showerhead and his lean body stretched and taut.

"Let go of the showerhead and turn around."

He turned and gave me a dark look of need, his hands clenched tightly at his sides. I handed him the soap. "Wash yourself."

I watched as he lathered the soap and ran his hands over his body. As his hands stroked his abdomen, I nodded approvingly. "Good, now your cock."

He slid his hands down and gripped his erection. He bit his lip as his hands stroked and washed his cock.

"Enough," I said. "Wash your legs, please."

He soaped his legs before ducking under the showerhead and rinsing clean.

"Now me." I turned my back to him and stood patiently as he lathered the soap and washed my back. His strong hands kneaded and rubbed, and I had to bite back my moan of need when he cupped my ass and squeezed. He knelt and washed my thighs and calves.

"Good boy." I turned around as he stood. "Keep going."

His eyes dark with desire, he washed my breasts. He spent long moments on my nipples, his fingers slick with soap as he pulled and rubbed them. It was taking every bit of willpower I possessed not to moan my approval.

I pushed his hands toward my abdomen and watched as he washed my wet flesh. He moved lower and stopped, giving me a questioning look. I spread my thighs in reply, and his hand dipped between my legs. This time I couldn't stop my moaning, and my hands gripped his arms tightly as he cleaned my pussy. I didn't stop him when he rinsed me clean of soap before sliding his hand back between my legs. He rubbed and stroked my clit and pushed one finger deep inside of me.

I had intended to tease him, but I suddenly, desperately needed him inside of me. I pulled away from him and leaned back against the shower wall.

"Fuck me, Liam. Fuck me right now," I demanded.

He lifted me, and I wrapped my legs around his hips as he braced me against the slick wall of the shower. I had a moment to marvel again at his strength before his cock pushed against my tight opening. He entered me in a silken glide, and we both cried out in pleasure.

"Mistress," he muttered against my throat.

I squeezed my hands around his broad shoulders. "Don't come until I tell you to. Do you understand?"

"Yes, mistress."

He buried his cock into my greedy body. His hips rocked against mine as his thick cock stroked my smooth inner walls. I was panting and moaning, heat sparking deep within my belly. When he reached between us and cupped my breast roughly, I shuddered and climaxed around his thick cock.

He moaned, his ass clenching as he pinned me against the wall. I could feel his cock twitching inside of me, and I squeezed my inner walls around him and tightened my thighs around his waist.

"Oh please, mistress," he groaned.

The part of me that planned to make him pull out without coming was lost under a sea of desire and an undeniable need to give Liam the same pleasure he had given me. I dipped my mouth to his ear and tugged hard on his earlobe with my teeth.

"Come, Liam. Come for me right now."

He plunged in and out, slamming my body against the shower wall with the force of his thrusts before his entire body shuddered, and he shouted hoarsely. He shook against me as he came, and he buried his face in my throat, panting harshly.

I stroked his back and stared at the water splashing onto his back as he continued to shudder with pleasure against my body. I was starting to suspect I didn't have it in me to be a professional Dominatrix.

CHAPTER 21

Thursday morning, I tried vainly to make sense of Liam's handwritten notes when my phone vibrated. I sighed and reached for it. No doubt it was Neil again. I had sent him a curt text on Monday reminding him that I had no interest in him. It slowed him down a little, but he still called at least once daily and sent texts.

I smiled when I saw Russ' number and hit the answer button. "Hello, handsome."

"Hi, Mae. Do you miss me?" Russ asked.

"Terribly," I said. "How are you?"

"Oh, pretty good. How are tango lessons going?"

"Fine," I said. Allie had such a busy social life that she wouldn't notice four weekends going by without me. But I had grown close to Russ and Steve and was forced to make up the tango lessons as a reason for not being around on the weekends.

"Fine? That's it." Russ snorted into the phone. You've spent two full weekends in individual and group lessons, and all I get is a fine?"

I laughed. "What can I say – I'm not that coordinated."

ELIZABETH KELLY

"You should pop by Sunday and show us some of your moves."

"Not a chance, Russ," I said. "I can't dance worth shit, even with lessons. I'm starting to think the instructor believes I'm completely useless."

Thank God he couldn't see my face. Russ would know I was lying in a heartbeat.

"Well, still come by on Sunday. We miss you. You've been busy at work during the week, and your weekends are nothing but dancing now."

"Um, I'm visiting my parents this Sunday," I fibbed.

"What about Monday night then?"

I smiled. "Monday night would be perfect. I'll bring the wine."

"Good. See you around six."

I said goodbye and hung up the phone before studying the paper. After a few minutes, I gave up on deciphering Liam's handwriting and decided to ask him. My office door was closed. I hadn't shut it. Liam must have closed it while I was talking to Russ. I would have to apologize for being loud and taking a personal call during company time.

I opened the door and stepped into Liam's office. "Liam, do you have a minute to review this document with me? I can't read your writing on this."

"Mae!"

"Oh, hi, Eileen." My stomach dropped. Eileen sat at one of the chairs across from Liam's desk. I forced a smile and darted a glance at Liam. If he felt the same dismay that I did, he hid it a hell of a lot better.

Eileen blinked a couple of times, looking uncertainly from Liam back to me before clearing her throat. "So, uh, you're Liam's PA?"

"I am," I said. "I'm sorry to interrupt. Liam, when you

have a moment, could you come see me regarding this document?"

"I will," he said.

I smiled awkwardly at his sister. "It was nice to see you again, Eileen."

"You as well." Eileen had gotten over her initial shock and was grinning at Liam and me. I escaped to my small office, shutting the door behind me and leaning against it. I had worked for Liam Knight for months and didn't remember ever seeing Eileen at the office. Four days after she caught me making out with her brother, she discovered I work for him. Christ almighty, I had the worst goddamn luck.

Fifteen minutes later, Liam opened my office door and entered the small space. I glanced up from my desk. "I am so sorry."

He shook his head. "It's my fault. Eileen dropped by without telling me. You were on the phone, so I just shut your door and hoped your conversation would last a while. I should have sent you a text telling you to stay in your office."

"Did you talk to her? Did you, um, tell her that she can't say anything?"

"I did. She'll keep it quiet. I also used it as an excuse for why we couldn't come by her house this weekend."

I swallowed the stupid and utterly pointless disappointment in my throat. It was better for us, better for *me*, not to go.

"Do you have lunch plans, Mae?" he asked.

I blinked at the quick change in subject. "It's probably not a good idea for us to have lunch together."

"It's work related. I wanted to go over the correspondence for the Duncalfe case with you. I'm not going to have time this afternoon," he said.

"Oh, right. I'm sorry." I blushed.

He shrugged. "It's fine. Besides, you're right. It probably isn't a good idea for us to go for lunch together."

"Probably not," I said.

"But we can order something and sit in the office with the door open while we work." He smiled at me, and I gave him a shaky smile in return.

"I'd like that," I said.

"I would, too. Do you like sushi?"

"Yes. And I know the perfect place to order in."

He grinned. "Great, you get the sushi, and I'll get the files."

* * *

"I'll need this entire section photocopied and this binder here as well." Liam pointed with his chopsticks at the sizeable black binder sitting beside me.

I popped another piece of sushi in my mouth and studied my notepad. "Do you need the documents from the tenth highlighted?"

"Yes, please."

"Sure. What's the time frame on -"

My cell phone buzzed. I glanced at it before giving Liam an apologetic smile. "Sorry."

"It's your lunch. Go ahead and answer it if you'd like."

I glanced at the number and rolled my eyes. "It's no one I want to talk to."

He stared questioningly at me. I shrugged. "Neil's been calling and sending me text messages since I ran into him at the charity event."

"He's called me a couple of times," Liam said.

I paused with my chopsticks in mid-air. "You're kidding me?"

"No."

"Why the hell is he calling you?"

He laughed at my indignant tone. "If I had to guess, he's desperate for business. He's left voicemails mentioning his availability to meet with me and that he believes we'd make excellent business partners."

"Christ," I sighed. "I'm sorry, Liam."

"Don't worry about it," he said dismissively. "It's not your fault."

He poked at the sushi in front of him with his chopsticks. "So, are you thinking of getting together with him?"

"God, no!" I said. "The guy's a sleazeball, and I'm better off without him."

He grinned at me, and I smiled back.

Ida stuck her head into the office. "Liam, are we still meeting at... I'm sorry, am I interrupting something?"

"No, just a work lunch," Liam said.

I smiled at Ida and stood, gathering the empty take-out containers as Ida stared silently at us. "I'll get started on the photocopying this afternoon, Mr. Knight, and have the other information to you by the end of the day tomorrow."

"That's fine. Thanks, Ms. Temple."

As I tossed the containers into the trash, Ida leaned against the doorframe. "Are you coming with us for Friday night drinks this week, Mae?"

"I've got other plans."

Ida grinned at me. "I heard you've been taking tango lessons. How are they going?"

"Honestly, I'm not sure I'm meant to be a dancer."

She laughed. "We can't all be twinkle toes. Talk to you later, Mae."

"Bye, Ida." I carried the binder and folders back to my office.

* * *

"TELL ME WHAT YOU WANT, LIAM."

"I want to lick your pussy, mistress."

I walked around him, smiling my approval at how he lowered his gaze when I stood before him.

It was Sunday afternoon. Liam knelt naked in the middle of the living room with the leather collar and cuffs around his neck and wrists. His hands were chained behind his back, and he inhaled when I reached out and ran my fingers through his dark hair.

"Look at me, Liam."

He stared up at me, his eyes glittering hotly. I smiled at him. "Do you like what you see?"

"Yes, very much," he said.

I glanced down at myself. I wore a tight, black leather corset with black panties and fishnet stockings attached to a garter. I had pulled my hair into a high ponytail and wore elbow-length leather gloves. Four-inch heels completed the outfit. It was Mistress Chelsea I was picturing when I picked out the outfit, and I wondered if Liam had noticed the similarities.

He would have, I decided. I smoothed my hand over my nylon-clad thigh, smiling a little at how his eyes followed my hand's motion. The sun shone on his dark hair, and I crossed to the large picture windows. I flicked the switch that lowered the blinds, and they covered the windows with a soft hum.

"I know we're out in the middle of nowhere, but just in case a family member decides to drop by."

He grinned. "Probably a good idea."

I walked to the couch and opened the small canvas bag sitting on it. I pulled out the black silk blindfold and the leather crop. The handle of the crop had black feathers on it, and as I walked back to Liam and stood before him, I could see the apprehension in his eyes.

"I'd never hurt you, Liam," I said.

"I know."

"I know your hard and soft limits and won't break them." I ran my leather-covered hand across his cheek.

"I trust you, mistress," he said.

"Tell me your safe word again."

"Red."

I bent and kissed him lightly on the mouth before standing behind him. "Close your eyes."

He closed his eyes obediently, and I draped the blindfold over his eyes before tying it behind his head.

"Stand up." I helped steady him as he climbed to his feet. I stood in front of him and stared at his cock. It was hard and thick, and my pussy ached and throbbed in response.

I used the leather end of the crop to trace the muscles in his abdomen. He jerked, his breath hissing out between his teeth, and I smiled a little.

"Relax," I soothed, rubbing my hand over his chest.

I moved behind him and stared hungrily at his ass. I ran the leather crop over it. He twitched again, his head turning helplessly.

"Your ass is amazing, Liam. Did you know that?" I asked.

He didn't reply, and I slapped him lightly on the ass with my hand. "Answer me."

"No, mistress. I didn't know that," he gasped.

I smiled again and leaned against his back, rubbing my leather-clad breasts against him. I slipped one arm around his waist and traced his abdomen with my fingers.

"It is. It's delectable, in fact. I want to kiss it, bite it," I paused and squeezed his right cheek, "spank it."

He gasped. "Mistress, I -"

I spanked him sharply on the ass, and he jerked wildly. "I didn't give you permission to speak, Liam."

"I'm sorry, mistress."

I studied his ass, staring at the red mark my hand had left as a panty-melting throb of lust went through me. "Do you like it when I spank you, Liam?"

He didn't reply, and I spanked him again. "Answer me."

"Yes, mistress," he moaned.

I grinned to myself before placing a soft kiss on his bare back. "I like it too."

I stripped off my gloves and ran my bare hand across his ass. He moaned, and I squeezed and kneaded his ass for a few minutes. I dropped my hand and frowned when he immediately tensed.

"I won't do anything you don't like, Liam." I rubbed his back. "Tell me your safe word."

"Red." He relaxed as I rubbed and massaged his broad back.

"What is it that you want?" I traced his lower back with my fingers.

"To please you, mistress," he said.

"Good." I used the feathered end of the crop to trace tiny circles across his ass. My eyes widened with delight at his reaction. I had to admit to myself that the sales clerk was right. I'd looked at the feather tuft at the end of the crop and thought it to be a bit cliché, but the woman had assured me it would be very useful.

"Spread your legs, Liam," I said.

He shifted his feet apart, and I ran the feather along the inside of his right thigh. He moaned, his hips thrusting forward. I flipped the crop and traced the inside of his left thigh with the leather. He stiffened, and his hands clenched into tight fists. He yanked at the chain that clipped them together.

"Shh," I whispered. I had no intention of using the leather end of the crop on him, but I couldn't deny I was enjoying his reaction. I flipped the crop again and traced the feather along both of his thighs and then across the heavy sac of his balls.

He cried out, and I ran the feather along his ass before slapping his ass so hard my hand stung. He muttered a curse as his body arched away from my hand.

I grabbed his hip and squeezed. "Did that hurt, Liam?"

"Yes."

"Do you want me to stop?" I traced the feather across his lower back before licking up his spine with my tongue.

He moaned and shuddered, and I kissed his shoulder blade. I made my voice slow and deliberate as I rested my hand against his ass. "Do you want me to stop?"

"No," he said.

I slapped his left cheek. "No, what?"

"No, mistress. I don't want you to stop."

"Good boy." I soothed his ass with light strokes of my hand. "Tell me what you want to do to me."

"I want to lick your pussy, mistress. I want to make you come. Please," he panted.

"Not yet," I replied and spanked him again.

He cursed like a sailor. I grinned and knelt behind him. I kissed and nibbled his ass as he released his breath on a low groan. He moaned when I pressed light kisses against the back of his thighs while I ran my hands up and down his calves. I stood and moved around to his front before bending and sucking one flat nipple into my mouth. He cried out again, his pelvis thrusting against me and his cock pressing against the leather of my corset.

"I like having you blindfolded," I said. "I like that you don't know where I'll touch you next or what I'll do to you. Do you like it?"

He hesitated, and I ran my hands over his chest. "Be honest with me, Liam."

"No," he said finally. "I want to see your face."

I grinned. "Just my face?"

"No, I want to see your tits as well."

I laughed and stepped back as I unhooked the corset. I dropped it to the ground, sighing with relief at releasing its tight constraints. I pulled and tugged on my nipples until they were rock hard, then stepped forward and brushed them against Liam's skin.

"Jesus Christ," he muttered. "Please, mistress."

"Please, what?" I reached around him, cupped his ass, and rubbed myself against his body. I could feel his cock throbbing against my stomach as he groaned and rocked against me.

"Please let me see your breasts, mistress."

"Not yet." I reached up and curled my fingers around his collar. I turned and tugged lightly on it. "Follow me, please."

He took a few faltering steps. I made a soft noise of encouragement as I led him towards the couch. I turned him and then pushed lightly on his chest. "You're in front of the couch. Sit down."

He sat down, and I pushed his thighs open wide before kneeling between them. I used the feather to lightly trace his thighs before running it down the shaft of his cock. He groaned and thrust upward, and I trailed the feather over his stomach.

He jerked and tried to move away. "Tickles," he grunted.

I grinned and repeated the movement until he twisted helplessly on the couch. His biceps strained as he pulled at the chain, and I traced them with the feather before running it over his entire upper body. When he was panting harshly and groaning uncontrollably, I finally stopped the torturous path of the feather.

He leaned back against the couch, his entire body shaking and twitching. I rubbed his thighs with my hands and waited patiently for him to relax. When his breathing had slowed and he wasn't quite so tense, I leaned over him and took his cock into my mouth.

He shouted my name and arched his body upward. I sucked hard on his cock, letting him pump his hips into my mouth for a few minutes before I released him.

"Please, oh please, mistress. Let me see you," he rasped.

I straddled his body and pressed my breast to his mouth. When he felt my nipple rubbing against his mouth, he opened it eagerly and sucked hard on the throbbing tip. I moaned and cupped his head, holding him against me as he sucked and licked.

Quickly, I untied the blindfold and dropped it on the floor. He blinked, and his pupils dilated as he stared up at me, his mouth still wrapped firmly around my nipple.

"Suck, Liam," I said.

He sucked hard until I was rubbing my panty-covered crotch across his naked cock and moaning. He switched to my left breast, rubbing my nipple against the roof of his mouth before he nipped it lightly with his teeth.

I moaned his name and ran my fingers up and down his arms. "What do you want, Liam?"

"I want to taste your pussy, mistress. Please let me." He gazed up at me.

I nodded and slid off his lap. I shimmied out of my panties, leaving the garter belt, stockings and shoes on before sitting on the couch. He slid clumsily to the floor and knelt between my thighs. He stared at my wet sex, and I widened my legs until he could see my swollen clit.

"Liam," I prompted when he continued to stare at it.

"If you uncuff me, I can use my fingers as well. You'd like that, mistress. I know you would." He gave me a hopeful look.

I smiled at him and stroked my fingers through his hair before tightening my grip and yanking hard. He grunted with pain as I stared at him. "I'll uncuff you when I'm ready. Now stop talking and put your tongue in my pussy before I spank you again."

He bent his head and buried his face into my wetness. He flicked his tongue against my wet clit, and I moaned and pushed hard on the back of his head. His tongue, wet and deliciously stiff, probed at my tight opening. I arched my hips when he slid it inside. He tongued me hard and fast before moving his lips to my clit. He sucked on the swollen pink nub, his tongue sweeping over it with short, firm strokes. I squeezed my thighs around his head and came hard against his mouth.

I collapsed against the couch, panting harshly as Liam leaned forward and nuzzled my breasts. "I love the way you taste, mistress," he said.

I smiled at him. "Do you want to fuck your mistress?"

He nodded, his grey eyes dark with need as I leaned over and kissed him. I could taste myself on his lips, and it sent another swell of desire through me. I reached down and pumped his cock with my hand. He moaned, his head falling back, and I kissed his throat. His stubble was rough against my lips, and I licked at it, liking the way it rasped across my tongue.

"You've been such a good boy. I'm going to reward you," I whispered into his ear, threading my hands through his hair and tugging lightly. "Would you like that?"

"Yes, mistress." He dipped his head and kissed my breast.

I pulled his head up until he was staring at me. "I'm going to let you fuck me however you want. Any position you'd like."

His nostrils flared, and he kissed me hard. "On your hands and knees," he muttered against my lips.

I shivered with pleasure and need. Secretly, I loved being fucked like that. I rarely indulged in it as I had always been drawn to submissive men. I didn't know if it was just the men I'd been with or submissive men in general, but they rarely wanted that position. Their preference was to have me on top. Despite being submissive, Liam was different. I knew instinctively that he liked the thought of me on my hands and knees as much as I did.

I reached behind him and unclipped the chain that bound his hands together. He immediately cupped my breasts, pulling hard on the nipples and pinching them. I moaned and shoved at his chest. "Let me up."

He moved back, and I slipped off the couch and onto my hands and knees. I spread my legs and stared at him over my shoulder. "I'm waiting, Liam."

He moved between my thighs. His hands caressed my large ass, kneading and squeezing as I arched my back and thrust it at him. "Liam," I moaned.

He guided his cock to my wet slit and pushed, encasing his entire length within me in one smooth stroke. I cried out, my muscles clenching tightly around him in response, and he took a deep, moaning breath.

"Wider," he said and pulled at my legs. I shifted them apart, letting him push my upper body to the hard floor as his cock surged even further into me. I cried out again, pressing my ass back against his hard stomach as his hands clamped around my hips. He held me firmly and thrust back and forth as I moaned and writhed beneath him.

"Oh God, Liam!" I groaned as his fingers grasped my ponytail. He pulled lightly, and I lifted my body, arching my back as he pressed against my lower back with his other hand.

"God, Mae. You're so fucking hot," he muttered. His hands slipped around to cup my breasts. His fingers pulled on my stiff and throbbing nipples, and I thrust furiously against him in response.

"I'm so close," I moaned as he plunged in and out of my wet and willing body. His fingers tightened on my nipples, pinching them hard, and the combination of pleasure and pain pushed me over the edge. I came violently, my inner muscles clamping down on his cock and holding him tightly in my body when he tried to withdraw.

"Mae, wait. Fuck, I can't…"

Liam shouted, his pelvis slapping up against my ass as he climaxed deep inside of me. He thrust back and forth roughly until we both collapsed on the floor. He rolled off of me, pulling me onto my side and spooning me and then kissed the back of my neck.

"Christ, Mae. That was fucking amazing," he said.

"I'm glad you liked it," I said.

He reached for the crop lying on the floor next to the couch. He ran the feather end down over my side, grinning when I shivered. "I'd like to try using this on you. What do you think?"

I nodded. "Yes, but maybe we could take round two to the bedroom? The hardwood looks great, but it's murder on the knees."

He laughed and rose gracefully to his feet before tugging me to mine. "Your wish is my command, mistress."

* * *

I STOOD BESIDE THE CAR AS LIAM PUT MY SUITCASE IN THE trunk. He closed the trunk with a bang and stood beside me before putting his arms around my waist and drawing me close.

"Thank you." I smiled at him.

"You're welcome." He leaned down and kissed me lightly. "I'll see you tomorrow at the office?"

"Yes." I patted his ass. "I didn't hurt you today, did I?"

He shook his head. "No, I told you – I liked it."

"I liked it too." I smiled at him.

He dipped his head and kissed me more thoroughly, sliding his tongue into my mouth as I clung tightly to his waist.

"Thank you, Mae. I'll see you tomorrow."

"Bye, Liam." I extracted myself from his gentle grip and climbed into the car. As I drove away, I looked in the rear-view mirror, but Liam had already disappeared into the house. I sighed. I had only one weekend left with him, and I was already depressed. After this weekend, things would go back to the way they were. I'd never again feel his arms around me or hear his voice rasping my name.

I could feel hot tears threatening, and I blinked them back rapidly. I was in love with Liam, but he wasn't in love with me. I was fulfilling a need for him, and after this final weekend, I would go back to spending weekends at my shit-ass apartment and trying not to think about my goddamn boss.

Bitter regret washed over me, but I shook it off. What was done was done. I was an adult, and I had decided to sign the contract. I wasn't taking the money, but I also wouldn't beg Liam for a real relationship. If that were what he wanted, he would have said something by now.

I sighed again and focused my gaze on the road ahead of me. A car, badly rusted and parked on the side of the road like a dead animal, was just up ahead. I slowed down, but the car was empty, and I drove on.

CHAPTER 22

"Goddammit, Neil. Leave me the fuck alone," I muttered under my breath as my phone chimed again.

It was Thursday night, and I had just finished cooking dinner when Neil started texting me. I sighed and read his latest one.

Mae, we need to talk. Call me right now.

No. Leave me alone, Neil. I texted back and tossed my phone on the table before taking a bite of chicken.

After only a few seconds, my cell phone chimed again. I considered heaving it across the room. I would have to change my number. This was starting to be stalker behaviour. I grabbed it, glanced at the screen, and dropped the phone in shock and dismay.

I spit the chicken out onto my plate. With trembling fingers, I picked up my phone as delicately as if it were a snake. I stared at the picture Neil had texted me and moaned softly, "Oh God, no."

It was a picture of Liam and me in his living room. Liam, his face in clear focus, knelt on the floor with his hands bound behind his back as he stared up at me. I realized with a numb panic that although my body, clad in the stockings and leather corset, was in the picture, my face wasn't. The image was cut off just above my breasts.

Of course, I thought hysterically, *he had to make sure he got all of Liam in the shot. He doesn't need my face.*

I moaned again and called Neil's number.

"Hello, Mae. I thought that might get your attention."

"How did you get that picture?" I whispered. My lips felt like they had been given a healthy shot of Novocaine, and I could hardly force the words out.

"You know what's weird, Mae? I've spent the last month thinking my life was fucked up beyond repair. My work life is – well, it's complicated – and my love life? Shit. It's been fucked since I kicked you out. I didn't know how good I had it until you were gone. It took me a while to realize it, but when I saw you at the charity event, I knew I had fucked up by letting you go," Neil said.

"The picture, Neil," I said. "How did you get it?"

"But it's like my mom always told me – when life gives you lemons, Neil, you make lemonade. That picture is my lemonade, Mae."

"Neil -"

"I've spent weeks trying to get Mr. High and Mighty Knight to return my calls. All I wanted was a few minutes of his time. I'm an excellent lawyer, Mae. I would be an incredible asset to your boyfriend's company, but he wouldn't even give me the time of day. That's pretty rude. Don't you think?"

I didn't reply, and he sighed deeply. "Here's the thing, Mae. I thought if I went to Mr. Knight's home and he had the chance to talk with me, he'd see what I was talking about. Only, I've had some financial difficulties as of late and had to trade in my BMW for a fucking rust bucket of a car. And wouldn't you know it – the goddamn thing broke down on me only a mile out from your boyfriend's home. Not a problem, I thought to myself. I was almost at his place anyway. It was a lovely day for a walk. Wasn't it a lovely day on Sunday, Mae?"

He paused and laughed. "I suppose you wouldn't know. You seemed to be pretty busy with some indoor activities. Anyway, I hiked my ass up to Mr. Knight's house, and wouldn't you know it – he already had company! You looked fucking hot in that leather corset, by the way, Mae. Why didn't you wear shit like that when we were dating? If you had, I might not have dumped your fat ass."

I was gripping the phone so tightly that my knuckles were white.

"Mae? You still there, sweetheart?"

"I'm here," I said hoarsely.

"Good, good. I snapped a picture real quick, and it's a good job I did because you ruined a perfectly good show by closing those damn blinds. It doesn't matter, though, because I think I got the shot I needed. Don't you?"

"What do you want, Neil?"

He laughed again. "What do you think I want, Mae? Money. It's what makes the world go round, isn't it? I'm sending that picture to your boss and letting him know that if he doesn't pay up, I'll forward the picture to every goddamn gossip site I can think of. What do you think the people in this city will say when they see Mr. Knight, a pillar of the community, on his knees wearing a dog collar?"

"I have money," I said quickly. "I'll give you fifty thousand dollars to delete that picture."

There was a surprised silence on the other end of the phone, and Neil cleared his throat. "How the hell do you have fifty thousand dollars?"

"What does it matter?" I said. "I'm offering you fifty grand to delete the picture."

He paused again. "I need seventy-five."

My mouth dropped open. I looked at the phone mutely for a moment before pressing it to my ear again.

"Mae? Did you hear me? I need seventy-five grand."

"I – I don't have seventy-five. I have fifty," I said.

"Then I guess I'll have to go to Mr. Knight."

"No!" I shouted. "I'll get you the money. If I pay you the seventy-five, will you delete the picture?"

"Of course I will," he said.

"How do I know that you will?" I asked.

"I guess you'll just have to trust me, sweetheart," he said. "Should I drop by tomorrow for the money?"

"It'll take me a few days to get the money together," I said shakily.

He grunted with disappointment. "Fine. I'm a generous guy. I'll give you until Wednesday to get the money. We'll go for dinner and get caught up. If you don't have the money, your boyfriend's reputation will be ruined by this time next week. You get me?"

"Yeah, I get you," I replied. "I'll have the money by Wednesday."

"Good. It was great to talk with you, Mae. I'm looking forward to dinner on Wednesday," Neil said.

I ended the call without replying and stared blankly at my dinner plate. I screamed and swept the plate off the table. It shattered on the floor, sending chicken and salad flying across the kitchen. I stared at the mess with wide eyes before my calm broke. I folded my arms across the table, dropped my head into them, and wept bitterly.

* * *

"Mae?"

"Yeah?"

"Please tell me what's wrong."

I sighed and rolled onto my side, away from Liam's gaze. It was Sunday evening, and I was leaving in an hour or so. I had spent the weekend at his place, but I was so nauseous and frightened I could hardly breathe. We had made love multiple times, but I didn't have the heart or energy to be his 'mistress'.

Our lovemaking was strictly vanilla the entire weekend. If Liam had found that odd, he hadn't said anything. Being in Liam's arms was the only thing that could make me forget about Neil and his blackmailing, but I was quiet and sick to my stomach whenever we weren't in bed. I couldn't eat, and I was constantly on the verge of these weird, almost hysterical crying jags. I had to run to the bathroom more than once before Liam saw the tears.

"I'm just sad because it's our last weekend together," I lied.

"I am, too." He rubbed my back. "I've enjoyed being with you, Mae."

"I've enjoyed it too," I said as the hot tears flowed down my cheeks.

He didn't say anything but continued to rub my back.

I took a deep breath, wiped the tears from my cheeks, and turned to face him. "Maybe it doesn't have to be our last weekend."

A delighted grin crossed his face. He squeezed my waist lightly. "Mae, I -"

"I'd be willing to extend the contract for two more weekends," I said. "Two more weekends for twenty-five grand."

The smile dropped from his face, and my heart broke as a guarded expression replaced it. "Extend the contract," he repeated.

"Yes." I gave him a small smile. "I'll be your mistress for two more weekends."

"For twenty-five thousand."

"Yes." I squeezed my hands together as he studied me carefully. Liam had been replaced by the distant and cold Mr. Knight, and I couldn't read his gaze at all. My stomach churned, and I tasted bitter bile in my mouth. I was very close to vomiting. If he didn't agree to extend the contract, I didn't know how I would get the money for Neil.

After a long moment, he nodded. "We'll extend the contract two more weekends."

"Good. I'm glad." I tried to smile at him.

"Yes, me too." He moved away from me in the bed, and I blinked back the tears.

"I was wondering if I could, uh…"

He raised one eyebrow. "What?"

"If I could get the money early. Like you did before," I said.

Something flickered in his eyes, something dark and painful.

I swallowed down more bile as he nodded. "Of course. I'll have the money for you by Tuesday. Does that work?"

"Yes."

"Good." He glanced at his phone before sitting up and throwing back the sheets. "I know it's a bit early for you to leave, but I have a long day tomorrow. Do you mind?"

I wanted to burst into tears. Instead, I said, "No, of course not. I'll get dressed and go."

"Thanks." He stood and, without looking at me, walked naked to the bathroom.

"Liam!" I said his name a bit hysterically, and he paused in the bathroom doorway.

"Yes?"

"I…"

Impatience crossed his features. I forced myself to smile. "Nothing. I'll see you tomorrow, okay?"

"Yes." He closed the bathroom door, and I heard the

shower turn on. I cried silently as I dressed and packed my suitcase. He was still in the shower when I finished, and although I wanted to say goodbye again, I left instead. Tears streamed down my face as I climbed into the car and drove away.

* * *

LATE WEDNESDAY AFTERNOON, I PUSHED BACK MY CHAIR AND rubbed my aching head. I had a throbbing headache, and my stomach was a tight bundle of nerves. I was meeting Neil for dinner after work and was anxious to have it over with. Liam was gone from the office all of Monday and most of Tuesday, and I knew he was avoiding me. He had returned to the office late Tuesday afternoon but had gone into a meeting almost immediately.

He was at his desk this morning when I came in and had returned my greeting politely but hadn't spoken to me since. All of our communication was by email or instant messenger. I had waited Monday and Tuesday for Liam to simply email me and tell me he had changed his mind about extending the contract.

I returned to my desk just before the end of the day on Tuesday to see an envelope propped against my laptop. My hands shaking badly, I ripped it open and couldn't stop the sigh of relief when I saw the money order for the twenty-five thousand. Liam had already left for the day, and I sobbed quietly until my face was hot and puffy, and I could barely breathe.

I stopped at the bank before work this morning and cashed the money orders. The cash was in my purse, a large wad of bills tucked carefully into an envelope and hidden at the bottom of my bag.

I checked my phone. Ten minutes to go, and I could leave.

I was meeting Neil at his favourite restaurant. He thought we were having dinner, but I would give him the money, watch him delete the picture, and get my ass out of there.

"Hello, Mae!"

I looked up to see Neil and Roxie in the doorway of my office. I stood hurriedly and grabbed my purse.

"What the hell are you doing here, Neil?" I said as Roxie blinked in surprise.

"Mae?" she said. "I'm sorry, I thought – I mean, Mr. Dorman said you were having dinner tonight. He asked me to bring him back to your office, and I didn't realize it would…"

"It's fine, Roxie. Thanks." I said stiffly.

She left as Neil entered my office. "Not bad for a PA, Mae. Not bad at all," he said as he admired the view out the window.

"Let's go, Neil," I gritted out. "We were supposed to meet at the goddamn restaurant, remember?"

"I know. I thought I would surprise you and stop by the office to pick you up." He held his arm out to me. "Shall we go?"

"Don't fucking touch me," I said.

He frowned. "No need to be rude, Mae."

"Shut the fuck up," I said. "Let's go."

I stormed out of my office and made a squeak of dismay, stopping abruptly. Liam had just entered his office and stared at us in shock as Neil stood beside me.

"Hello, Liam. It's good to see you." Neil grinned at him.

"What are you doing here?" Liam asked tersely.

"Didn't you hear?" Neil put his arm around my shoulders. "Mae and I are giving it another go."

Liam's eyes widened. I tried to pull away from Neil. His arm tightened around me, and his hand squeezed my shoulder.

"Isn't that right, Mae?" Neil said pointedly.

"Yeah," I said as I fought not to vomit right there in Liam's office.

"We're going for dinner. Unless, of course, you need my little sweetheart to work late?" Neil asked.

Liam shook his head. His mouth was a thin line, and he had a look of disgust on his face as Neil guided me toward the door of the office.

"Good to see you again, Liam," Neil said. "We should have dinner sometime, discuss business."

Liam didn't reply, and Neil smiled down at me. "C'mon, sweetheart. I'm starving."

* * *

"The meatloaf is excellent here. You should try that." Neil said as he perused the menu.

"What do you need the money for, Neil?" I asked. "You've never had money problems before."

"That's none of your goddamn business, Mae." He glared at me before looking down at the menu again.

I dug through my purse and pulled out the envelope of cash. I placed it on the table and pushed it across the smooth surface. "Let me see you delete the picture."

Neil glanced at the envelope and reached for it. I placed my hand on it. "The picture, Neil. Let me see you delete it."

"How do I know the money is in there?"

I opened the envelope, showing him the cash inside. His eyes lit up, and he gave me a large smile. "That's my girl."

"The picture," I said.

"Right, right." He pulled his phone out and showed me the picture. I watched as he hit the delete button.

"How do I know you haven't made a copy?" I asked.

He shrugged. "Like I said before - you'll just have to trust me, sweetheart."

I let go of the envelope, and Neil slipped it into the breast pocket of his suit jacket before picking up his menu. "What are you having to eat?"

I was already sliding out of the booth, and he stared at me in surprise. "Mae? Where are you going?"

"I'm not having dinner with you. I don't ever want to see you again. Do you understand, Neil? Don't call me, don't text me, and don't fucking come by my apartment or the office ever again. Do you get it?"

"Yeah, I get it," he said.

"Good."

"Have a great day, Mae." He winked at me, and it took all my willpower not to throw my glass of water at his head.

"Fuck you, Neil."

* * *

"May I speak with you, Ms. Temple?"

I looked up from my desk. It was almost quitting time on Thursday, and this was the first time Liam had spoken to me all day. Hell, it was the first time I had seen him all day.

I nodded. "Of course."

He had closed my office door, and a trickle of apprehension went through me. He folded his arms across his chest and stared silently at me.

I couldn't stand the silence any longer. "Liam, I'm not -"

"I've changed my mind about extending the contract. I won't require your services this weekend or the next," he said.

My heart dropped into my stomach, and I stood up quickly. I started toward him, and he took a step back. "Don't, Ms. Temple."

"I'm not seeing Neil," I said. "He was lying."

"Are you not? That's good." He glanced at the heavy watch on his wrist.

"Liam, please. Let me explain," I said.

"There's nothing to explain. I told you before that a contract between a Dom and a Sub was nothing more than a verbal agreement. I've changed my mind about continuing our... contract."

"I didn't mean to hurt you," I said.

"You haven't," he said dismissively. "There is, however, the matter of the twenty-five thousand dollars. I'll need that back."

My face paled. I grabbed at my desk when my legs threatened to give out on me. "I – I've already spent it."

A look of surprise crossed his face before he rearranged his features into a calm mask. "Have you? That was quick."

"I'm so sorry." I took a deep breath and squeezed the edge of the desk. "I'll pay you back. I swear."

"On a PA salary and with your current debt load?"

"I'll get a second job," I said. "I can pay you a thousand dollars a month, plus I'll pay you interest."

He stared at me for so long that the colour drained from my cheeks. He was going to say no, he was going to demand all the money back immediately, and I had no idea how I would –

"Fine," he said suddenly. "A thousand a month. I'll expect it by the fifteenth of the month. Does that sound fair?"

I nodded. "Yes. Absolutely. Thank you so much, Liam."

His look would have frozen an entire island. "I think it's best if you call me Mr. Knight from now on."

My heart shattered. I swallowed down the loud sob that wanted to escape from my throat. "Of course. I'm sorry."

"Good night, Ms. Temple."

He turned and left my office, closing the door behind

him. I sank into my chair and stared blankly out the window. Liam was disgusted by me. I thought loving him and knowing he felt nothing more than lust was awful, but this was infinitely worse.

I considered running after him and telling him the truth. Telling him about the picture, Neil blackmailing me, and that I was in love with him. I stood up before coming to my senses and sinking back into the chair.

Liam didn't love me. I unintentionally brought Neil into Liam's life, but it was still my fault. If Liam found out that Neil had that picture, if he knew that my ex-fiancé could reveal his secret, his disgust would turn to pure loathing. He would fire my ass from the firm, and then I'd really be screwed.

Tears dripped down my cheeks, and I wiped them away angrily. I had cried enough. It was time to grow up.

* * *

AFTER A SLEEPLESS NIGHT, I WALKED INTO THE OFFICE THE following day, determined to make the best of the situation. I forced a cheerful smile at the receptionist. "Good morning, Betsy. How are you?"

"Good, thanks. Ida's looking for you." Betsy was giving me a strange look.

"Is there something wrong?"

She widened her eyes innocently and shrugged. "How would I know? I'm just the receptionist."

I frowned again as the phone rang. Betsy reached for it. "She told me to tell you to go straight to her office."

I hurried toward Ida's office. I passed Christine and Roxie and gave them a distracted smile. "Morning, ladies."

They stared silently at me, and with disquiet growing in my belly, I nearly ran to Ida's office. I knocked on the door and stuck my head in. "Ida? You wanted to see me?"

"I did." She motioned for me to come in. "Shut the door behind you, please, Mae."

I did what she asked and sat in the chair in front of her desk. "Is there something wrong?"

"Have you been online this morning?" she asked.

I shook my head. My knees were starting to tremble. "No, I haven't."

"Gloria Franklin posted a very revealing picture on her website late last night," she said.

"Oh God," I whispered. Ida swung her computer screen toward me, and for a brief, terrifying moment, I thought I might vomit. I stared in terror at the screen.

My mouth dropped open, and I nearly laughed with relief at the picture of Liam and me kissing outside his home. It was grainy and a bit out of focus, but there was no denying it was us. Neil must have been hiding in the goddamn trees outside of Liam's house when I left Sunday. I had a mental picture of Neil hiding in the trees, his camera phone flashing as he snapped photos of us like demented paparazzi, and a hysterical grin crossed my face.

"This isn't funny, Mae," Ida said sharply. "Do you have any idea how much trouble you're in?"

"Ida -"

"You said you weren't dating him." Ida was absolutely and utterly furious with me.

"I'm sorry, Ida."

"You lied to me, Mae. You looked me in the face and lied to me," she snapped.

Technically, I hadn't. Liam and I had never dated. I was just his very expensive prostitute. I couldn't tell that to the HR manager, though, so I apologized again. "I'm sorry. I couldn't tell you the truth, Ida."

She sighed. "Dammit, Mae. Why the hell did you have to fuck up so badly?"

"We're not – we're not dating anymore."

"It doesn't matter. It's too late now. I have no choice but to fire you."

I swallowed with difficulty. "Ida, please. I need this job. Couldn't you just switch me to another lawyer?"

"No."

I blinked back the tears. I would be damned if I cried in front of Ida. "Please, Ida. I really need this job."

"You should have thought of that before you slept with your boss. You're fired, Mae," she said.

I stared down at her desk as she stood and walked to me. Her hand squeezed my shoulder. "I really am sorry, Mae."

"Yeah, me too," I said. "Does – does Liam know?"

"Yes. I called him this morning, told him about the picture, and that I was firing you."

"Did he fight for me? Did he try to convince you to let me keep my job?" I asked.

She didn't hesitate. "No, he didn't."

CHAPTER 23

T hree Months Later

"Christ, my feet hurt." I collapsed on the couch with a soft groan. Steve muted the television and grabbed my legs, swinging them up and resting them on his lap.

He kneaded the bottom of my feet, and I groaned with appreciation. "Damn, that feels great."

"You know what I want in return, gorgeous," Steve said.

I reached into my bag lying on the floor and pulled out the bag of coffee beans. I tossed it into his lap and, still rubbing my foot with one hand, Steve picked up the bag of beans with his other hand and inhaled deeply.

"That's the stuff." He grinned at me and massaged both of my feet again. "You working at the coffee house sure has its advantages, Mae."

I smiled at him. "You and Russ have let me live with you for nearly three months. Free coffee is the least I can do."

He shrugged. "We've liked having you live with us."

I closed my eyes as his fingers kneaded the bottom of my heel. Since being fired from Knight and Associates, I worked as a receptionist for a construction company during the day and as a barista at my former coffee house in the evenings and weekends. With the cut in pay at my day job and the money that I owed Liam, I couldn't afford even my shitty bachelor apartment. Russ and Steve had encouraged me to move in with them, and they were kind enough to cut me a break on the rent.

Even with the two jobs, I was barely squeaking by, and my dream of owning my own coffee shop had gone out the window. I sighed and stared at the ceiling as Russ entered the living room.

He collapsed in the chair across from us and loosened his tie. "How are my bitches doing tonight?"

Steve rolled his eyes, and I threw a pillow at him as Russ laughed and took a swig of beer. "I've missed you too."

"How was work?" Steve asked as I tugged my feet from his grip and sat cross-legged on the couch.

"Fine. Another charity event, another three hours sitting in the car waiting for Mr. Knight."

I hugged my knees, and Russ stared sympathetically at me. "Sorry, Mae."

"It's fine. You can say his name in front of me, Russ. I'm over him."

Russ and Steve both laughed. I gave them a dirty look. "Shut it. I am."

"No, love, you're not." Steve put his arm around me and squeezed roughly. "You're just as in love with that dickhead now as you were when he fired your ass."

"He didn't fire me," I said. "Ida fired me."

"Yeah, yeah." Steve stood and grabbed Russ's beer, taking a long swallow before kissing Russ and heading toward the kitchen. "I'm gonna grab a beer. Do you want one, Mae?"

"No, thanks. I'm going to bed soon."

Russ and I stared silently at each other for a moment.

"How is he?" I asked.

He shrugged, picking at the label on his beer bottle. "Quiet. I mean, not that he talked much before, but he's a goddamn mute now."

I stared at my hands. "Who did he take as his date tonight?"

"No one. He doesn't take anyone to these events anymore, Mae. You know that."

I shrugged. "Yeah. But sooner or later, he'll start again."

"Why do you want to know? It's better to forget him," Russ said gently.

"I know. I'm worried about him. He's all alone."

Russ snorted. "You're worried about him. Christ, Mae. You're too soft-hearted for your own good. You're working two jobs, you're practically starving, and I could pack my entire wardrobe in the bags under your eyes, and you're worried about the millionaire in his big, lonely mansion."

"I'm not starving," I said.

"Whatever, Mae. Have you looked in the mirror lately? You've lost like thirty pounds."

I glared at him. "I'm just swamped and not that hungry, okay? And it's more like fifteen pounds, and trust me, I could stand to lose some more."

Russ shook his head. "Get on the scale. If you haven't lost thirty pounds, I'll eat that entire bag of coffee beans."

"Shut up, Russ," I said.

"Seriously, Mae. We're worried about you. You need to stop moping over Mr. Knight and get back out there. You're a pretty girl. You'll have no trouble finding someone."

I stood up. "I'm heading to bed. I'm tired, and I'm working at both jobs again tomorrow. Good night, Russ."

"Good night, Mae." Russ gave me a worried look as I dropped a kiss on his head and left the room.

Halfway to my room, I realized I had left my bag on the floor and headed back. I could hear Steve and Russ talking softly, and I stopped outside the room when I heard my name.

"She's fine, Russ," Steve said. "She just needs more time."

I eased closer to the open doorway.

"I'm worried about her," Russ said.

"I know you are, honey. She'll be okay. She's a tough girl," Steve said.

"He asked about her tonight," Russ said.

My heart beat so fiercely that I could barely hear them over the sound of it in my ears.

"I was driving him home, and he was as quiet as he normally is. Then, out of the blue, he asked me how she was. He hadn't said a word about her in three months, and he suddenly wanted to know if she was still living in that shitty apartment of hers."

"Really?"

"Yeah. I told him she was living with us now because she couldn't afford her place anymore."

"What did he say?"

"He was surprised. He seemed to be under the impression that Mae had come into some money. Did she say anything to you about an inheritance or something like that?" Russ asked.

"No," Steve said.

"Anyway, he wanted to know if she had found another job. I told him she was working two jobs and doing just fine."

"Will you tell her that he asked about her?" Steve said.

"No, I don't think so. He didn't react to anything I said, and I don't want Mae to get her hopes up, you know? She needs to move on," Russ said.

When Steve didn't reply, I heard Russ move across the room and sit on the couch beside him. "Do you think I should tell her?"

"No. I don't. It's not like they'll start dating again. Whatever happened between them must have been pretty ugly."

"Yeah," Russ said. "She won't tell me what happened. I've dropped hints to get her to open up about it, but she won't budge."

"She won't tell me either. And I've straight out asked her to tell me," Steve said.

I heard Russ's soft groan and knew Steve was massaging his neck. "Will she be okay, Steve?"

"Yeah, honey. She will. She's tough."

I turned and made my way through the dark hallway to my bedroom. I collapsed on the bed and stared at the ceiling. Liam had asked about me, and although I tried not to over-think it, my heart felt a little lighter for the first time in three months.

* * *

I HIT SEND ON THE E-TRANSFER, THEN CHECKED MY MESSAGES, staring at Liam's number. Every month after I sent him his payment, I was tempted to text him a quick note. So far, I'd resisted, but it grew more difficult with every payment. What would be the point of messaging him? He wouldn't respond because he was finished with me. I was just a thousand dollar payment that hit his bank account on the fifteenth of every month.

I needed to stop thinking about him and wishing things were different. And while I was at it, maybe I could stop compulsively Googling him. I leaned back in my chair, drowning out the sound of the other people in the coffee shop. I had ten more minutes on my break and sipped at my cup of water. My feet hurt, my back ached, and I still had another two hours before my shift was over. I loved working at the coffee shop, but the 14-hour workdays were killing me.

"Get used to it, Mae," I said. "You've got at least five more years of this."

The owner, Hilda, plopped into the armchair next to me. "Hey, Mae."

"Hi, Hilda." I started to stand, and she put her hand on my arm.

"Sit down, darling. You've still got ten minutes left on your break."

I relaxed in the chair as she stared thoughtfully at me. "We're selling the business, Mae."

My mouth dropped open. "What? I'm sorry to hear that."

Hilda laughed. "I'm not. And neither is George. We've been running this place for fifteen years, and we're more than ready to retire. We're moving to Florida and baking in the heat."

"Good for you." I smiled at her. "I'm going to miss you, though."

"We'll miss you too. Listen, George and I were talking, and we want to give you the opportunity to buy the business."

My mouth dropped open for a second time, and she grinned with amusement. "Close your mouth, darling. It's terribly unladylike."

"I don't know what to say," I said.

"Say yes. You love this place, and you're excellent with the customers. You have a good head on your shoulders and know the business inside and out. I know about your plan to start your own shop. Why start from scratch when you don't have to?"

A thin sliver of excitement washed over me. I stared at

the coffee shop, picturing in my head the changes I would make and imagining what it would be like to own the place. I allowed my small, sweet daydream to continue for another minute before I forced myself back to reality.

"I would love to buy the place," I said. "Unfortunately, I can't afford it."

"I'm sorry to hear that, Mae," Hilda said. "There isn't someone you know who would be willing to invest? The business is solid."

An image of Liam flashed in my head. "No, there isn't." I stared at her with genuine regret. "I wish I could afford this place. It's my dream, you know?"

"I do know." Hilda leaned forward and squeezed my hand. "Don't worry, Mae. You're young and determined. You'll have plenty of time to save and start your own business."

"Thanks, Hilda." I tried not to let my dejection show. It would take me years to pay off my debt and save up for my own business, and I had no one to blame but myself.

I glanced at my watch. "I'd better get back at it. Good luck in selling the business, Hilda."

"Thanks, darling."

* * *

"Russ, there is no asparagus in here." I rummaged through the fridge as Russ chopped up the chicken.

"There is. I think it's at the back."

I moved the package of mushrooms and a head of lettuce that had seen better days. "Ah, here it is."

I pulled the asparagus from the fridge and put it on the counter. I cut the ends off as my phone buzzed. I reached for it, glanced at the screen, and gasped so loudly that Russ turned toward me. "Mae? What's wrong?"

"N-nothing. I – I have to make a phone call. Please, excuse me."

I fled the kitchen to my bedroom, shutting the door behind me and dialing the number with shaking fingers.

"Hello, Mae."

"You said you deleted the picture, you son of a bitch," I snarled.

"Yeah, I lied," Neil said.

"We had a deal!" I shouted at him. "I give you the money. You delete the picture!"

"Shut up and listen to me, Mae!" Neil shouted back. "Or I swear to God, I'll send this picture out tonight!"

I took a few deep breaths as panic settled in my stomach like a stone. "Neil, I -"

"I need more money, Mae. Another fifty thousand."

"I don't have it," I said.

"I don't care. I need the fifty thousand, or everyone in this city will see that picture."

"You got me fucking fired by sending that goddamn picture of me kissing Liam to that stupid gossipy bitch Gloria! I don't have the money. I can barely afford to eat," I said.

"Then ask your boyfriend for it."

"He's not my boyfriend. You destroyed that relationship, remember?"

"Fine. Then I'll send the picture to Knight and get the money myself," Neil said.

"No!" I shouted. I could hear the panic in my voice. "I – I'll get you the goddamn money. Just give me some time."

"You have until Friday. I'll pop by the coffee shop and get it from you."

"How do you know I'm working at the coffee shop?" I said.

"I've been keeping tabs on you, Mae. I still think there might be a chance for us to get back together."

"Fuck you, you crazy asshole!" I shouted.

"Friday, Mae. I'll come by around seven. Have the money for me, or I send the picture to Gloria." Neil ended the call.

I stared blankly at my phone before throwing it across the room. My heart pounded madly in my chest, and my breath rushed in and out of my lungs in hard gasps. Today was Sunday. I had five days to get another fifty grand. It was impossible. Neil would send that picture to Gloria, ruining Liam's reputation, and it would be all my fucking fault.

There was a weird buzzing in my head, and it didn't feel like there was enough air in the room. I couldn't seem to slow down my breathing, and I panted harshly as my knees started to shake.

Dimly, I was aware of Russ gripping my arm. "Mae? Mae, you're hyperventilating, honey. Sit down on the bed. C'mon…"

He half-dragged, half-carried me to the bed, and I collapsed on it. I started to lie back, and he put a rough hand on the back of my neck and pushed my head between my knees. "Deep breaths, honey. In through your nose, out through your mouth. Nice and slow."

I took deep breaths, listening to Russ' voice until the buzzing in my head had stopped, and I no longer thought I might faint.

"Better?" Russ said.

I nodded, and he helped me sit up before kissing me on the forehead. "Tell me what's going on, Mae."

"N-nothing," I whispered.

"Bullshit. I heard you shouting, and you just about fainted on me. Tell me what's wrong."

"I can't," I said.

"You can," he said. "I'm your friend, and I love you, and we're not leaving this room until you tell me what's wrong."

I took a shaky breath. "I'm being blackmailed."

* * *

"I don't think you have much of a choice, Mae. You have to tell Mr. Knight," Russ said half an hour later. We had moved to the kitchen, and he poured me a cup of hot tea.

"No." I stared into the tea. "This is my fault, Russ. If it hadn't been for me, Neil would never have gone after Liam."

"It's not your fault. How many times do I have to tell you that?" Russ sat beside me and took my cold hand in his warm one. "What if you don't give him the money? Is the picture that bad? What exactly were you and Mr. Knight doing?" he asked delicately.

"I told you before - I'm not sharing that with you." I pulled my hand from his.

"Okay," he said. "I'm sorry."

"No, I'm sorry," I said. "I know you're only trying to help."

"You have to tell Mr. Knight," he repeated.

"I can't!" I cried. "Liam is already angry with me. He'll hate me if he discovers my ex-fiancé has this picture. I can't live with that. I can't have him hating me. Don't you understand that?" I was starting to hyperventilate again.

"Okay, calm down. We'll figure out something." Russ rubbed my back as I dropped my head into my hands.

"I'm not dragging you into this, Russ," I said. "I'll talk to Neil on Friday. I'll convince him not to release the picture even without the fifty thousand."

"I don't think that will work," Russ said.

"It has to," I said.

CHAPTER 24

"Hello, Mae. You're looking terrific. You've lost weight." Neil smiled at me and leaned in to kiss me on the cheek.

I jerked away from him and glanced around before muttering, "Don't fucking touch me."

He stared at me with genuine hurt. "I pay you a compliment, and that's how you act? When did you become such a bitch?"

"Shut up." I led him to a table in the far corner of the coffee shop. We sat across from each other, and he smiled expectantly at me.

"Do you have my money, Mae?"

"Tell me why you need it."

"I told you it's none of your business. Do you have my money or not?"

"Neil, listen to me." I leaned forward and stared desperately at him. "I don't -"

Liam joined us, his face grave, and sat in the chair beside me. I stared at him in shock. He carried a large envelope in one hand and placed it on the table before him.

"Good evening, Mr. Dorman," he said politely.

My face white, and my body shaking, I continued to stare at Liam. It was the first time I had seen him in three months, and despite my fear, I could barely resist the urge to touch him. Liam gently squeezed my cold, trembling hand as if he had read my thoughts.

"Everything will be fine, Mae," he said.

"So, you decided to call your boyfriend, huh, Mae?" Neil said.

I shook my head. "No, I -"

"I want to see the picture," Liam said.

Neil frowned at me. "Mae didn't show it to you?"

"Let me see it," Liam repeated.

Neil shrugged and brought out his phone. He showed Liam the picture, pulling the phone back protectively when Liam reached for it.

Liam rolled his eyes. "I doubt this is the only copy you have."

Neil flushed and handed over his phone. Liam studied the picture carefully as tears slipped down my face.

Liam handed the phone back to Neil before glancing at me. He reached out and brushed the tears from my face. "Don't cry, Mae."

He turned back to Neil. "Fifty thousand dollars is a lot of money, Mr. Dorman."

"You can afford it," Neil said.

"Yes, I can," Liam replied. "Why have you waited so long to ask us for money?"

Neil frowned at me. "I didn't... did you not tell him?"

My ability to talk had abandoned me, and I could only shake my head mutely.

Neil snorted. "Three months ago, Mae gave me seventy-five grand to keep my mouth shut about your little fetish."

Liam returned his gaze to me. I stared wide-eyed at him

as he sighed. "That's why you wanted the twenty-five thousand."

"I'm so sorry," I said. "I didn't want you to find out, but I didn't know how else to get the money."

When he didn't reply, I stared desperately at him. "I didn't mean to hurt you. I'll pay back all of it, not just the twenty-five but the fifty, too. I don't care how long it takes or what I have to do. I'll pay it back."

Neil grinned. "Oh my God, this just gets better and better. You borrowed the seventy-five from him but didn't tell him what it was for. God, I really have missed you."

He reached out to touch my hand, and Liam snarled, "Touch her, and I'll break your arm."

Neil jerked his hand back. "Fine. But seeing as you now know, I think the price for my silence has just gotten a little larger. A hundred grand should do it."

I swallowed thickly. "Neil, you can't -"

"Hush, Mae," Liam said gently. He raised my hand to his mouth and lightly kissed my knuckles.

"A hundred and seventy-five thousand is a lot of money for a single picture." Liam stared at Neil.

"Maybe. But if this picture gets out, your career is over. We all know it. Now, are you writing me a cheque or not?" Neil said.

Liam regarded him gravely as he opened the envelope and slid a plain, manila folder from it. "Before I write the cheque, I believe I have something you might be interested in seeing."

I watched numbly as he opened the folder and spread the glossy photos across the table. I stared at the pictures of Neil at one of the local casinos. As Liam continued to spread the images, I saw a black-and-white shot of Neil entering a motel with a stacked blonde wearing very little clothing at his side.

I glanced up at Neil. His face had gone white, and he was gripping the table's edge tightly. "Where did you get these?"

"Does it matter?" Liam shrugged dismissively.

Neil took a deep breath. He was obviously struggling to regain his composure and succeeded after a moment. "These pictures mean nothing. I'm not the first lawyer who likes to play blackjack, nor am I the first lawyer to hire a whore."

"I suppose you're right," Liam said. "Of course, not many lawyers use their clients' trust money to fund their gambling addiction or their prostitution habit."

My mouth dropped open, and I stared at Neil as he flushed a bright red. "You have no proof of that."

"Actually," Liam said mildly, "I do." He pulled some documents out of the folder and pushed them across the table toward Neil.

Neil scanned them, the red slowly fading from his face as he looked them over. "How – how did you…"

"How did I do this?" Liam asked. "As you've pointed out, I have a lot of money at my disposal. It makes it easier to hire people to dig up information on scum like you. Of course, you made it much easier for them by gambling and fucking any woman who walked by you every night this week."

He smiled at Neil. "I'm surprised it took you three months to burn through the seventy-five grand Mae gave you. You're not a very good gambler, and you have expensive tastes in women."

"You goddamn son of a bitch!" Neil gritted out. "If you think you can -"

"Shut up, Mr. Dorman," Liam said quietly. "I'm about to offer you a deal that will allow you to keep your career and stop you from going to prison. You'd be wise to keep your loud mouth closed and listen carefully."

Neil's mouth shut with a snap, and Liam smiled at me before squeezing my hand again. "I'll keep this information about your various indiscretions to myself if you delete the photo."

"Deal," Neil said.

Liam's smile was small and bitter. "I don't doubt that you'll keep the photo in a desperate attempt to extort more money later from us. I'll warn you now – if you try to contact either of us again or if a copy of that picture is released to the public, I'll release the information I have. Releasing that picture might destroy my career, but you'll be imprisoned for fraud. Do I make myself clear?"

"Yeah, I get it," Neil said.

"Good." Liam gathered the photos and documents and piled them neatly in the folder. "I believe our business is finished. Good evening, Mr. Dorman."

With a final angry look at me, Neil stood and left the coffee shop. I exhaled in a harsh rush as Liam turned to me.

He regarded me solemnly for a moment. "You look tired, Mae."

"I haven't been sleeping very well the last few days," I said.

He looked me up and down. "You're too thin."

I laughed shakily. "Yeah."

He still held my hand, and I looked down at our linked fingers. "How did you know?"

"Russ came to see me Monday morning."

"Goddammit, Russ," I said wearily.

He shook his head. "Don't be angry with him, Mae. He did the right thing in coming to me. Why didn't you tell me about the photo and that Neil was blackmailing you?"

"Because it was my fault," I said. "If it hadn't been for me, Neil would never have -"

"It isn't your fault," he said fiercely. "Don't do that to yourself."

I swallowed and glanced around nervously. Hilda gave us

a curious look, and I made myself smile normally and wave at her. "How did you know that stuff about Neil?"

He shrugged. "I figured Neil needed the money for something. I hired a team of private investigators, and it took them less than two days to dig up the information."

"You're kidding me," I said.

"They're very good at what they do."

"How – how much did it cost to hire them?" I asked.

"Why?"

"Because I'll pay you back whatever it cost. This is my -"

"Stop!" He squeezed my arms lightly. "This isn't your fault. Do you hear me?"

I nodded. "Yeah, okay."

"And I want you to forget about paying me back the twenty-five grand. I don't want another penny of it from you. I'll give you back the three grand you've already paid me," Liam said.

"No," I said. "I'm repaying you the money, Liam. We had an agreement, and I didn't live up to it."

"I'm not taking any more money from you. This discussion is over," Liam said. "Why did you pay him the money?"

"What do you mean?" I asked.

"Your face wasn't in the picture. No one would have known it was you," he said.

I blinked at him. "I – I couldn't let him ruin your career, Liam. Everything you worked so hard for would be destroyed because of my stupid, goddamn ex-fiancé. I couldn't let that happen."

We sat in awkward silence for a few minutes. Truthfully, I was waiting and praying that Liam would say he loved me. That he missed me and wanted to be with me. As the seconds spun into minutes and he only sat silently, I knew it wouldn't happen. I was such a fool.

"My supper break is almost over," I said.

"It was good to see you again, Mae."

"It was good to see you too." I made myself smile. "Thank you for – for your help."

"You're welcome."

I stood up and slipped by him. I heard his chair scrape back, and then he called my name.

I turned back to him. "Yes?"

"I…" he hesitated, and I gave him an encouraging smile, but he just said, "Nothing. Take care of yourself, Mae Temple."

I swallowed back my tears and nodded. "You too, Liam."

* * *

SATURDAY EVENING, I WAS WIPING DOWN THE TABLES IN THE coffee shop when Hilda came striding into the store. I smiled at her, a little surprised to see her. She usually came in on Saturday mornings to work on the books and order inventory.

"Hey, Hilda. How are you?" I swiped some crumbs from the table and picked up the empty coffee cup as she grinned at me.

"Awesome, as I'm sure you know!" she said.

"Uh, what do you mean?"

"What do I mean…? The business – we've sold it," Hilda said with a confused look at me.

"Already? Wow…that was quick." I tried to give her a genuine smile, but it felt stiff and unnatural. I knew in my heart that I couldn't afford to buy the business, but deep down inside, I had held onto a glimmer of hope.

Hilda cocked her head at me. "Mae, you didn't know?"

"No, how would I?"

"Well, because your friend bought it. I thought he would have told you."

"My friend?"

Why on earth would Russ buy the coffee shop? I thought stupidly. *And where did he get the money from?*

"Yes." Hilda was starting to look uncomfortable.

"But why would Russ buy the coffee shop?" I asked. Russ and Steve had been in the shop numerous times, and Hilda always gave them free coffee.

"Not Russ. Mr. Knight," Hilda said.

My mouth dropped open, and I stared in bewilderment at her. "What?"

"I – you mean he didn't tell you?" Hilda said.

I sunk into a chair. "Liam Knight bought this coffee shop."

"Yes." Hilda sat down in the chair across from me. "I mean, it's not official, obviously. He came in this morning and said he'd seen the 'for sale' sign in the window when he was in yesterday. He gave us a very generous offer, and we accepted. The paperwork is being completed on Monday."

She hesitated. "Is there something wrong, Mae? Mr. Knight seems to be on the up and up. George and I Googled him, and he's done very well for himself."

I shook my head. "No, no, it's nothing like that. I'm just surprised that he bought it, that's all."

"We were too. I mean, what use does a lawyer have with a coffee shop? That's why George asked him."

"What did he say?" I asked.

Hilda stared thoughtfully at me. "You really don't know, Mae? He bought it for you."

My shock nearly dropped me from my chair. "You are fucking kidding me."

At her look of disapproval, I said, "Sorry, Hilda."

"You know I hate vulgarity, darling."

"I know. I'm sorry."

She chewed at her bottom lip. "Oh dear. Obviously, I've ruined his surprise. I'm so sorry, Mae."

I didn't reply, and she patted my hand. "How long have you and Mr. Knight been a couple?"

"We're not," I said.

She laughed. "Right. I saw how you looked at each other last night, and the man bought you a coffee shop. Seriously, how long have you been dating?"

I swallowed and stood up. "Not for that long."

Hilda stood and squeezed my arm. "I'm sorry I've ruined your surprise, darling. But I'm super glad you've found someone like Mr. Knight. You deserve to be happy."

"Thanks, Hilda."

She squeezed my arm a final time and headed for the coffee bar as I wiped half-heartedly at the table. What the hell was Liam doing?

CHAPTER 25

I sat cross-legged on the bed and stared fixedly at the text message I was about to send Liam. I knew he wasn't at home. Russ left an hour after I got home to drive Liam to another charity event. After pacing my bedroom for a couple of hours, I had composed, deleted and then composed and deleted a second time before typing the message I now stared at.

Hi, Liam. Hilda told me that you were purchasing the coffee shop. I wondered if we could get together and talk about it. Let me know. Thanks, Mae.

I sighed and deleted the text. This was ridiculous. I needed to talk to Liam but couldn't text him about this. I would call him tomorrow and ask him to meet with me. I shut off the light and crawled into bed. I stared at the ceiling, my mind whirling and my heart aching, and tried to sleep.

* * *

"MAE!"

I sat straight up in the bed, staring blankly at the door to my bedroom. I glanced at the alarm clock. It was just after two, and I was dreaming of Liam. It was so realistic that I actually thought I had heard his voice. I flopped back on the bed. I needed to –

"MAE!"

I nearly fell out of bed in my hurry to get to the door. There was no doubt that it was Liam's voice bellowing for me. I ran out of my bedroom and down the hall.

"Mae! Where are you?" Liam hollered.

I could hear Russ shushing him frantically as Steve came stumbling out of his and Russ's bedroom and stared blankly at me. "What the hell is going on?"

"I have no idea," I said.

We entered the living room, and I stared in surprise at Russ standing in the middle of the room, supporting a weaving Liam.

"Mae!" Liam grinned boyishly at me. "Hi, honey!"

I walked toward them and grunted in surprise when Liam threw his arm around my shoulders and leaned heavily against me. Russ tried to pry him upward, and Liam shook him off before kissing me on the top of the head. "I've missed you."

I urged him toward the couch. "Here, Liam. Come sit down."

"Sure!" He staggered toward the couch and nearly knocked me down when he stumbled. Russ and Steve hurried forward and helped him to the sofa. He collapsed against it with a loud sigh and patted his leg. "Sit on my lap, sweet thing."

Russ and Steve laughed, and I scowled at them. "This isn't funny. Russ, why did you bring him here?"

Russ shrugged as Liam tugged on my arm. I sat beside him and shivered when he put his arm around me and nuzzled my neck affectionately. "Liam, wait a minute."

He stroked the side of my breast through my tank top, and I slapped his hand lightly. "Behave yourself."

"Yes, Mae."

He sat back, his fingers tracing circles on my bare upper arm as I stared at Russ. "Russ?"

He shrugged again. "He insisted I bring him back here. He came out of the charity event sober but had a bottle of whiskey with him. He had me drive him around for an hour or so while he drank most of the bottle, and then he made me drive him here to see you."

"Made you?" I said.

"Yes," Russ said. "He said if I didn't, he would fire me."

"Liam! You did not threaten to fire Russ."

"I totally did," Liam said shamelessly. "I wanted to see you, Mae."

"You could have just called me," I said.

"I thought this was more romantic." He winked at me.

"You thought threatening to fire my friend was romantic?"

He snickered. "I wouldn't have fired Russ. It's not my fault he's so gullible."

Russ grinned. "My bad."

I glared at Russ, who held up his hands. "The man wanted to see you, Mae. He said he had something important to tell you."

"What?" I looked at Liam.

"Well…" He glanced at Russ and Steve. They stood in the middle of the room, their arms around each other while they watched us with bright interest.

"Maybe we should go somewhere private," I said.

Liam shook his head. "Nope. I want everyone to know this."

"Liam -"

He grabbed my arm and turned me to face him. "I bought you a coffee shop today."

Russ nudged Steve. "Damn, baby. You've never bought me a coffee shop."

"True. But I did take you to Disneyland last year," Steve said.

"Good point." Russ motioned for Liam to continue. "Go on, Mr. Knight."

"Thank you, Russ," Liam said with careful dignity. He cleared his throat. "I bought you a coffee shop, Mae."

"I know, Liam. Hilda told me earlier tonight. You – you shouldn't have done that, honey."

Russ snorted in exasperation. "What the hell, Mae? The man buys you a coffeehouse, and all you can say is, 'You shouldn't have done that'? Seriously, girl."

"Shut it, Russ." I gave him a warning look that he completely ignored.

"So why did you buy her a coffee shop, Mr. Knight?" he said.

"It's a wedding gift." Liam smiled broadly at me before stifling a yawn.

Steve gasped in surprise, and Russ gaped at me. "You're getting married?"

"I - "

"Who the hell are you marrying?" Russ asked.

"She's marrying me," Liam said indignantly. "Who else would she be marrying?"

"He asked you to marry him?" Russ and Steve shouted in unison.

"No!" I rubbed my forehead as Liam stared at me in confusion.

"Yes, I did," he said. "Didn't I?"

"No, honey. You didn't," I said.

"Really? I'm sure I came here to tell you you were

marrying me. I mean, ask you to marry me."

"Oh my God. He is downright adorable when he's completely wasted," Steve said to Russ.

"I know, right?" Russ said delightedly.

"I bought you a coffee shop," Liam repeated.

"Liam, you -"

"You don't believe me?" He gave me a wide-eyed look of dismay before struggling to his feet. "I can prove it. I have a preliminary agreement signed by Hilda and George." He reached into his suit jacket pocket and fumbled out a piece of paper. It fell to the ground, and he bent over, nearly braining himself on the coffee table in the process, and scooped it up.

"Steve." Russ elbowed Steve, who was staring with avid interest at Liam's ass.

"What? The man has a great ass," Steve said.

Liam grinned at him. "Thank you. Mae likes my ass too. She says it's delectable. She likes to spa-"

"Okay! Time to get you into bed!" I stood and took Liam's arm.

Liam threw his arm around my waist. "Lead me to your bedroom, mistress. I'll go quietly."

Russ and Steve both laughed, and I scowled at them. "Help me get him to my bedroom."

Supporting Liam between them, they helped him weave his way to my room. They sat him carefully on the bed, and Liam nodded to them.

"Thanks, boys. We'll try not to be too loud."

Steve laughed again as I blushed furiously.

"Oh my God, Mae. If you don't marry him, I will kick your ass." Russ grinned.

"Thank you for helping him. We'll see you in the morning," I said.

Russ and Steve left the bedroom, shutting the door softly behind them. I loosened Liam's tie and pulled it over his head before helping him out of his suit jacket. I folded it neatly, placed it on the dresser, and unbuttoned his shirt.

He put his hands on my hips and smiled at me as he yawned again. I stripped off his shirt and pushed lightly on his chest.

"Lie back, honey."

He obeyed, and I quickly pulled off his shoes and socks before unzipping his pants and tugging them down his body.

"Okay, under the covers." He rolled over and crawled under the sheet and quilt, sighing contently when I joined him.

"Hello, mistress." He pressed his lips against my neck, and I shuddered with pleasure.

"Go to sleep, Liam," I said.

"I've missed you," he said.

"I've missed you too." I kissed him, and he smiled sweetly at me.

"I love you, Mae."

"You're drunk, honey." I smiled at him.

"Drunk on love," he said so solemnly that I couldn't help but giggle.

He stroked my face and ran his thumb over my mouth. "Do you love me?"

"Yes," I said. "I love you, Liam."

"I'm sorry I got you fired and that I was such a prick to you. I was hurt and angry, and I was a complete asshole."

"It's okay." His hand cupped my breast through my tank top, and I found it difficult to concentrate.

"You're too thin, Mae." He ran his hand down my side. "I don't like it."

I brushed his hair back from his forehead. "Go to sleep, honey."

"I bought you a coffee shop," he murmured. "It's my wedding present to you."

"Thank you, honey. It's a lovely gift." I rubbed his back as his eyes drifted shut and his body relaxed into the bed.

I thought he had passed out when his eyes suddenly popped open. "I love you, Mae."

"I love you too."

"Good. Stay with me?"

"Always. Go to sleep now."

CHAPTER 26

"How's your Prince Charming feeling this morning, Cinderella?" Russ asked when I walked into the kitchen the following day.

"He's still passed out in the bed."

Russ handed me a cup of coffee. "So, are you going to marry him or what?"

"He was drunk last night, Russ."

"So what? The guy obviously wants to marry you."

"People say all sorts of things when drunk," I said.

Before Russ could reply, Steve strolled into the kitchen. "Morning, my lovelies."

"Hey, baby. Are we still on for the farmer's market this morning?"

"Yep. We should get going if we want to beat the crowds. Besides, your boss is awake and in the shower. I imagine he and Mae have some stuff to talk about."

"Yeah, like a wedding date, honeymoon location, a big or small wedding…" Russ grinned at me.

"Shut up, Russ."

Steve laughed. "Try not to make too much noise when *talking,* okay? We've got nosy neighbours."

"Shut up, Steve."

He laughed again and kissed me on the forehead before he and Russ left. I took a few sips of my coffee and returned to the bedroom. I was sitting on the bed when Liam entered the bedroom, wearing just a towel around his waist. My mouth dried up at the sight of his damp, naked skin as he sat next to me.

"Hi, Mae."

"Hi. How are you feeling?"

"Okay. A bit of a headache," he said.

"Yeah, I bet."

He stared down at his loosely clasped hands. "I'm sorry, Mae."

"It's fine. It isn't like I haven't been drunk in front of you," I said.

He shook his head. "No, I'm sorry for how awful I was to you. I was angry with you, and I treated you horribly. Everything you did, you did to protect me, and I hurt you. I'll never forgive myself."

I cupped his face, forcing him to look at me. "You didn't know what was happening. I should have told you about Neil and what he was doing. I don't blame you for your reaction."

"It doesn't excuse my behaviour and I -"

I kissed him. He kissed me back immediately and pushed me backward onto the bed. He cupped my breast almost frantically and kissed me with a fierce kind of desperation that took my breath away.

"I'm so sorry. I'm so sorry," he muttered against my mouth as his fingers found my tight nipple and rubbed lightly.

"Shh," I said. "Make love to me, Liam. Please."

I pulled my T-shirt over my head and wiggled out of my

shorts as he stared at me with dark lust. When I was naked, he reached out and traced my abdomen with the tips of his fingers, running them lightly across my trembling skin.

I took his hand and pushed it between my thighs. It was too long since I had felt his touch, and I was in no mood for teasing. He stroked my soft skin and then rubbed his finger lightly across my clit. I gasped and tugged his towel free. I reached for his cock, stroking it until it was rock hard and throbbing under my touch.

As his fingers circled my clit, he dipped his head and sucked on my nipple. I moaned and squeezed his cock until he gave his own moan of pleasure. I was soaking wet already, and I urged him between my thighs.

"Now, Liam. I can't wait," I demanded.

"Yes, Mae," he murmured as he rested his cock against my tight opening. He slid into me, and I moaned as his thickness stretched and pressed against my inner walls.

"Oh God, Liam. I've missed this," I moaned. I squeezed my pussy around his cock, and he groaned with need.

"Stop, Mae. I'm so close already," he gritted out.

I smiled at him and licked his jawline, relishing the rough scrape of his stubble against my tongue. He moved within me with long, deep strokes, resting his hands beside my head as I arched my hips into him. I kissed just below his earlobe, took a deep breath, and whispered, "I love you, Liam."

He stared down at me. "I love you too."

Tears slid down my face, and he kissed them away. "Please don't cry, honey."

"I love you," I repeated.

He kissed me as he continued to push gently in and out of my warm body. "I love you."

I reached and took his hands, linking our fingers together as his hips thrust faster. I matched his rhythm, my breath quickening and my core throbbing and aching as he brought me closer and closer to my climax.

With a sudden, soft cry, I stiffened beneath him as my orgasm rushed through me. He squeezed my hands and thrust deep into me. Warmth flooded through me, and I wrapped my shaking legs around his hips and clung to him as he rested against me.

After a few minutes, he rolled off me, and I turned on my side to face him. I stroked his face as we stared silently at each other.

"Do you remember what happened last night?" I finally asked.

"Yes."

"Really?"

He gave me a sheepish look. "I remember it in great detail, unfortunately. I made a fool of myself in front of Russ and Steve."

I grinned at him. "They thought you were adorable."

He kissed my forehead. I stared up at him. "What else do you remember?"

"I remember asking you to marry me," he said.

I couldn't stop the smile from crossing my face. "More like telling me I was marrying you."

He groaned and covered his face with his hand. "I'm so sorry, Mae."

I pushed him on his back and straddled him before pulling his hand away. "Are you sorry for asking me to marry you or that it was the least romantic proposal ever?"

"I don't regret asking you to marry me."

My smile widened as he gave me a wry look. "I do regret that it wasn't romantic, that I was drunk, and that I forgot to give you the damn ring."

"You bought a ring?" I leaned over him.

"I did. It's in my suit jacket."

With a soft shriek of delight, I slithered off of him and hurried naked to his jacket. I rifled through the pockets and smiled excitedly when I found the blue velvet box in the inside pocket. I opened it and caught my breath. A silver ring with the biggest diamond I had ever seen was nestled inside.

"Oh, Liam," I breathed, "it's so beautiful."

"Do you like it?" he asked.

"I love it." Holding it tightly, I closed the box and climbed on top of Liam again.

"Try it on," he encouraged.

I hesitated and then balanced the box on the middle of his chest. "Ask me again, Liam. Properly this time and while you're sober."

He grinned and stroked my bare thighs with his warm hands. "Let me up, then."

"What for?"

"So I can get down on one knee. You said properly, remember?"

I shook my head. "Nope. You naked and under me is perfect. Now, ask me again before I spank you for your disobedience."

"Yes, mistress." He popped open the ring box.

He stared at me, his eyes filled with warmth and love, and smiled. "I love you, Mae Temple. Will you marry me?"

I leaned down and kissed him. "Yes, Mr. Knight. I will."

EPILOGUE

Two Years Later

"Hello, gorgeous."

I looked up from wrestling with a bag of coffee beans and grinned. "Hello, Russ."

"Are you trying to open that bag of beans or beat it into submission?"

I snickered as Christa wandered over and took the bag. "Here, Mae. Let me help."

"Thanks, Christa." I smiled at her.

"Mae, I was wondering if I could have next Friday off? My boyfriend and I were thinking of camping for the weekend," Christa asked.

I nodded. "I don't think it'll be a problem. Just let me check the schedule, and I'll get back to you by tomorrow. Okay?"

"Yes, thanks so much." Christa poured the beans into the grinder, and I stepped out from behind the counter and hugged Russ.

"How's business going?" he asked.

"It's awesome, like always."

Russ glanced around the crowded coffee shop. "You've done a great job, Mae."

"Thanks, Russ." I wiped my hands on my apron. "Now, are you here for free coffee or just to chat?"

"Mostly for the free coffee, but it's good to see you too," he said as Christa slid his usual across the counter. He took a sip and sighed happily. "Damn, that's good."

"We're trying out a new bean. Do you like it?"

"Yep. It's a keeper. Steve and I wondered if you and Liam wanted to join us for dinner on Saturday night. Steve has a rare night off, and it's been a while since the four of us have played drunk Boggle."

I laughed. "I'll check with Liam, but it sounds good to me."

"Awesome." Russ took another sip of his coffee. "So, you heard the news about your dirtbag ex-fiancé, right?"

I frowned. "No, what news?"

"Are you kidding me? It's all over the news and the gossip sites. Gloria Franklin had a huge article about it this morning."

"You know I stay away from her stupid site, Russ," I grumbled.

"Considering all the crappy articles she posted when you and Liam first got married, I don't blame you."

"Is she still posting them?" I'd promised myself I wouldn't look at gossip sites about Liam and me and stuck to it.

He shrugged. "Only when you attend charity events together."

"Which is every other week." I rubbed my forehead.

Russ shrugged. "Eventually, Gloria will get tired of it. Anyway, I can't believe you haven't heard about Neil. Seriously, Mae. It's all over the news."

"I've been here since five this morning." I shrugged. "Why is Neil suddenly so popular?"

"He was arrested this morning. I guess old Neil has been using his clients' trust money to gamble and indulge in a little hanky-panky with some pretty pricey 'ladies of the evening'."

My face paled, and I stared dumbly at Russ. He frowned and reached out to grab my hand.

"Mae? What's wrong?"

"Nothing, I -"

"Hello, honey."

Liam's deep voice spoke behind me, and I whirled around, wrapped my arms around his waist and rested my head against his broad chest. "I'm so glad you're here."

He kissed the top of my head and smiled at Russ. "Hello, Russ. Do you mind giving us a moment? I dropped by to chat with Mae about something."

Russ nodded. "You bet. I invited you and Mae over Saturday night, so maybe we'll see you then?"

Liam rubbed my back. "Sounds good."

"Bye, Mae."

"Bye, Russ. We'll see you Saturday."

As Russ left the coffee shop, I took Liam's hand and led him to my office in the back room. It was a small room, barely big enough for me, and it seemed even smaller, with Liam's large body wedged between the desk and the wall. I didn't care. I needed him, and like so often in the last two years, he was there.

"Russ just told me that Neil's been arrested for fraud."

He rubbed my back soothingly. "I know. That's why I'm here."

"What are we going to do? What if he – he releases the picture? Nothing is stopping him from emailing the damn thing to that jerk Gloria," I said.

285

Liam shrugged. "If that happens, we'll handle it together."

"Handle it? How on earth will we handle it, Liam?" I squeaked out.

He smiled at me. "We'll make a joint statement, reiterating our love for each other and acknowledging that as a happily married couple deeply in love, we occasionally enjoy playing adult games."

I blinked at him. "Are you – will that work to save your reputation and the firm's?"

"I think so," he said. "People love you, Mae."

"What do you mean?"

He grinned and kissed me. "You've avoided the gossip sites, but I haven't."

I gaped at him in shock. "You look at the gossip sites?"

He laughed. "Yeah, every once in a while. The point is – people love you. That Gloria woman might say nasty things, but no one else does. I don't think they'll be all that scandalized if they see the photo of us. They love that a normal woman is married to -"

He stopped, a blush rising in his cheeks, and I couldn't stop the grin from crossing my face. "A Greek God like you?"

He rolled his eyes. "They have it wrong, Mae. I'm lucky to be married to you."

"Damn straight you are," I said.

He laughed and squeezed my hip. To Liam's delight, I had slowly gained back the pounds I'd lost until I was at my usual weight. "Anyway, if Neil does release the picture, we'll deal with it together, okay?"

"Okay. I love you, Liam."

He hugged me again. "I love you too, Mae."

"Will you be late tonight?" I asked.

"No. Why, do you have something in mind?" He cupped my breast.

"I thought we could play a game," I said sweetly.

He grinned. "I like the sound of that."

"Good." I reached around him and slapped him lightly on the ass. "I'll set up the Boggle game and wait for you."

He groaned, and I arched my eyebrow at him. "Hey, I'm not suffering another humiliating defeat at the hands of Russ and Steve. You need to practice."

He leaned down and nuzzled my neck. "And what do I get if I win?"

I smiled cheekily at him. "I'll let you tie me to the bed for a change."

He nipped my earlobe and gently squeezed my breast. "You might regret that."

"You're assuming you're going to win."

He laughed. "I love you, Mae."

"I love you too, Liam."

Keep reading for an excerpt from Elizabeth Kelly's novel, "Shameless"

SHAMELESS EXCERPT

My car dying was the final straw. As the engine sputtered, choked, and coughed, I steered it to the side of the dark, silent road, shut it off, and rested my forehead on the steering wheel. The hot tears slid down my cheeks, tears I had desperately held back for hours. I let loose with a primal scream of fury and despair that echoed in the quiet interior of my car.

I screamed until my voice was hoarse. Until the rage and sorrow and utter disbelief that had been crowding my chest finally dissipated enough for me to take my first deep breath in hours. Panting harshly, I banged my fist against the dead car's dashboard before reaching for my purse.

I didn't have my cell phone. Of course, I didn't have it. I'd left it at home, determined not to have anyone interrupt my night of seduction. I planned on making Jordan turn his off as well. I wanted the night to be perfect, and hearing his damn phone chirping every five minutes wasn't a part of the perfect night.

I sighed and wiped at the tears still flowing down my

face. Crying wasn't going to help. I needed to get my fat ass out of this car and back to that bar I had passed a few miles back. I hadn't given it much thought at the time, just a quick glance at the garish neon sign blinking in the darkness as I drove past it. Now, it was my only chance.

If I had been thinking clearly, I might have decided to wait in my car. I might have taken my chance with the next person who drove down that deserted country road. But my mind was still reeling, and my heart was still breaking, and I wanted nothing more than to be back in my tiny, lonely house. I used to hate that house. I dreamed nightly that Jordan would invite me to live with him in his perfectly acceptable townhouse. But now I wanted my home with a desperation born of panic and a desire to pretend my entire world hadn't been blown apart around me.

I grabbed my purse and my keys and climbed out of the car. I slammed the door harder than I needed to before trudging down the road. It was cold, and I pulled my thin wrap tightly around my curvy body. I glanced at my shoes, cursing myself in my head. I'd be lucky if I could even walk back to the bar in the damn things. They were stilettos and excruciatingly uncomfortable to walk in. Of course, I had worn them tonight intending to be fucked in them, not walking in them.

I put my head down and walked faster, teetering a little on the damn heels before catching my balance. The cold wind knifed across my body. I wasn't dressed for the weather. I tugged at my too-short dress and tried to use the wrap to cover my bare arms completely.

It was pointless. The wrap was poor protection against the wind. I wished bitterly that I was wearing my usual yoga pants and cardigan. At least then, I'd be warmer.

Of course, one didn't seduce their fiancé in yoga pants

and a cardigan, did they? No, they seduced them with six-inch stilettos, stockings, barely-there underwear, and the quintessential little black dress.

At least, I had assumed one did. After walking in on what I did, obviously I was mistaken. Or maybe it wouldn't have even mattered. Jordan might have been alone, taken one look at my chubby body poured into this ridiculous dress, and rejected me like he had so often in the last six months. And why wouldn't he? He was handsome, with a perfect body and a metabolism that allowed him to eat whatever the fuck he wanted. My overly curvy body and my constant struggle to lose weight had often been an annoyance to him.

It has nothing to do with you, Maddie. You know that, right? He lied to you. He hid his true self and strung you along for four fucking years. You're better off without him.

A sob escaped my throat, and I wiped savagely at the fresh tears. I needed to forget Jordan and his lies and concentrate on getting home.

* * *

If I hadn't been so cold, if my feet weren't blistered and bleeding, I would have kept right on walking past the bar. Bikes and nothing but bikes filled the parking lot, and the building appeared on its last legs. It looked rough and dangerous and everything I had avoided my entire life but if I didn't get out of the wind soon, I really was going to freeze to death.

My entire body trembling from the cold, I climbed the splintered wooden steps and stared at the giant of a man blocking the front door. He was bald with tattoos scattered across his skull, and he looked me up and down as I cleared my throat.

"Um, can I go in?" I asked.

The man grunted, and I squeaked in surprise when he reached out and touched my dark hair. He gave me another once-over before stepping aside and opening the door.

"Entertainment's here, boys!" he shouted. I stepped back when I heard the roars of approval coming from within the bar.

"Go on, girl. Ain't no point in being shy now." The man leered at me before grabbing my arm and nearly shoving me into the bar.

I stumbled in my heels, reaching out and grabbing onto the nearest table in a desperate attempt to keep from falling flat on my face. I breathed a sigh of relief at the warmth of the bar. I was anxious to find the ladies' room to remove my shoes and rub some warmth back into my frozen toes. If I were lucky, maybe they'd have some Band-Aids I could slap on my bleeding blisters.

I glanced up, my face paling at the sight before me. The place didn't look like a typical bar. It had a long, curved bar with a mirror behind it and rows and rows of liquor bottles, and there were a few pool tables scattered about, but there were only a few tables, and most of the seats were torn, sagging couches and dirty overstuffed armchairs. But it wasn't the décor that made my blood run cold. Besides the bartender, the entire place was filled with men and only men. They were all big, tattooed, and absolutely dangerous look-ing, and every single one of them was staring at me like I was a glass of water and they were dying of thirst. I took a lurching step backward.

"I'm sorry. I – I think I'm in the wrong place."

I turned to flee. I didn't care how cold I was or how much further I had to walk. I had made a terrible mistake coming to this place.

"Where do you think you're going, pretty little bitch?" A man snagged my arm, pulling me to a stop.

He squeezed my arm as I stared up at him. He had long blond hair tied back in a ponytail and was built like a truck. He studied me briefly before his face broke out into a wide grin.

"Only one tonight, boys, but I reckon she's got enough meat on her bones to handle us. Don't you?" he shouted.

The men in the room laughed, and I pulled against his grip. "I'm sorry. This was a mistake, I don't -"

"Shut up," the man said. "We ain't paying you to talk."

He yanked my wrap away before reaching for my large breasts. Without stopping to consider the consequences, I slapped him as hard as I could across his face.

His head rocked back, and he stared at me in surprise before touching the blood on his lip. "You'll pay for that, you stupid bitch."

He raised his arm, and I cringed back. Before he could slap me, a hand caught his arm and yanked him away.

"Back the fuck off, Jenkins. She belongs to me."

"The fuck she does, Riley," Jenkins said.

"The fuck she doesn't," Riley said.

I stared numbly at the man standing next to Jenkins. He was a mountain of a man, and even though I was over six feet in my heels, I still felt short next to him. He wore jeans and a tight blue T-shirt. A black leather vest clung to his broad shoulders, and tattoos covered his thick neck. His dark hair was cut short, and my eyes lingered on the scar that was visible on his left temple. His nose had obviously been broken a few times. He pushed Jenkins back before taking my arm and yanking me into his embrace.

I had a quick, fleeting glance at his dark blue eyes before his mouth claimed mine. He shoved his tongue into my

293

mouth as his hands gripped my ass, and he pressed my pelvis into his.

He was incredibly warm, and my frozen body instinctively pressed into him, seeking out his heat like a bee to a flower. As his tongue licked and stroked mine, I was shocked to hear my soft moan and even more surprised at the flicker of lust that lit in my belly. In all of my twenty-eight years, I had never once been kissed like this. I had never been so utterly and completely owned by a man's mouth, and my hands clutched at his broad shoulders as I returned his kiss shamelessly.

He curved his tongue under my upper lip and sucked hard on it, eliciting another soft moan before he tore his mouth from mine. I stared dazedly at him, not entirely willing to believe that it was his erection I was feeling against the curve of my belly. He gave me a warning look before sighing loudly.

"I told you not to drop by tonight, Kitten." There was an edge to his voice as he squeezed my waist, his fingers digging into my flesh. I knew instinctively that this man and his claim that I belonged to him was the only thing that would save me tonight.

"I'm sorry, baby," I said. "My car broke down, and I didn't know where else to go."

He sighed again, a *Can you believe the shit I have to deal with?* sigh, before turning to face the others. He kept his arm around me, pressing me tight against him as he waved his hand at the men in the bar. "Boys, this is Kitten. Kitten, these are the boys."

The men stared silently at me, and I licked my wind-chapped lips. "It's nice to meet you."

One of the older men with a long dark beard shot through with streaks of grey bellowed laughter. "There ain't no way in hell this pretty little filly would ever be seen with your ugly mug, Rye."

Riley scowled at him. "What the fuck is that supposed to mean?"

"He's sayin' you're ugly, boy." Jenkins clapped him on the back before giving me a once-over. "And this bitch ain't your type."

"How the fuck would you know what my type is?" Riley raised his eyebrows at him. "And stop looking at her like that, or I'll rip your fucking eyeballs out of your head. Got it?"

"Jaysus, boy." Jenkins gave him an exaggerated look of hurt. "Cool your jets. I didn't know she was your woman. Fuck, you never talk about her."

"Maybe because I didn't want you fucking leering at her like the goddamn pervert you are." Riley took my hand and led me toward the door. "C'mon, Kitten."

"Where do you think you're going?" A short man with a large beer belly and long white hair stood from one of the couches.

"I'm gonna take my woman home, and then I'll be back," Riley said.

"We got business to take care of," the man said.

"Yeah, I know. I won't be long."

The man shook his head. "She can stay."

"Frank, she doesn't need to -"

"I said she can stay. Unless," Frank cocked his head at Riley, "she don't know how to keep her mouth shut. Do you trust your little *kitten*, Riley?"

I started to tremble. Riley had stiffened against me, and there was something in how Frank looked at him that made my stomach churn.

"I trust her," Riley replied.

"Then there ain't a problem with her staying," Frank said.

Without speaking, Riley led me toward one of the dirty,

worn armchairs. He sat down and pulled me roughly into his lap, pressing me back against his chest. My dress had ridden up until the tops of my stockings were showing. He rested his hand on my thigh, his fingers stroking the thin band of flesh that was peeking out from above the stocking.

I pulled on the bottom of my dress, trying to tug it down, and he grunted with disapproval before pushing my hand away. "Don't, Kitten."

The rest of the men were ignoring us now. A few of them had returned to playing pool while the others were conversing in small groups. Only Frank was still staring at us. I gave him a nervous look as Riley slipped his other hand under my long, dark hair and held the back of my neck in a firm grip.

He continued to stroke my smooth thigh, and I pushed down the new bite of lust. I was in deep trouble, and now was not the time for my libido to rear its ugly head.

"I have to use the bathroom," I whispered.

He pushed me to my feet and led me toward the back of the bar. I followed him meekly, my hand gripping his. I staggered a little when he led me down a dark hallway. He glanced back at me, his eyes unreadable in the dim light, before opening a door on the left.

"You have two minutes."

I hurried into the bathroom. I realized with surprise that I really did have to pee, and I eyed the dirty toilet with distaste before layering the top with toilet paper. I peed quickly, sighing with relief as my bladder emptied, then flushed the toilet and lurched my way to the mirror. I gripped the sink and stared at my reflection. My face, always pale to begin with, was deathly white, and my bright red lipstick was smeared.

I turned on the tap and used the water to wash my hands and scrub the remains of my lipstick from my lips and face.

My hands were shaking badly, and my feet were screaming at me.

There was a small stool in the corner of the room, and I limped my way to it before sitting down and slipping off my shoes. My feet practically shrieked *hallelujah,* and with a small groan, I massaged them gently. I was just inspecting the blood-soaked blister on the back of my right heel when the bathroom door banged open, and Riley walked in.

I shrank back as he slammed the door shut and squatted before me. He held my chin in a firm grip. "Who are you?"

"N-no one," I whispered.

"What are you doing at this bar?"

"I told you – my car broke down, and I just wanted to use a phone to call a tow truck, that's all. Please, let me go. You can slip me out the back or something, okay?" I pleaded.

"There isn't another place around for miles. You'll freeze to death."

"I'll walk back to my car and stay there until morning. Someone will come by, and I'll use their phone," I said.

He gave me a grim look. "The only people who will drive by are the men out there. Do you want them stopping to help you?"

I shook my head and blinked back the tears as Riley rubbed at his forehead. "Fuck. What's your name?"

"Maddie."

"Listen up, Maddie. The only way you'll survive this night is by doing everything I tell you to. Understand?"

I was so scared my throat had gone bone dry, and I couldn't squeak out a reply. He squeezed my chin. "The men out there are brutal and dangerous. If they think you're not who I say you are, they'll rape you, beat you, and leave you for dead. Do you understand?"

"Y-yes," I said.

"I can't let you leave out the back. If I do that, they'll beat

297

the shit out of me and then find you and hurt you. Your only chance - *our* only chance - is to keep pretending that you belong to me."

"Why are you doing this?" I asked.

He hesitated before glancing at the bathroom floor. "You remind me of someone. Someone sweet and innocent who I failed to protect. And I'll be damned if it happens again."

"Who?" I said.

He frowned at me. "What?"

"Who do I remind you of?"

"It doesn't matter. Just keep your mouth shut and do whatever I tell you. Do you understand?"

"Yes."

He studied me carefully, and alarm flooded my nervous system when his eyes dropped to my large breasts. My dress was ridiculously low cut, and he got more than an eyeful of my cleavage.

"Christ," he suddenly muttered. He forced his gaze to my face, and my thighs trembled at the look of pure need on his face. I stared at his mouth, those full lips that had touched my own and made me forget that I was in a room full of dangerous, terrifying men.

Don't be ridiculous, Maddie. Someone like him would not find someone like you attractive.

No, he definitely wouldn't. Even though he wasn't conventionally attractive, something about him called to me. I had no trouble believing he could easily have whatever woman he wanted. His body was pure muscle, and the scar on his face only made him more mysterious and attractive.

It was absolutely the wrong moment for my lust to come roaring back to life, but apparently, I had zero control over it. I wanted him to kiss me again. I wanted to feel his hands on my breasts and his cock in my pussy while he whispered dirty things in my ear and –

"Fuck, Kitten. You've got your need written all over that pretty little face of yours," he groaned.

I jerked in surprise when he dropped to his knees in front of me and yanked me forward. His crotch pressed against me, and my eyes widened when I felt the hard evidence of his arousal.

"Wha- what are you doing?" I squeaked.

"Giving you what you want," he growled.

ABOUT THE AUTHOR

Elizabeth Kelly was born and raised in Ontario, Canada. She moved west as a teenager and now lives in Alberta with her husband and a menagerie of pets. She firmly believes that a person can survive solely on sushi and coffee, and only her husband's mad cooking skills prevents her from proving that theory.

For more information about Elizabeth, check out her website at

www.elizabethkelly.ca

facebook.com/EKellyBooks
instagram.com/elizabethkelly_author
amazon.com/Elizabeth-Kelly/e/B00EOHZ0MS
bookbub.com/authors/elizabeth-kelly

ALSO BY ELIZABETH KELLY

Tempted Series

Tempted

Twice Tempted

Forever Tempted

Breathless

Tempted Trilogy (Books 1-3)

Red Moon Series

Red Moon

Red Moon Rising

Dark Moon

Alpha Moon

Pale Moon

The Recruit Series

The Recruit (Book One)

The Recruit (Book Two)

The Recruit (Book Three)

The Recruit (Book Four)

The Recruit (Book Five)

The Recruit (Book Six)

The Shifters Series

Willow and the Wolf (Book One)

Ava and the Bear (Book Two)

Katarina and the Bird (Book Three)

Porter's Mate (Book Four)

Bria and the Tiger (Book Five)

Rosalie Undone (Book Six)

The Dragon's Mate (Book Seven)

Rise of the Jaguar (Book Eight)

The Assassin and the Bear (Book Nine)

Elora and the Crow (Book Ten)

The Draax Series

Reign (Book One)

Rule (Book Two)

Rebel (Book Three)

Surrender (Book Four)

Survive (Book Five)

Salvation (Book Six)

Harmony Falls Series

Sweet Harmony (Book One)

Perfect Harmony (Book Two)

Forbidden Harmony (Book Three)

Redeeming Harmony (Book Four)

Absolute Harmony (Novella)

Beautiful Harmony (Book Five)

Reckless Harmony (Book Six)

Seasoned Romance Series

Bet Your Heart on Me (Book One)

Take a Chance on Me (Book Two)

Place Your Trust in Me (Book Three)

Individual Books

The Necessary Engagement

Amelia's Touch

The Rancher's Daughter

Healing Gabriel

The Contract

A Home for Lily

Saving Charlotte

Shameless

The Fairy Tales Collection

Broken

An Unlikely Seduction

Holiday Romance

The Christmas Wife

The Christmas Rescue

The Christmas Nanny

The Christmas Boss

Sordid Games